© Michael Muller

© Stewart Simons

JASON SEGEL is an actor, a screenwriter, and an author. Segel wrote and starred in *Forgetting Sarah Marshall*, and also co-wrote Disney's *The Muppets*, which won an Academy Award for Best Original Song. Segel's other film credits include *The End of the Tour*; *I Love You, Man*; *Jeff Who Lives at Home*; *Knocked Up*; and *The Five-Year Engagement*. On television, Segel starred in *How I Met Your Mother*, as well as *Freaks and Geeks*. He is the co-author of the *New York Times* bestselling Nightmares! series— *Nightmares!*; *Nightmares! The Sleepwalker Tonic*; *Nightmares! The Lost Lullaby*; and *Everything You Need to Know About Nightmares! and How to Defeat Them*. *OtherLife* is his third novel for young adults.

KIRSTEN MILLER lives and writes in New York City. She is the author of the acclaimed Kiki Strike books, the *New York Times* bestseller *The Eternal Ones*, and *How to Lead a Life of Crime*. *OtherLife* is the seventh novel Kirsten has written with Jason Segel. You can visit Kirsten at kirstenmillerbooks.com or follow @bankstirregular on Twitter.

Praise for the LAST REALITY series

BOOKS BY JASON SEGEL
AND KIRSTEN MILLER

Otherworld

OtherEarth

OtherLife

OTHERLIFE

JASON SEGEL
KIRSTEN MILLER

ROCK THE BOAT

A Rock the Boat Book

First published in Great Britain & Australia by Rock the Boat,
an imprint of Oneworld Publications, 2019

ISBN 978-1-78607-678-6
ISBN 978-1-78607-679-3 (ebook)

Interior design by Stephanie Moss
Printed and bound in Great Britain by Clays Ltd, Elcograf S.p.A.

Oneworld Publications
10 Bloomsbury Street
London WC1B 3SR
England

Stay up to date with the latest books,
special offers, and exclusive content from
Rock the Boat with our newsletter

Sign up on our website
oneworld-publications.com/rtb

THE SIMULATION

They say the water's deep out there. The floor of the ocean plunges a few hundred feet from shore. There could be anything at the bottom, and we'd never suspect it. Waves lap peacefully against the rocks lying scattered across the beach. I watch the swells rise and fall. And I wait. At any moment, a beast no human's ever encountered could rise from the depths, water cascading off its reptilian scales. The last thing I'd lay eyes on would be the sole of a giant, clawed foot coming down from above. The odds of a monster attack are slim, of course, but these days they're definitely not zero.

"You've been watching too many of those OtherEarth ads, Simon," says a voice beside me. "That crap can't be good for your noodle."

I don't need to look over. I know who's there. I can even picture the clothes he's wearing. His outfit never changes. It's always the same suit, accessorized with a fedora and a foul-smelling cigarette.

I glance down at his checked pants. They're made of a fabric that probably feels like a ziplock bag in this heat. "Don't you own a pair of shorts?" I ask my dead grandfather.

"Sure." He's instantly wearing a pair of flamingo pink Bermudas. The rest of his outfit remains the same. His legs are bluish white and covered in thick, dark hair.

He takes off his fedora and fans his face with it. The sun reflects off the enormous nose that inspired the nickname they gave him—the Kishka. I've never been able to figure out what he is. Ghost? Hallucination? Cerebral hemorrhage? Whatever the case, the graphics are awesome.

The Kishka rests his bony elbows on the balcony's railing, and we both stare out at the sea. "Thinking about the other you?" he asks. "The one inside the simulation?"

Of course I am. He always knows what I'm thinking.

"I can't stop wondering what'll happen when they turn him off," I say. "Do you think he'll be scared?" I'd be terrified if I were in his shoes. He won't even know how lucky he is that he doesn't have to live through the things I have.

"I don't know, son," the Kishka says. "If you ask me, we should all be scared. None of this was meant to be. Humanity's out in uncharted waters now. There's no telling what kind of shit we're gonna see."

I hear footsteps on the wood behind me, and I turn to see Kat walking toward me across the deck. She's wearing a simple sundress, her copper curls surrounding her head like a halo. I swear to God, I've never seen anyone so lovely. Sometimes it's hard to believe she's human. Towering over her is the magnificent mansion we've called home for the past month. Its ornate wooden bones are as white as a skeleton that's been bleached by the sun.

The Kishka vanishes the instant Kat leans in to kiss me.

"Were you talking to your grandfather just now?" Kat asks softly, her lips still close to mine. That's reason four thousand and two that I love her. She believes in things she's unable to see.

Before I answer, though, I check the open windows of the house behind her to make sure no one is eavesdropping. "Yeah."

"Any words of wisdom?"

"We're all in deep shit," I say, eliciting an exaggerated sigh of disappointment from my girlfriend.

"You know, Simon, I really expect a little more optimism from *the One*."

I groan theatrically. Ages ago someone called me *the One*, and I haven't heard the end of it yet. "Did you come here just to torture me?"

"No." Kat grins mischievously. "I came to tell you that Busara's out of the simulation."

I stand up straight. "Just now?" I ask, and she nods. I wonder if that's why the Kishka was here. I wonder if somehow, he knew.

Busara and Elvis are huddled together on one of the white sofas in our hostess's grand colonial-style living room. The fans that hang from the teak ceiling are circling, and everything seems to be moving in slow motion. I watch a fly do a halfhearted loop-de-loop. Even the insects get sluggish in this heat. Things are starting to get particularly hot on the sofa, so Kat clears her throat.

Elvis and Busara instantly scoot a few inches apart. I honestly don't know why they bother. Everyone knows they've been together since the day they met. But now that Busara's mother is here on the island, they've been acting skittish, like a couple at an eighth-grade dance.

"Simon!" Busara cries out cheerfully when she sees me. She's been in the simulation for over twenty-four hours, and they do say absence makes the heart grow fonder, but her enthusiasm seems a bit much. She's overcompensating for something.

"Is it done?" I ask bluntly.

"Yes, and the operation was a resounding success," Busara informs me. "Wayne showed up. When he saw me there, he was mad as hell."

Kat snickers. There's no one she hates more than her step-father. "I bet."

"So they don't know what really happened to us?"

"Nope," Busara tells me. "Our secret is safe."

Along with the relief comes a nagging anxiety. There are so many questions I want to ask. But I'm not sure I want to hear the answers.

Busara's watching me like she knows something. "Your face looks better," she says.

There are mirrors everywhere in this place. I know what I look like. I preferred the bruises around my eyes when they were a lovely purple. Now they're an unsettling green. "Thanks," I respond.

"She's just being polite. It's not that much better," Elvis says. "But you weren't very good-looking to begin with, so it really isn't much of a loss."

I love that Ukrainian head case. He gives me the truth, no matter how brutal. And that's how I like it. I don't need the facts polished or prettied up.

I glance over at the nearest mirror. A large white bandage covers my nose. Before the doctors could fix it, they had to break it again. One had the chutzpah to ask if I was interested in making a few improvements. I told her no, of course. Without the nose I was born with—the glorious schnoz I inherited from the Kishka—I wouldn't even know who I am.

My nose will heal in time. I'm still not so sure about the rest of me. The Company had me for two whole days. There's no telling what they've done.

I remember being at the Waldorf Astoria. I was there in flesh and blood. I experienced it all firsthand. I know what happened. But what came afterward makes me question every memory I have.

In my mind's eye I can still see Kat standing over me. We're in a suite inside one of New York's most expensive hotels, and she's just pulled me out of Otherworld. She shouts at me to get up, we have to get out. I can see the terror on her face. In the space of a second, I'm on my feet. Kat has me by the hand and she's dragging me to the door. But it's too late. Wayne and his men are already there.

Elvis and Busara aren't in the room. I don't know where they are, and I hope like hell they've managed to escape. Wayne sends two of his men down to the lobby to search for them. Then he rolls up his shirtsleeves and turns to me.

What followed is a blur. The next thing I remember is passing an old woman in the hallway of the hotel. She clapped a hand over her mouth and pressed her back to the wall when she caught sight of my face. I'm sure I was hideous. Wayne really knows how to throw a punch. And there wasn't much chance he'd miss with his men holding my arms behind my back.

The Company men took us out through the hotel's secret garage—the one royalty and presidents use. I figured my hours were numbered. By the end of the day, my body would be found floating facedown in the harbor. My only thought was how to save Kat. But the Company had no intention of killing either of us—at least, not right away. We had something they wanted to take from us first.

Kat and I were smuggled into the Company's headquarters in a Manhattan skyscraper. There we were strapped down, and strange white helmets with no visors were placed on our heads. I don't know how long mine was on. As soon as it began humming, my thoughts turned to static, and I lost all track of time.

It wasn't until later that I found out what they did to us. The Company had extracted at least a month's worth of memories from Kat and me. I doubt the tech in the helmets had been thoroughly tested. There's no telling what the process did to my brain. I think it's safe to say that the Company wouldn't have minded much if the extraction had killed us. They were desperate to discover what Kat and I knew.

After we escaped, they tried to use the data they'd collected to determine what actions we might take next. So they ran a computer simulation using the memories they'd stolen. My skin still crawls just thinking about it. While my body lay there helplessly, the Company invaded my brain. Wayne now knows almost everything that happened to Kat and me between April and May. He saw our first kiss back at home in New Jersey. He was watching over us whenever we slept side by side. I hope he enjoyed the part where I shot him. That's one memory I'll never get tired of reliving.

But the Company didn't see everything. With the help of Elvis and our current hostess, Busara was able to access the simulation, which had to run in real time. She took on her own double as an avatar. She didn't change much in the simulation. Wayne needed to think everything was happening just as it had. Busara only made a few tiny tweaks to our story. But those tweaks ensured that, even with all the data they've stolen, there's no way the Company can predict our next step.

Busara stands up and takes me by the arm. Elvis says nothing, but they've clearly discussed whatever Busara intends to do. She guides me outside to the same railing where I've been standing all day. I think they all assume that I'm soothed by the ocean. They don't know I've been watching and waiting for the next attack.

Busara lets go of my arm and shoves her hands into the pockets of her linen jumpsuit. It's a signal of sorts—an alert that some straight talk is on the way. Like Elvis, Busara rarely minces words. I trust her now—and I've almost forgiven her for getting me into this mess.

"Elvis told me you've been worried about our doubles—and what happened to them when the simulation ended," Busara says.

"What made them any less real than the Children?" I ask. We risked our lives to save the sentient residents of Otherworld. But we did nothing to spare our own digital clones.

Busara gazes out across the ocean. In profile she resembles an ancient queen. "I don't know how to answer that question," she tells me. "But I can tell you that it was an act of mercy to end the simulation." She turns and catches my eye. "Something went wrong with your double, Simon. The simulation wasn't a perfect copy. He'd lost touch with reality—"

"Reality?" I butt in.

"Okay, let me rephrase," Busara replies. I listen to the waves as she decides what to say next. They're all so careful with me these days. "Your double told me Earth and Otherworld were colliding in his head. He was seeing Otherworld beasts in Central Park. The goat man from the wasteland showed up inside the Museum of Natural History. All of it was driving him nuts. The guy was in mental agony. I don't think he could have survived much longer."

I suppose that makes me feel a little bit better. I only see the occupants of Otherworld in my dreams. If they started showing up here, I'd probably throw myself in the ocean. "So he was pretty messed up?"

"Yeah," Busara said. "It had gotten so bad that he'd started having conversations with your dead grandfather."

I stare at the horizon. "Really? That bad?" I say.

THE ISLAND

I've discovered the perfect definition of love. You know you're in love when you trust someone enough to let her know you might be losing your mind.

"Stop. You're not crazy." Kat wraps an arm around my shoulder and whispers in my ear. Then she pauses and reconsiders. "Well, not in *that* way."

Kat and I are down by the cove. It's a horseshoe-shaped strip of beach surrounded by tall rocks. A school of blue fish darts away as we approach the water, past the sea urchin colony that makes swimming perilous. When the tide is out, the ocean barely covers their sharp black spines. I sit down on the damp sand and Kat joins me. This is the one part of the island where I experience something like peace. Nothing has changed here for thousands of years. With the waves crashing against the cliffs, we can't be overheard. Along with the balcony, it's one of two places on the property Kat and I go to talk. She's pretty sure every room in the house is bugged. It's not that I don't trust our hostess. I don't trust *anyone*. After you've had your brain invaded and your memories recorded, you really start to value your privacy.

Kat's wild hair is flowing in the wind. The sun's turned her skin a deep bronze and brought out every freckle. "Thanks, but having my girlfriend say I'm sane is like hearing my mom say I'm handsome," I try to joke. But I can't manage a smile. Busara's words have been haunting me all day. She thought the other me was too nuts to survive.

"I'm not joking, Simon," Kat insists. If I weren't in such a shitty mood I'd laugh. When Kat gets serious, she could take over the world. "There's nothing wrong with your brain. I think the Kishka is a feature, not a bug. Most people don't listen to their intuition. Yours takes on human form and talks like a gangster from the 1960s."

That deserves a kiss, though I'm still not sure I believe her. When we're done, I change the subject. I'm tired of discussing my mental illness. "Let's go for a walk," I say, standing up and reaching out for her hand.

The air here smells like Thanksgiving every day of the year. Two centuries ago, the entire island was a nutmeg plantation. That's all we've been told, but it's impossible to ignore the history lurking underneath that fact. Slaves constructed the beautiful old house in which we've been staying. Men, women and children were forced to work in the groves. This entire place was built with cruelty and misery. Not many people live on the island these days. The ones who tend the gardens and operate the gun towers are probably paid well. Our hostess says she treats them like family. She'll need their loyalty when the trouble comes.

Elvis says places like this have become the ultimate status symbol for the ultrawealthy. Every multibillionaire now has a fortress where they can hide from their fears. Some worry about water wars. Most are waiting for the poor to take up arms. Our hostess lives in terror of global economic collapse. That's why she's constructing a remote island stronghold. The old colonial mansion is just for show. Eventually it will be turned into an office and guesthouse. Her real home will be built into the rocky mountain in the center of the island. I haven't seen the work site—none of us has. I doubt Abigail would give us a tour if we begged. I suppose we belong to the class who'll soon turn against her. She does make a pretty good case for her vision of the future, I gotta say. She can tell you exactly how a rise in the price of pork belly will eventually end with the extinction of the human species. Knowing what I do, I'd say extinction is the least of our worries.

"Are you ready to go back?" Kat asks. I think it's her way of asking if I'll be okay.

"We told Elvis and Busara we'd be back in an hour. We've only been gone fifteen minutes."

"Not to the house," she says. "Back to New York."

I look around at the sparkling white sand, turquoise water and vibrant jungle. "Yeah," I say. I can't fucking wait to get off this island. The whole place gives me the creeps. Whatever happened here in the past will never wash away.

We turn to make our way back and see a woman walking toward us, wading through the foamy edges of the waves. She's watching her feet as if waiting for the sand to open up underneath them. Her cheerful yellow dress is at odds with her somber expression.

That was one of the other tweaks Busara made to the simulation. She hid her mother's whereabouts from the Company. After her husband disappeared, Nasha Ogubu and her daughter moved to the East Coast. Busara enrolled in school in Brockenhurst, New Jersey, but her mother's life seemed to stall. She's still struggling to adapt to an existence without her husband.

Convincing Nasha to join us on the island wasn't as hard as Busara expected. Getting her mother to visit James Ogubu's avatar in Otherworld has been a whole different story. Before he died, James uploaded his consciousness into an avatar. Aside from a body, everything that made him human is in Otherworld. Busara keeps asking Nasha to go see him, and her mother always refuses. She seems to think James's avatar is a ghost—a bit of lingering energy that's taken the form of a man. She says it's not how she wants to remember her husband.

Nasha Ogubu offers a warm smile when she sees us on the beach. Then she silently carries on. All she ever does is endlessly walk the island, as if the grief will overtake her if she ever comes to a stop.

Kat and I reach the mansion's living room just as a movie screen is descending from an opening hidden between the two-hundred-year-old ceiling beams. I start to wonder what the evil slave-owning bastards who once ran this island would have done with technology like ours. Then I realize it's a stupid question. The answer is all around us. Technology has changed. Humanity hasn't. We're still the same species that tortured and terrorized its own kind. Now we just use different tools.

"Welcome back." Busara's trying to play it cool, but the way she's eyeing me says everything.

"Nervous breakdown averted?" Elvis asks, and I have to laugh. What else could I do? "Good. 'Cause I'm not sure I'd want to find out what kind of mental health facilities might be available here on Paranoia Island."

"Stop!" Kat snickers as she puts a finger to her lips.

"Oh, come on," Elvis replies. "You think it's news to anyone? Besides, if she's spying on us, she deserves to hear it."

The subject is making me anxious. Crazy or not, our hostess is not someone to be toyed with. Anyone who builds a fortress like this is a person who takes herself *very* seriously. "What are you guys planning to watch?" I ask to change the topic.

"The Company just released two new OtherEarth ads," Busara says. "One's for the regular game. The other is for the exclusive disk version. It was sent to potential clients and got leaked to the press."

I take a seat on the arm of the sofa. The Company has produced six ads for OtherEarth so far, and sixteen million sets of the augmented reality glasses have been preordered. That's almost twice the number of people who live in New York. Soon the entire island of Manhattan will become a giant playground. Unlike virtual reality, which makes you leave your world behind, augmented reality merely adds layers of fantasy to what you ordinarily see. You can hunt down aliens in Central Park or explore Manhattan in 2300.

It's all fairly harmless—until you sync the OtherEarth glasses with a disk. Like the disks used in Otherworld, they allow you to experience a fantasy with all five senses. But with OtherEarth, those fantasies take place here on Earth. And you get to pick the "people" who'll share them.

Busara clicks the Play button on the remote, and the screen lights up. The first OtherEarth ad starts with a view of the ocean on a sunny day. Then something black appears on the surface, like the back of a massive whale. It keeps rising as the camera pulls back. The Statue of Liberty appears. This is New York Harbor. A pair of burning red eyes emerges from the murky gray water, and the beast they belong to continues to grow until it towers over the Statue of Liberty. All we can see is its massive legs as it crushes the statue beneath one of its feet. The camera trembles as the beast issues a deafening roar and makes a beeline for the Freedom Tower, leaving a wake of rubble through lower Manhattan.

"OtherEarth," says the announcer. "It's your world, only *better*. Available August fifteenth."

"Meh," Elvis says dismissively. "I'm not so impressed by this one. I mean, the Company could create any monster they want, but they have to steal their ideas from a twentieth-century Japanese film? Lame. Give me thirty minutes and I'll come up with a million better ways to destroy Manhattan."

I get the sense that Elvis has spent a lot of time pondering the subject. It's hardly a testament to his psychological health, but at the moment, I'm far more concerned about my own mental state. I'm wondering why I've been staring at the ocean since I got to this island, waiting for something to rise out of it. I played the Godzilla game after Alexei Semenov's brother gave me the Other-Earth headset. Maybe that's how the giant reptile got stuck in my brain. Maybe not.

"Let's have a look at the next ad," Busara says.

A beautiful sunset appears on the screen. We see a man resting on a chaise longue, looking out over a city that resembles Los Angeles. The scene's shot from behind—we can't see the man's face. But it's clear from his salt-and-pepper hair and opulent surroundings that he's an older man of means. He picks up a pair of glasses from the table beside him and puts them on.

I hear Busara gasp.

"What the fuck?" Elvis shouts.

I feel the sofa bounce as Elvis jumps to his feet, but I don't take my eyes off the screen for a second.

A woman has appeared in the chair beside the man in the ad. Her face remains out of sight, but even from behind, her close-cropped hair and deep brown skin look all too familiar. She holds out a hand to the man and he takes it. The camera pans in on the hands as she caresses his thumb with her own. It's like half the commercials you see for erectile dysfunction—except the women in those ads are real. In OtherEarth you can order up any companion you like.

"OtherEarth," says the same announcer. "You can *feel* the difference."

The commercial ends. The screen goes black. No one in the room says a thing. Elvis is standing frozen in the center of the room. Then the spell breaks and he spins around.

"How did they get footage of Busara?" he demands. I don't think I've ever seen him this agitated before. He looks like he's going to explode.

"We don't know for sure that it's me," Busara says calmly.

"Trust me. I've spent a lot of time staring at you from behind.

That was *you*." Then Elvis stops. "Shit, that sounded bad. Sorry."
He's been trying to cut back on the dirty jokes. We all know it's
been hard for him. I don't think any of us really care; we're just
impressed he's making the effort.

"Let's not get bent out of shape. The Company's trolling us,"
Kat says. "They don't know what we have. It's all psy-ops. They're
doing their best to freak us out."

"Well, ding, ding, ding!" Elvis shouts. "Guess what! We have
a winner."

"Come on, Elvis," Busara says. "It's not that big a deal. There's
a reason they didn't show my face. They didn't have enough footage to re-create it."

"I think he's jealous," Kat stage-whispers to Busara. "He wants
to be in an OtherEarth ad too."

I turn to Busara, who's struggling to hide a grin. I'm far too
anxious to be amused. "You're sure they don't know about Max?"
I ask.

Her grin fades. "Positive. In the simulation, your mother gave
you George Reynolds's name and told you he was the lawyer defending the homicidal director. You got back to the hotel and
showed it to me. I took the name and number and said I'd call for
you, but I never did. There's no way the Company could know
what Reynolds sent us in real life."

"They saw the list Alexei Semenov gave me, though? The one
with all the OtherEarth users who ended up dead or in jail?"

Busara frowns, annoyed by my line of questioning. "I did
everything exactly the way we planned it, Simon. I let them see
Semenov's list so they'd chase the red herrings. What's going on?
You don't sound like you trust me."

"I trust you," I tell her. And I do. "I've just got a really bad feeling about all of this. I think—"

I stop abruptly when I hear the clicking of stiletto heels. We all know who it is. The four of us spin around in unison.

A deeply tanned blonde dressed in ivory silk is approaching. It's impossible to say how old she is—or to guess what she might once have looked like. The world's best surgeons have transformed her into a feline beauty who's both attractive and terrifying. Having gotten to know Abigail Prince during our stay, I'd say that's exactly the look she was after.

Abigail focuses her gaze on my face. She always speaks to me as if I'm the only person in the room.

"Good afternoon," she purrs. "I'm afraid we have a problem."

MAX

The last time I saw my mother in person, we were at the American Museum of Natural History in Manhattan. She gave me some money and George Reynolds's phone number. The lawyer had recently acquired a new client—a well-known movie director who'd tried to murder an actress. At the time of his arrest, the director had been wearing a pair of chunky black glasses.

I called the lawyer as soon as I got back to the hotel. And as soon as I told him why I was calling, he promptly hung up on me.

Thirty minutes later, there was a knock on the door of our suite at the Waldorf. A porter handed me a plain white envelope. Inside was a single piece of paper, and on that paper was a name and a phone number. *Abigail Prince.* At the very bottom were two sentences scribbled out by hand: *Destroy the note and envelope immediately. Don't make any more calls from your room.*

I could have kicked myself for being so stupid. It had taken a lawyer only half an hour to track me down. The next time, it could have been the Company at the door, not a porter. After I showed Busara what had arrived, I ripped the paper and envelope to shreds and flushed both down the toilet. I was about to get Googling when Kat and Elvis emerged from Otherworld. The distraction saved us. Later, after the Company searched our room, they checked our browsing history and call logs. Thankfully, Abigail Prince wasn't on them.

When Kat and I were captured, Busara and Elvis didn't know where to turn. Then Busara took a chance and reached out to Abigail Prince, a discount-store heiress who happens to be the tenth richest person in America. Abigail paid a team of mercenaries to free Kat and me from the Company, then whisked us all to her private Caribbean island. It wasn't just a good deed, of course. I doubt Abigail ever feels driven to do the right thing. No, she wanted our help getting her hands on one of the few things her money can't buy her—the freedom of her beloved and only son, Max, who's wasting away in a jail cell in Queens, awaiting trial for murder.

Abigail may be one of the wealthiest people on earth, but if you're in the under-twenty crowd, her son, Max, is the Prince you're likely to know. By age sixteen Max Prince had ten million YouTube followers. Every thirteen-year-old in the United States could probably recite one of his play-throughs by heart. Unfortunately, his fame didn't break through with older audiences until he murdered his stepfather in the most gruesome way possible.

A maid found Abigail's fourth husband, a former captain of the Argentinian national soccer team, chopped into bite-size pieces in Max Prince's bathtub. There was no doubt regarding the identity of the murderer. Everyone on the planet knew Max and his stepfather had despised each other. And in case that wasn't proof enough, Max was found lounging next to the bathtub in a pool of his stepfather's blood.

Ordinarily, such a gory family homicide might cause a rift between mother and son. Perhaps that was the intention. But Abigail Prince stuck by her heir. She knew he couldn't be responsible for his actions. She was certain the Company had framed him.

If I'd heard Abigail's story a year ago, I would have dismissed it as another rich mother making excuses for an overprivileged, fucked-up son. (A dynamic I happen to know all too well.) Max has never spoken a word in his own defense—in public or private. In fact, when his mother visits him, he rarely speaks at all. Which seems kind of odd for someone who made millions insulting strangers and cracking dirty jokes at his stepfather's expense. But I could have explained that away too—if it hadn't been for one piece of evidence that made me take Abigail Prince seriously. The maid who discovered the crime scene claimed that Max Prince was wearing black glasses when she found him. Yet the police report makes no mention of them—and Max Prince has 20/20 vision.

There's also Max's relationship with the Company to consider. He'd been among the first to purchase the once-coveted, limited-edition Otherworld headsets. Before the game was shelved by the Company, views of his play-throughs had broken all of his previous records. Forty million people had watched Max slay a hundred-headed monster in a realm known as Lerna. After that, the Company began to court him as a spokesperson.

Max didn't need the Company's money, and he didn't want his fans to think his opinions were paid for. But he got to be friendly with several of the Company's lead engineers. He even claimed he'd been given a tour of a secret innovation lab. Shortly afterward, Max showed his mother a pair of chunky black glasses. He told her it was a game that would change the world.

Then something happened. Max went silent. He stopped posting videos. He wouldn't answer his phone. He sent his staff away. When Abigail turned up at his apartment one morning, he answered the door in clothes that looked like they hadn't been changed in days. They were soaked through with sweat, and Max's face was bright red. He was wearing the glasses he'd shown her. And he had something attached to the back of his skull. He took the glasses off, reached out and poked her as if to confirm she was real. Then he slammed the door in her face.

The next day, Max murdered his stepfather.

Abigail is convinced the Company was somehow responsible. No one else has bought her theory. Max confessed to the crime. He had a motive. He was caught *literally* red-handed. But I believe Max was framed for murder. All of us do. The Company set him up because he knows something. Unfortunately, we can't call, email or text him. If we want to find out what it is, we'll need to visit Max in person. Now that the simulation is over, we'll be flying back to New York to see him.

But there seems to be a new problem with the plan. Abigail Prince takes the remote out of Elvis's hand, switches over to satellite television and scrolls to CNN. A reporter is stationed in front of a

Midtown skyscraper, talking to the camera, his face somber. In the background, dozens of police officers stand guard behind yellow crime scene tape. I see the reporter place his index finger on his earpiece. He bows his head for a moment while he listens; then his eyes shoot back up to the camera. He looks shaken.

"I apologize for the delay. We've just gotten word from Columbia Presbyterian Hospital that Scott Winston is still in surgery for injuries he sustained less than two hours ago. To repeat, Scott Winston, billionaire, philanthropist and tech pioneer, is in critical condition after a shooting outside Chimera Corp, the wildly successful software company he's run for over ten years."

"Wow," Kat gasps.

I'm too shocked to respond. Winston is one of the tech world's best-known names, and Chimera is a leading developer of multimedia and creativity software. Winston was twenty-three when he started the business. For six months, he was the youngest CEO in America. Then nineteen-year-old Milo Yolkin founded the Company. The two "boy geniuses" were good friends for almost a decade. Their relationship is said to have soured last year after Winston questioned Milo's mental health in a television news interview.

Abigail holds up a perfectly manicured fingernail. "Wait for it," she tells us. There's more to come.

"The perpetrators of this brutal assassination attempt are still at large this afternoon," the reporter continues. "Armed with what the police believe to be 3D-printed guns, they ambushed Winston on this busy Midtown street. The two of them were caught on camera by a passerby."

The news show cuts to footage from a smartphone. The

camera is wobbling, and you can hear its owner squeal with excitement as she captures a video of the famously handsome billionaire emerging from his company's skyscraper. Then a Vespa speeds into the frame and comes to an abrupt stop. A female is driving, with a male on the seat behind her. They point what look like plastic guns at Scott Winston and his bodyguard. When their bullets hit the mark, the assailants toss the weapons and the female steps on the gas. Winston drops to the sidewalk, and his bodyguard throws himself across the CEO's chest. But it's too late for a human shield to be of use. The glass windows behind them have shattered and the building's walls are splattered with Winston's blood.

As the assailants wheel the Vespa around to make their getaway, the camera captures their faces clearly. It's Kat and me.

Holy shit. I can't breathe.

"The assassins have been identified as Katherine Foley and Simon Eaton of Brockenhurst, New Jersey. According to residents of Brockenhurst, both disappeared from town six weeks ago, two months short of their high school graduation. The pair's friends and parents haven't seen them since, but facial recognition software has allowed us to determine their whereabouts on another memorable day."

A static picture appears on screen. It's a smartphone snapshot. Milo Yolkin is positioned on the bow of the Staten Island Ferry, about to take his final plunge. In the photo, several Good Samaritans are rushing to grab him while a couple leans against the boat's railing, smirking at all the commotion. Once again, it's Kat and me.

"We've confirmed that Eaton and Foley were on the Staten

Island Ferry the day Milo Yolkin, the Company's twenty-nine-year-old founder, committed suicide. Whether they played some role in Yolkin's untimely demise remains to be seen. But Eaton does have a well-documented history of animosity toward the tech industry. Two years ago, he was arrested for hacking into RoboTech, a company that manufactures robot toys for kids. Eaton reprogrammed the toys to deliver terrifying threats, scaring hundreds of small children before the products were recalled."

"Hey!" Elvis cries out. The robot hack was his handiwork. I think he's a bit pissed that I ended up with the credit. "It was a warning, not a threat!"

"Shush!" Abigail orders.

"Today Scott Winston was Simon Eaton's latest target," the reporter continues. "But police believe Winston may not be Eaton's last. They're asking anyone with any knowledge of either Eaton's or Foley's whereabouts to contact the authorities immediately."

Abigail switches off the television and stands in front of us with her arms crossed. She's looking at me like I'm a little kid who's been caught pooping in the bathtub. I'm getting the feeling she thinks we're somehow to blame.

"That wasn't us," I mutter.

Abigail shakes her head as if I'm hopelessly stupid. "For God's sake, of course not," she says. "There's no way off this island without my authorization. What I want to know is how they did it."

"Videos like that are called deep fakes," Elvis explains. "Similar software's been around for a while. It's like Photoshop for video. I've heard the Chimera Corporation was set to introduce some next-level tech, but I've never seen anything this good. You'd need a lot of video footage to replicate someone that well."

"We should have known this would happen." Kat looks over at me. "If the Company can create a virtual world, they can sure as hell edit us into an iPhone video."

"This changes everything," I mutter.

"For you, maybe. Not for me. We made a deal," Abigail says. "I want to know what the four of you are planning to do next."

That, I gotta say, is an *excellent* question.

WANTED

"I'm here with Olivia Dalio, a student at Brockenhurst High," says the television reporter. "Olivia, you were a schoolmate of Simon Eaton and Katherine Foley, is that correct?"

Olivia keeps her face tilted at a weird angle. I think she wants the camera to catch her good side, but she looks like the recipient of a bad head transplant.

"Yes, that's right," Olivia confirms.

"Did you ever see any sign that they might be capable of such a heinous act?"

"Oh, yeah," says Olivia. "Simon's definitely dangerous. He once overheard me talking to a friend about Kat, and he got all up in my face and threatened to hack my phone."

Kat switches off the television. "Awww," she says, planting a kiss on my cheek. "Did you really do that for me?"

Kat seems to be handling our newfound fame pretty well. I'm still reeling from the shock. The biggest manhunt in years is taking place in the United States. Kat and I have hit the top of the Most Wanted list. We've been watching the coverage from two thousand miles away, on an island in the Caribbean. The portraits the police are painting make us look like evil incarnate. We've even taken the blame for the building collapse that nearly killed Kat. They say it was a trial run—we were testing explosives. They haven't bothered to explain why Kat was one of the victims.

Our homes have been raided. Every kid in our school has been interviewed. People I've never even seen before have weighed in on our sociopathic tendencies. It's truly a next-level doxxing. Kat and I will never be able to go home again—not that either of us ever planned to. I'm sure the residents of fancy-pants Brocken-hurst are mortified by the exposure. If there's a silver lining to this bullshit, it's that. Oh, and watching my father try to avoid the television crews parked outside his office. That's given me some genuine pleasure. They haven't gotten to my mother yet. I wonder where she's been hiding out.

I have to hand it to the Company. They've really outdone themselves. Their doctored videos are playing nonstop on all channels. I look at myself every day in the mirror, and even *I'd* swear one of the assassins was me. The Company must have scanned our bodies while they stole our memories. I wonder if our doppelgängers are anatomically accurate.

The Company didn't stop there, either. They gave us motives. I'd almost forgotten social media existed, but Kat and I both left behind old accounts that were hacked. That's where they posted our manifesto. I don't know who they hired to write it, but they did a fabulous job. It's beautifully written. The Unabomber meets F. Scott Fitzgerald. In the manifesto, we warn the world that technology will eventually destroy humankind. The talking heads on television have all called it insane. I believe every goddamned word of it.

People still seem to think the world will end with an explosion of some sort. Or armed revolutions. Or environmental collapse. But that's not how it's going to happen. The world as we know it will end when there's no longer a line between the real and unreal. When we can't trust our eyes. When seeing is no longer believing—and taste, smell and touch don't help much either. The Earth itself isn't in danger. The planet will always be fine. It's humanity that's screwed. Technology will destroy us the day we can't tell the difference between what should matter and what shouldn't.

Most people out there have no idea how close we are to that day. Watching the Company's videos, I realize we're even closer than I thought.

Abigail says she expects us to have a plan by tomorrow. Despite everything, we have to save Max. Every cop, security guard and vigilante in the United States is on the hunt for Kat and me. And yet somehow, we need to get into a prison in one of the most densely populated zip codes in America to talk to a famous murderer.

Abigail's a billionaire. She's accustomed to ordering the impossible. Who knows what she'll do to us if we can't deliver? I wouldn't be surprised if she loaded us all onto a rubber raft and set us adrift in the middle of the ocean. If I've learned nothing else over the last few months, it's that you really shouldn't trust billionaires. Anyone who's stashed away that kind of loot doesn't give a damn about you unless you happen to be one of their heirs.

* * *

For the past few hours, Busara has been setting up a security camera and laptop with facial recognition software. Kat is online, researching disguises. Elvis is sitting at the table, surrounded by wires and electrodes. I've been pacing back and forth in front of the windows. A man with a giant schnoz is nervously chain-smoking cigarettes by a tree outside. He knows something is coming. He doesn't know what. I don't bother to alert my friends. They wouldn't be able to see him anyway.

"When are you going to give us a demo?" I ask Elvis, pointing to the hat he's been tinkering with for the past few hours.

He looks up with annoyance, and I expect him to tell me to go away. I probably deserve it. This isn't the first time I've asked. "As soon as I'm sure it's going to do what I want it to," he says. "Abigail's got a pretty impressive tool closet, but she didn't have everything I was looking for. I've had to improvise. If it doesn't work, I promise you, bro, I'll come up with something else."

I'm not sure Elvis realizes how much trouble we're in. "If it doesn't work, Abigail's going to feed us to the fucking sharks."

"Look, if I can't come up with a solution, I'll go to New York by myself," Elvis says. "Nobody's going to recognize me. I'm the only one of us without a digital double. The Company hasn't made my face famous."

I swear to God, you'd think the kid had a death wish. He's always volunteering for suicide missions. I suspect it's because Busara always refuses to let him go.

"Not going to happen." Busara saves him again. "If they have footage of me, they have you on tape, too."

"Doubt it," says Elvis. "I'm *very* careful."

"We're all going to New York," I say. "If Elvis's gadgets don't work, we'll just have to depend on our disguises."

This elicits a hearty laugh from Elvis. "You can't hide with that nose," he says. "The Company would see right through the disguise."

"What are you talking about?" I snap back instinctively, surprising myself. It's been a long time since I felt sensitive about my schnoz. "There are other big-nosed people in the world, you know."

"That's not what he's saying," Busara says. "Fooling people is one thing. Tricking cameras is much harder. The Company's facial recognition software can see through most disguises. There are certain things each of us isn't able to hide. In your case it's your nose."

"How many cameras in New York City use the latest facial recognition software?" I demand.

Elvis and Busara both burst into laughter. "You have no idea, do you?" Elvis says. "Everywhere you go, they know who you are. Banks, office buildings, post offices. They're all watching you. Hell, half the stores in Manhattan use facial recognition to snoop on their customers."

Kat looks up from her work with a worried grimace. "So we're stuck here until we figure out how to beat the software?"

We're in a room that was made for Instagram. A light, fragrant breeze makes the candles flicker and rustles the leaves in the nearby jungle. Most people would want to stay here forever. We're supposed to leave the day after tomorrow, and I can't bear to be stuck here a moment longer.

"Will you guys stop with all the praise and encouragement?" Elvis says. "My head's going to get too big for this cap."

Elvis puts the baseball hat on and adjusts the brim. Busara doubles over laughing the second she sees it. The only hats on the island were stuffed inside a cooler we found among the fishing supplies. This one says MASTER BAITER.

"You chose *that* one?" Busara sputters.

It's hard to tell whether Elvis's frown is sincere. "I picked the one that best fit my interests and personality," he says. "You don't like it?"

"Just don't let my mom see you wearing that. I told you—she's seriously old-school. I've never even heard her curse," Busara replies. "So does this mean you're ready?"

"I'm always ready, sweet cheeks," Elvis replies with a saucy wink.

God, these two are nauseating. Never in a million years would I have imagined them together. A little over a month ago, I would have sworn that Busara was more robot than human. I still can't believe she fell for someone who once lived on a diet of Slim Jims and Doritos while he hacked into toy companies. Now Elvis's sense of humor is a little less filthy, and the rest of him is cleaner than ever. He's showered nearly every day since he's met Busara. That in itself is a minor miracle.

And there's no doubt the two of them make an amazing team. Busara points the camera at Elvis, who shifts from one pose to the next. She studies the image on the computer screen, adjusts Elvis's hat, looks back at the screen and nods.

"See what you think," she says, turning the laptop to face Kat and me.

This time I have to laugh. The face on the computer is one I'll always remember—but it doesn't belong to Elvis. The hat he's wearing makes the camera see a completely different guy.

"Whoa!" Kat's eyes flick back and forth between Elvis and the screen. "Who is that dude?"

"It's a douchebag named Brett Hamilton," I say. "Elvis and I knew him at boarding school. As I recall, he once reported Elvis for creating unsanitary conditions in the dormitory."

"That's not what matters," Elvis sniffs, as if offended that I would question his motives. "All that matters is that Brett is a law-abiding citizen of roughly the same age who's never been arrested and has every reason to be in the New York area."

"And who did you pick for me?" I ask. If the answer is the one I'm expecting, I'll know I've chosen the ideal best friend.

"Mark Cunningham."

"Yes!" I pump the air with my fist. "Thank you!" When I was first sent to private school, Mark Cunningham dedicated his senior year to inventing new ways to insult my nose.

"I have no idea why that would excite you," Elvis says in his best Brett Hamilton impression, "but I'm glad I could bring some joy to your otherwise miserable life."

Kat walks over to Elvis and lifts his hat. Three small LEDs have been attached to the underside of the brim. "How does this work?" she asks.

"The LEDs project a pattern of light onto your face," Busara says. "People can't see it, but cameras pick up on it. It makes them read a different face."

"And you can make these for all of us?" I ask.

"Sure," Elvis replies. "The hard work is already done."

"So does that mean you don't need any help from the rest of us?" Busara asks.

"Nope," Elvis says with a sigh. "As usual, I can save the day on my own."

"Glad to hear it." Busara turns to us. "If he's working, I'm going to Otherworld to see my dad."

Since we arrived on the island, she's visited her father whenever she's gotten a chance. I know she worries that he's lonely. Usually Busara goes on her own. Sometimes she takes Elvis. Tonight she turns to me and Kat.

"Either of you want to come?"

THE WHITE CITY

Hidden somewhere in Russia is the black box that hosts Other-world. After Alexei Semenov's death, his brother took charge of it. I have a feeling the location of the server was one of the things the Company was hoping to learn when they downloaded my memories. Thankfully, I have no clue where it is.

No one knows where Alexei's brother is, either. All we know is that he's spent a good deal of Alexei's fortune buying up all the limited-edition headsets that the Company produced. A virus destroyed most of the two thousand they'd sold. But there are still a few die-hard fans out there who've been trying to hire engineers to fix them. Rumor has it that the younger Semenov is happy to turn to his brother's extensive collection of *kompromat* to blackmail anyone who might need an incentive to sell.

But as it turns out, the virus didn't infect every headset. By the time the virus was set loose in Otherworld, Max Prince had already moved on to OtherEarth, the *next* big thing in gaming. His three Otherworld headsets were collecting dust on a shelf while the virus was rampaging. As a result, they survived unscathed, and Max's mother has graciously made the headsets available for our use.

The four of us keep our avatars in a high-rise apartment inside Otherworld's White City. I haven't polled my friends lately, but I for one have zero interest in visiting any of the realms. I'm not even sure if they still exist. Otherworld belongs to the Children now. I wouldn't be surprised if Milo Yolkin's "accidents" have torn down everything he created and started their world all over again.

I don't think any of us would visit Otherworld at all if it weren't for James Ogubu. That's where his avatar lives—though I still don't know if the word *live* can be applied to his existence. The flesh-and-blood man is dead and gone. Only his consciousness survives, uploaded into his Otherworld avatar. After the virus wiped out the headset players, we guided Ogubu's avatar to the White City from Imra. The White City's been abandoned for ages. It's dull and lonely, but it's safe—and Ogubu's avatar must be protected at all costs. If he dies in the game, there will be no starting over.

I enter Otherworld and find Busara and her dad stationed across from Kat on the sofa. The Ogubus are listening quietly as Kat fills James in on recent events. They both sit with their spines perfectly straight and their hands clasped in their laps. Their faces remain expressionless while their black eyes glimmer with interest. I've never seen a daughter who bears such a striking resemblance to her father. I see nothing of the soft, voluptuous Nasha in her.

"So you're going to use disguises and devices to visit this young man in prison?" James Ogubu sums it up once Kat has finished. "Does your mother know about all of this?" he asks Busara.

I see him frown when his daughter laughs at the mere idea.

"But she *is* on the island with you," he follows up.

"Of course," Busara says.

The answer seems to give him some solace. "You're going to a great deal of effort to see this Max Prince. What do you imagine he's going to tell you?" James asks.

"We're not sure," Busara confesses.

"The Company has been testing the OtherEarth disk on men in New York," I say. "Several of them have ended up dead or under arrest for assault or murder. Max Prince's mother is convinced her son has some kind of proof."

"What do you think the Company's end game might be?" James Ogubu asks. "This is different from the Facility. They've taken an enormous risk testing their product out in the open in this way. What do you suppose they're after?"

"They want to make money," Kat says. You can practically hear the *duh* in her voice.

James Ogubu blinks. "How well do you know your stepfather, Kat? Do you think money is what drives him?"

I once sat in a boardroom with Wayne Gibson and the Company's board of directors. You never would have guessed which man was in charge. The other guys all wore bespoke suits and watches that cost more than the average house. Wayne had on a pair of Dockers and a button-down shirt that looked like he'd bought it on sale at Walmart.

"I couldn't say," Kat responds.

"Well, I only met the man a few times," says James Ogubu. "But he didn't strike me as the sort who's driven by a desire for the finer things in life."

Ogubu is right. When Wayne moved to Brockenhurst, he could have bought a mansion. Instead he chose to fix up an old shack in the woods. I don't think living large is his motivation.

"Wayne wants power," Busara says.

"Certainly," her father agrees. "But why? How does he intend to use it?"

The two girls are stumped once again. "I don't know," Kat says.

James Ogubu smiles. "I'm glad to hear you admit it. Only dangerous people believe they have all the answers."

I get the sense he's trying to tell us something, but I can't figure out what it is.

"Perhaps if you got to know your stepfather a bit better, you might figure out what he wants."

"I'm not sure that's an option," Kat says. "It's not like he's going to answer my calls."

James Ogubu turns to his daughter. "You should ask your mother what she thinks. She's an excellent judge of character. Among other things."

"Mom?" Busara replies as though the suggestion makes no sense. These days, her mother looks to her for help—not the other way around. That must be what Busara's thinking when her eyes suddenly widen with horror. "Oh my God! What am I going to do with Mom when the rest of us go back to New York? We can't leave her on the island with Princess Paranoia."

"I wouldn't worry too much about your mother," James replies. "You haven't known her as long as I have. Nasha is the ultimate survivor."

I should join the conversation, but something outside the window has caught my eye. The lights in a nearby building are flashing as the décor in one of the apartments changes. Modern, rustic, tatami mat, log cabin. The ability to change the décor was one of the perks provided to residents of the White City. They could choose from a vast menu of options. A few blocks away, another apartment begins flashing. I'm confused. There shouldn't be anyone else inside the White City.

I look back over my shoulder to see James Ogubu watching me. I get the sense he's been waiting for one of us to notice the lights. Kat and Busara catch on and swivel to face me.

"There are people out there," I say. "Who are they?"

"Not people. *Children*," Ogubu says. "They began moving in months ago."

"Months ago?" Busara asks. "But I was here *this morning*."

When James Ogubu looks down at his daughter, he reminds me of the Clay Man, the avatar Busara once used here. Now that I think about it, I'm sure that isn't a coincidence. Busara's father has always been her hero. There was a time when she would have happily sacrificed me to save him. "Your morning was a long time ago," Ogubu replies.

Our world and Otherworld are out of sync. Time moves much faster here. But since we brought James Ogubu to the White City, we've had no way to judge how fast it's passing. Until now, nothing's ever changed.

Kat, Busara and I all gather at the window. A third of the neighboring apartments now appear to be occupied.

"I've been worried this would happen," James Ogubu says.

"Worried? Why?" Kat asks. "The buildings went to waste for so long. Why shouldn't the Children make use of them?"

"It's not the buildings that concern me," Ogubu tells her. "It's the technology that was left behind in them. The Children are about to take a giant leap forward. Like humans, they are still a young species. I don't know if they're ready."

"Humans are a young species?" I ask. "The Children started showing up less than a year ago Earth time. We've been around for millennia."

"Yes, and three hundred years ago, there wasn't a human on Earth with indoor plumbing," Ogubu replies. "Today we're creating new worlds. We aren't ready for the responsibility. Neither are the Children."

I'm the first to remove my headset and hop off my multidirectional treadmill. It's dark in the game room. With the headsets on, there's no need for lights. I can hear the soft hum of the treadmills' motors and Busara's muffled words as she says her goodbyes to her father. Outside, the night sky is filled with stars. The constellations passing over us are the ones the pharaohs saw. The same ones our ancestors drew on the walls of their caves. They'll still be there, I think, when our species finally destroys itself.

I head for the living room, where Elvis is working. He yelps with surprise when I appear in front of him.

"What the hell, Simon," he says, clutching his chest like an old man. "I thought you were going with the girls to Otherworld."

"I did," I tell him. "I was there for at least an hour."

"You literally left ten seconds ago," Elvis tells me.

"Time is speeding up there," I tell him. "And the Children are moving into the White City. They're using the technology that was left behind."

"Yikes." Elvis grimaces. "That shit's going to get ugly."

"James Ogubu said the same thing—without the profanity."

"Not surprised." Elvis returns to his tinkering. "Great minds think alike."

"Since I'm back early, is there anything I can do?"

Elvis sighs and points to a chair and slides one of the hats over. I think he was looking forward to some time alone. "Sit down and get to work. If we get these done fast enough, we may be able to leave in the morning. This time it's our world that needs to be saved."

UNDER SIEGE

I'm standing on one of the bridges that cross Brooklyn's Gowanus Canal. The brown, frothy water below reeks of chemicals and
sewage. The sun is rising over the city, and I can hear helicopters
in the distance. I feel more at peace here than anywhere on Abigail's island. I don't want to go back.

"Something's happening," says the Kishka. "Abigail shouldn't
have brought you to this island."

"I don't like it, either," I say. "But where else could we have
gone?"

The Kishka turns his eyes to the sky. "It's starting to look like
you jumped out of the frying pan and into the fire."

The helicopters are getting closer. There are three of them
coming—slick black machines that can dart like dragonflies. The
peace is long gone now. My anxiety is building. They're coming
for us.

"Wake up, Simon," the Kishka orders. "Wake up now."

My eyes instantly open. The pale light of dawn is filtering through the shutters. I can still hear helicopters in the distance.

I shake Kat awake. "Get dressed," I tell her as I pull on my jeans. "The Company's coming."

"What?" Kat asks groggily, wiping the sleep from her eyes. "How do you know?"

"The Kishka told me," I say. I can't think of another explanation to offer. It does the trick. Kat leaps out of bed and into a sundress she left in a pile on the floor.

The sound of the helicopters is growing louder, but they're not here yet. I have a hunch they'll use the garden as a landing pad. If not for the Kishka's warning, we'd all be dead soon.

Kat and I hurry to wake the others and find them already up and rushing toward us, Busara's mom in the lead. She's fully dressed in a black tracksuit, her braids pulled back in a no-nonsense bun.

"Have you seen Abigail?" she asks.

"No," Kat says.

"Damn it, where did that woman get to?" Nasha mutters. "Come on then, follow me," she orders the rest of us.

"Where are we going? What's going on?" Busara's the only one asking questions. The rest of us follow without argument. This is not the Nasha Ogubu I've come to know. But whoever it is, she clearly knows what she's doing.

We stick close behind Nasha as she leads us out of the house and into a grove of nutmeg trees on the north side of the garden.

The helicopters are overhead now, and the bright beams of light cast from their bellies are dancing on the lawn. If one of those beams was aimed at the grove, we'd be instantly exposed. I'm starting to wonder if we should have trusted Nasha. The safest route would have taken us out toward the ocean. Instead, we're plunging deeper into the center of an island that's on the verge of being invaded.

I'm about to ask where we're going when Nasha stops, reaches down and pulls up a perfectly camouflaged trapdoor. There's a set of stairs underneath.

"Go," she orders. The helicopters are getting closer. The rest of us hesitate.

"What's down there?" Busara is staring at her mother as if she suspects an impostor.

"A safe room," Nasha says. "Now go!"

At the bottom of the stairs is a wall that appears featureless aside from a biometric lock. Nasha closes the trapdoor above. In the dark, the lock's screen glows green. Nasha presses her palm against the screen and the entire wall slides to the side. The room beyond is lit by screens showing footage from security cameras posted all around the island.

"How the hell did you know this was here?" Elvis voices the question we're all thinking.

Busara flinches when she hears her boyfriend curse in front of her mother.

"What did you think I was looking for on all my walks around the island—flowers and seashells?"

Busara's jaw has hit the ground. Her eyes follow Nasha as her mother switches on more lights. There are bunk beds against one wall, food rations stacked against another. We have everything we need to live underground for a week.

"But how—" Kat starts.

"You think a woman like Abigail Prince wouldn't have safe rooms hidden all around the island?" Nasha says, cutting the question short. "Until her fortress is completed, she's a sitting duck."

"Yeah, but, Mom—" Busara keeps blinking like she can't trust her eyes.

"How about we get through this first," her mother answers, pointing up at a screen that shows helicopters descending. "Once the guests are gone you can all ask your questions. If you're lucky, I'll answer a few of them."

I don't know if I can wait that long, honestly. The curiosity might kill me. How did she find the safe room? How did she just open the door?

Busara steps closer to the screens. "Do you think it's the Company?" she asks me.

There are no markings on the aircraft, as far as I can see. The three of them are identical—jet-black with tinted windows.

"Yes," her mother responds before I can open my mouth. "It's the Company."

As soon as the helicopters touch ground, soldiers begin to spill out. Dressed in head-to-toe black, their faces covered, they all look like ninjas on steroids. That's probably exactly what they are. I count fifteen of them before all but two disappear, fanning out in every direction. Within seconds, there's a rattle of gunfire in the jungle. The irony is rich. Abigail wanted to be prepared. But when the invasion arrived, her fortress was still under construction.

The remaining ninjas position themselves on either side of an open door on the helicopter nearest the house. A man in Dockers and a blue button-down shirt steps out. As he walks toward the house, the ninjas follow him. Wayne looks like he's done this kind of thing before.

A figure in a long white nightgown appears in the door of the house. Abigail rushes out, fleeing in the direction of the safe room, her blond hair and silk robe fluttering behind her. She's too late.

"Shit," Nasha says. "Why didn't she wait in her room like I told her!"

One of the ninjas has captured Abigail and is dragging her toward Wayne. I see her shouting over the helicopters. I can't hear a word she's saying, but it's pretty damned obvious she's not happy.

The helicopter engines begin to die down, and the sound of Abigail's voice rises above them.

"Who the hell are you? What are you doing here? Do you know who I am? Are you from the Company? Give me my son, you evil bastards!" She turns her head back toward the house. Standing outside, two of the workers who were hired to protect the island have appeared. "Help me!" she shouts to them. Both instantly drop to their knees, their hands held high in the air.

Wayne pulls a gun from a holster clipped to the back of his pants. There are two loud bangs, and the workers both slump to the ground. A pair of ninjas step over the men's bodies and disappear inside.

"Put Ms. Prince in the chopper," Wayne orders. "Lock her up good. We have work to do."

Abigail is dragged kicking and screaming toward the helicopter. The silk of her nightgown glows in the moonlight. We watch in silence as the men strap her into a seat and leave her behind.

"What do they want from Abigail?" Busara asks.

"I don't know, but we can't let them take her," Kat replies.

Before Nasha has a chance to stop her, Kat is up the stairs and racing across the lawn toward Abigail. I head after her.

"Simon, no!" Nasha shouts after me.

But I have no choice but to follow. Kat doesn't really need my protection. There just won't be any point in living if she gets shot.

We find Abigail immobilized inside the chopper, and Kat immediately begins loosening the restraints. There's no telling where Wayne's men have gone, but they'll probably be back soon.

"Stop!" Abigail insists. "If you free me, they'll know you're here. They'll search until they find you."

"Why are they taking you?" I ask her. "What do they want?"

Abigail clutches my forearm, her fingers digging into my flesh. Without makeup, she looks like a ghost. "It doesn't matter. You have to hide. Let them have me. Just promise me that you'll save my Max."

The security cameras across the island went out at some point in the night. The monitors in the safe room show nothing but snow. When I open the trapdoor, I can hear waves lapping against the shore. The sun is peeking above the horizon, and the soft purple light of daybreak reveals what at first appears to be a peaceful scene. The birds are calling to one another, and the breeze carries the fragrance of nutmeg. Then I notice a body lying at the foot of one of the trees. Another is stretched out across the path that leads to the mountain. Wayne's men killed everyone.

"We have to get off the island." Kat's awake.

That much is obvious. If anyone finds us here, they'll blame this on us too.

SPIES

I have no idea what's going on. You'd think I'd have gotten used to the feeling by now, but it's driving me completely nuts.

Shortly after dawn, a boat appeared off the coast of Abigail Prince's island. It stayed on the horizon, as though its crew wanted to keep a safe distance. Can't say that I blame them. Flies were already gathering on the corpses scattered around the garden. By midday the bodies were going to be ripe and fragrant.

Nasha stood at the shoreline, her posture perfect, a hand shielding her eyes from the sun. Soon I could see an orange raft skipping toward us over the waves. I'm sure my friends were wondering the same thing I was. Someone had come to get us. We had no idea who it was. Nasha did, but she refused to tell us. She said the world would be safer if we didn't know.

When we all loaded onto the dinghy, I found myself sitting across from Busara. Never once during the trip did she glance at me. She was gripping Elvis's hand so tightly that the tips of his fingers had lost all color. Her eyes were glued to Nasha as if she were waiting for someone to rip off a mask. I don't think she's taking her mother's transformation well.

We're about halfway across the water now, and the boat is coming into full view. It's bigger than I realized, at least a hundred feet from bow to stern. Slate gray and unmarked, it appears to be some sort of military research vessel. There are two massive deck cranes, and a bridge atop the ship's superstructure that has three-hundred-and-sixty-degree views. There's no crew in sight. The boat silently bobs up and down on the waves like a modern-day *Marie Celeste*.

Nasha is sitting beside the man who's captaining our raft. The only thing remarkable about him is how unremarkable he is. When I close my eyes and try to picture him in my head, all I get is a broad nose and sandy blond hair. His navy-blue shirt and pants have no recognizable style. I don't have a clue what nationality he is. I haven't once heard his voice.

I think we may have made a huge mistake hitching this particular ride. I look over at Kat, and I can see it in her eyes. She thinks so, too. It's been obvious for quite a while that Nasha Ogubu is not who we thought she was. We know nothing about her. But whoever owns this boat must know exactly who *we* are.

Once our raft has been lined up alongside the ship, someone above tosses a rope ladder down to us. Nasha grabs the closest rung and begins to climb. The rest of us refuse to budge.

Our blandly boyish captain offers a hand to Busara. She won't take it.

"Why are you waiting?" Her mother has paused to peer back down at us.

"I'm not getting off the boat unless you tell us who you are," Busara said firmly.

Nasha huffs with frustration. "For God's sake, Busara, I'm your *mother*," she says. "You honestly think I would put you in danger?" The four of us remain seated. I am perfectly happy to keep Busara company on the raft. Nasha must sense that no one's going to take that for an answer. "Who I was before I became your mother is an altogether different story," she adds.

"Will you tell us who you were back then?" Kat asks.

"I'll tell you what I can," Nasha promises.

Nasha and James Ogubu have the ultimate meet-cute story. It's a real shame no one else will ever get to hear it. He was a brilliant engineer. She was a spy sent by her employer to learn everything she could about him. Nasha won't tell us who that employer was. A reasonable guess would be the CIA. The Kremlin would be equally reasonable. But I wouldn't rule out industrial espionage, either. Every tech company in the world plants spies in their competitors' operations.

Of course, just as you'd expect, the engineer and the spy fell madly in love. Which apparently didn't prevent Nasha from continuing to report back to her employer. She retired from the espionage game when their daughter was born with a heart defect. After that, Nasha spent seventeen years taking care of her family—only to be pulled back into service the day Wayne Gibson showed up at the Company.

Everyone in the spy business knows Wayne, it seems. For years, he ran US Cyber Command—a fact that came as a surprise to all of us, including his stepdaughter. His mission was to protect the United States from cyber terrorism. When he took the job, he probably expected the bad guys to be hackers from hostile nations. Over time, he came to believe that the biggest threat to America came from the inside.

No one in government seemed to be paying attention to what our own tech companies were creating. The CEOs all claimed they were inventing things that would change the world. They never mentioned that their innovations might just as easily destroy it. The leaders of the tech world didn't give a damn what would happen if a person's voice could be copied or their appearance digitally duplicated. The only thing that mattered was boosting their stock price.

Then came an incident that sent Wayne sailing right over the edge: an engineer from an American biotech corporation disappeared mysteriously. For a while, it was feared she'd been kidnapped by a hostile rogue nation. The woman had been the genius behind an artificial parasite designed to settle inside the human brain and allow its host to be controlled remotely. It was just an experiment, the company said. The parasite had never been tested on humans. No one knew if it would actually work. It had taken over a week for the engineer's employer to report her missing. Turned out the woman had run off on a spirit quest to India. But the incident was enough to scare Wayne Gibson into action.

Unable to get the government to act, Wayne went public. He spoke to the biggest news organizations in the country, accusing the tech companies of endangering the United States of America. Then one day he stopped talking. Milo Yolkin offered him a position leading security at the Company—and to everyone's surprise, Wayne took it. Some thought he'd been lured by big money. Others thought Milo had offered him a chance to reform the tech industry. Nasha wasn't buying either explanation.

"I knew what my husband had invented, and I knew what the Company could do. They were able to create new worlds. Download memories. Imprison people's minds in virtual prisons. I also knew Milo Yolkin was unhinged. He'd clearly become addicted to Otherworld. The Company had turned into a giant security risk. At the time, I thought there were only two reasons Wayne Gibson would join. He was planning to either blow the whistle on the Company—or take it down."

"But he didn't do either," Busara says.

We're all huddled together around a table in the crew's cramped dining area. I've been scanning my surroundings, looking for anything that might identify the ship's owner. There's nothing. No logos, no emblems, no writing of any kind. Even the crew themselves don't offer any clues. They work silently. Whenever Nasha makes a move, they instantly dart away, like a school of fish avoiding a shark.

"No," Nasha responds. "In fact, Wayne appears to be doing everything he can to save the Company. We don't understand why he's acting the way he is."

"Face it. Wayne Gibson has gone over to the dark side," I say. "He's murdered dozens of people. He forced hospital patients to beta test Otherworld disks. There are at least five men in New York who've either died or killed another person while testing OtherEarth. Wayne told me progress was worth the sacrifice."

"And I'm sure he meant it," Nasha says. "Wayne's a career military man. He's been trained to believe in sacrificing lives for the common good."

The way she says it leads me to think she might believe it too. I suddenly suspect she'd gladly sacrifice me for the common good.

"Soldiers know they're putting their lives on the line," I say. "Wayne's been sacrificing civilians. A lot of them have been kids."

"Yes, he appears to be willing to accept a great deal of collateral damage," Nasha agrees bluntly. "That's one reason we're extremely interested in finding out what Wayne's up to. We're hoping you'll be willing to help. We need you to talk to Max Prince."

She stops, as if waiting for an answer. The four of us share a long look. No one appears terribly convinced. Finally, Busara clears her throat.

"Who do you work for?" she demands, her voice cracking.

Nasha shakes her head. "I can't tell you that, sugar."

"Then why should we trust you?" Kat asks.

"We risked exposing our operation to rescue you and Simon from the Company," Nasha says. "I'm sure you realize they would have killed you."

"Abigail Prince paid people to rescue us," I argue. "What did you and your employer have to do with it?"

"Abigail didn't know it, but she hired *us*," Nasha says. "We've been overseeing this entire operation. We were the ones who put you in touch with Abigail in the first place."

"No, you didn't." I know that much for certain. "A friend of my mother's gave us the number."

Nasha raises her eyebrows as if it's hard to believe I could be so naive. "And you didn't find it at all odd that a lawyer was able to track you down and deliver the message within half an hour of your call?"

I think I'll just shut up now. I'm obviously way out of my league.

"I don't understand," Elvis says. "Why do you need our help? If you're convinced Max Prince knows something, why don't you go speak to him yourselves?"

"We have," Nasha says. "He refuses to say a word."

"Why did you think he would?" Busara asks bitterly. "He doesn't have any more reason to trust you than we do."

Sighing, Nasha reaches under her seat and pulls out a thin laptop. "You need more proof of our goodwill." She cracks open the computer and types in a password. Then she turns the screen to face us. A different video is playing in each quadrant.

"What the hell!" Elvis cries, pointing at the upper right quadrant. There's a man on the screen. He's cooking what appears to be an omelet, wearing a frilly apron—and nothing else.

"Friend of yours?" I snicker.

"That's my dad!" Elvis shouts, just as his father turns his back to the camera, revealing a pair of hairy butt cheeks. "Oh my God! Turn that off before my mom comes in!"

Nasha reaches over and clicks off the feed. It's nice to know there are limits to Elvis's deranged sense of humor.

"What are you doing to my parents?" he demands. Then Busara grips his arm and puts a finger to her lips. Three videos are still playing on the screen. My eyes have landed on a small, pretty woman with dyed-red hair that's gray at the roots. She's sitting on a sofa with her feet tucked beneath her. There's a book in her lap and a cup of coffee in her hand. Behind her is a large picture window that offers a view of a vast green forest with mountains in the distance. I can see a few goats milling about nearby.

Kat leans forward, her face inches from the screen. When she turns back around, I can't tell if she's relieved or terrified. Probably both. "That's my mom, but where is she?" Kat asks. "Wayne told me he'd had her committed to a mental institution."

"He was lying," Nasha said. "We've been taking care of your mother since you were in the coma. She's in a safe house in Eastern Europe."

"Eastern Europe?" Kat repeats. "Would you mind being a *little* more specific?"

"I'm afraid it would be unwise to disclose the exact location. If you were to fall back into Company hands, Wayne could extract that information and use it against you."

Kat's lips stay sealed. She's not going to argue. But she isn't satisfied with the answer. She grabs the computer as if determined to figure it out for herself. But the moment her eyes drop to the screen, they dart away from the feed coming from Europe. Kat taps the lower left quadrant of the screen. "Simon! Look! It's your dad."

"Do I have to?" I ask.

"And your mom!" she says, pointing to the next video.

This time I lean in. The moment I see her, I'm convinced the image is fake. I've known Irene Eaton for eighteen years, and I've seen her in jeans maybe two or three times. Yet the woman I'm supposed to believe is my mother is walking across an apartment I don't recognize wearing ripped jeans, boots and a black T-shirt. She doesn't even look like the same person.

"Nice try," I say. "You got the hair right, but that's not my mom."

"It is," Nasha says. "Your mother's life has changed a great deal since you last saw her. She doesn't have much need for her old wardrobe these days."

Okay, *that* makes me nervous. I'm pretty sure my mother owned at least one Chanel suit that she loved like a second child. "Why not?"

"She resigned from her law firm. And she no longer lives with your father. She's devoted her life to helping you."

"Me? She doesn't even know where I am."

"She has an idea," Nasha says. "We've let her know you're in good hands. She's aware that we're keeping an eye on you. I'm sure she suspects we're keeping an eye on her as well."

I sit back and study Nasha. Despite her black spy gear, she's as pretty and poised as a TV mom. She's even wearing little diamond studs in her ears. Never in a million years would I have expected any of this from her. I suppose it's served her well throughout her career. The best spies are always the ones no one ever suspects.

"So you and your employer are spying on all of our parents," Kat says. I can hear the suspicion in her voice.

"To keep them safe," Nasha assures us.

That's the innocent explanation. I can think of a few others.

"And to let us know you can get to them whenever you like," Kat adds.

"We aren't trying to threaten you," Nasha says. "We won't interfere with your parents' lives unless the Company makes a move against them."

"What if we decide we don't want to give you any information?"

Busara demands. "Will your employer hurt their mothers and fathers?"

"Of course not," Nasha replies. "But we may choose to reallocate the resources that are currently devoted to their protection."

"You're saying you'll leave our parents in danger," I translate.

"We are not the ones who endangered your parents. It is not our duty to protect them. We are helping them in the hopes that you will return the favor and help us."

The only sound in the room is that of the ship's engines. Everything seems even more complicated than it did on Abigail's island. I catch Kat's eye and she gives me a nod. She's in. Elvis nods as well. Busara isn't looking at any of us. She's glaring at her mother.

"Did Dad know who you really are?" she asks. "Did he know who you work for?"

Nasha's expression doesn't change. Her face remains a mask. But something flickers in her eyes. "Yes," she says.

"That's why you won't go see him in Otherworld, isn't it?" Busara asks. "He must feel as betrayed as I do right now."

"Did he say that?" Nasha waits for her daughter's response, but Busara stays silent. "I didn't think so." Nasha stands up and peers down at the four of us. "I'm going to give you some time to consider our offer. I'll be back in an hour."

She leaves the tablet lying on the table, the videos of our parents still playing on its screen.

TOUCHSTONE

Elvis and Kat are hunched over the tablet, trying to figure out where Kat's mother might be hidden. Elvis says the goats look Romanian.

"See how well groomed they are?" he asks, tapping the screen with a finger. "Romanians *really* love their goats."

Busara shows no interest in the videos. Why would she? Her parents are both accounted for. But something is clearly wrong with her. She's staring at the wall with a blank expression. I don't think she's moved an inch since her mother left.

"What are you thinking about?" I reluctantly drop down beside her. I'm *really* not the right person for this operation, but it looks like no one else is going to volunteer.

Busara sits with her hands in her lap, her eyes still on the wall. "I'm thinking that I never knew my mother," she says.

The grief in her voice takes me by surprise. The way she says it, you'd assume that her mother was dead. I have a hunch that pointing out that Nasha Ogubu is alive, well and probably eavesdropping on our conversation won't do much good. So I wisely opt to keep my mouth firmly shut.

"I was nine when my parents found out I was sick," she continues. "My father immediately disappeared into his lab. I knew he was searching for some way to help me, and I thought he was a hero. But my mother was the one who really saved me. That whole time, she barely left my side. She would sit on the side of my bed and tell me about all the things that happened to her when she was growing up in Africa. A snake crawled into her bed one night and she tossed it right out the window. Another time she outwitted a band of poachers who were stalking the local elephants. I thought she was exaggerating, but I loved all her stories. The lesson was always the same. She told me she never gave in to fear because she knew she was bound for big things. She told me I shouldn't be scared because I was too."

"She was right," I tell Busara.

"She was full of it. The mother I loved never really existed," she says. "She's probably not even from Africa. I'm sure all the stories were bullshit."

"Maybe. But the person sitting on the side of your bed was real," I point out.

Busara finally turns to face me. "The person sitting on the side of my bed was there to spy on my father. The loving-mother part was just a disguise."

"Remember what Elvis said about disguises?" I ask. "He said there are things about each of us that we aren't able to hide. He was right. And those are the parts of us that are the most real. Think about it. You couldn't hide that you'd fallen for Elvis." I pause just long enough to hear the punch line of what I can only assume was a dirty goat joke. "Even though I'm still having a hard time believing it."

"He tries to be funny because he wants people to like him and he worries his intelligence will set him apart," Busara says. "But Elvis is a genius."

"Oh, I know. And for the record, he says the same thing about you. He saw it even when you were doing your best to act like a robot. That's the other thing you can't hide, Busara. You are bound for greatness. Your mother figured it out before you were ten years old. It doesn't matter if none of those things really happened. The lesson of all her stories was true."

"The lesson was that I'd grow up to be like her," Busara says softly. She's watching Elvis on the other side of the room. There's real fear in her eyes. "Simon, what if I *have*?"

"Then you are exactly who you're supposed to be."

The way Busara raises her eyebrow when she turns to me, there's no doubt she is her mother's daughter. "Who are you?" she asks. "And what have you done with Simon?"

"Believe me, I'm as surprised as you are," I tell her. "But this is a subject I happen to know something about. Do you know what this is?" I tap my giant nose.

"Your bizarre claim to fame?"

"It's the thing I can't hide. Until I was twelve, I had no idea where it came from. I didn't look like anyone in my family. It made me a mark for every bully in school. Then one day I found a picture of a man who looked just like me. He'd been a gangster in Brooklyn. They called him the Kishka because of his nose."

"Your grandfather," Busara says.

"Yeah, and that was the moment everything started to make sense. Before that I'd been a weird-looking kid who lived in a fake château in Brockenhurst, New Jersey. But that wasn't who I really was. I was the heir to the Kishka."

"And this is something you're proud of?" Busara grins. "That your grandfather was a criminal?"

I shrug. "So they say. He died a long time before I was born. Kat once told me that meant I could imagine him however I wanted. I guess to me he's a reminder of who I really am."

"The One?" Busara laughs out loud at her own joke.

"Yeah, yeah, not funny," I grumble, though I'm glad she's recovered her sense of humor.

"Sorry," she says, biting her lip to keep from laughing again. "This is some pretty profound stuff you're spouting. If you don't watch it, you're going to make me a believer too."

"Yeah, whatever. But do you get what I'm trying to say? Your mother already showed you who she really is. She sat on the side of your bed and told you stories that saved your life. That's the kind of love that can't be faked."

Busara crosses her arms and slumps back against the cushions. "I'm still mad," she huffs.

"You deserve to be," I tell her.

"I don't trust her."

"I don't either."

"So why are you giving me this little pep talk?" Busara asks.

"Because I don't think your mother would ever do anything to harm you. Everything else about her may be fake, but I know her love for you is real. And that's the one thing that makes me feel okay about all of this."

"We don't even know who she works for and you want to help her."

Want isn't the right word. I don't want to know people like Nasha. I want a normal life with Kat. I want to go to college and eat Hot Pockets and not have to worry about the fate of the human race.

"I don't think we have much of a choice," I say.

THE STEPFATHER

When Nasha returns, she's changed into a gray sweat suit that looks like something they'd hand out at the FBI Academy. Busara scowls at the sight. I think the outfit's more proof that this isn't the mother she knew. She doesn't say a word, but she's on full alert. If Nasha makes one wrong move, Busara's likely to bail.

A man enters the room behind Nasha, a tall pile of gray sweat suits in his arms. He deposits them on the table and then leaves, closing the door behind him.

"Thought you might appreciate a change of clothing," Nasha says. "There are showers as well, if you'd like to use them."

After spending the night in an underground bunker, I would kill for a shower. Maybe that's what Nasha has in mind.

"Have you had enough time to think things through? Are you all on board?"

I've been given the honor of speaking for the team. "Yes," I tell her.

"You too?" Nasha looks down at her daughter, who offers a curt nod.

"But this arrangement isn't going to be one-sided," I add. "You get us in to Rikers to see Max Prince, and we'll let you know what he says. But first you need to tell us everything you can about the situation."

"Fair enough." Nasha sits down. I wasn't expecting it to be quite so easy. "Shall we talk about why Max murdered his stepfather?"

No one who visits Otherworld believes that it's Earth. Even the comatose patients the Company kidnapped knew they'd been transported somewhere else. At least one of them was convinced Otherworld was heaven. A lot more of them probably thought it was hell. But they knew there was no way they were on their home planet. Even when you can smell, taste and touch Otherworld— even when it can kill you—it's hard to believe that any of it is real.

OtherEarth is a different story. It's the world you see all around you—just wrapped in a different skin. With the glasses on, it's hard to know where the game ends and the world begins. But Max Prince wasn't just playing OtherEarth with glasses. He had a disk that not only taps into all five senses, it allows you to customize your experience. You can decide what—or who—you want to see.

The first time I tried OtherEarth, I conjured the actress Judi Dench. I could smell her perfume. I could have reached out and touched her. With an OtherEarth disk and glasses, Dame Judi

Dench's clone seemed one hundred percent real. That's the draw, of course. That's also exactly what makes the game so deadly.

Nasha Ogubu says the organization she works for has identified seven men who've either died or gotten themselves into serious trouble while playing OtherEarth. Alexei Semenov gave me the names of five of them.

The first man to expire while playing OtherEarth died of a heart attack in a bathroom stall in Manhattan's Bryant Park. He wasn't physically prepared for what he'd asked the game to generate. His family threatened to sue the Company—until they were shown a video of the custom experience he'd chosen. Whatever it was must have blown their minds. The man was buried without a funeral. All talk of lawsuits ended immediately.

A famous Hollywood director named Grant Farmer almost became the first man to kill. Nasha says he became obsessed with his latest star. When the woman rejected his advances, good ole Grant decided to replicate her in OtherEarth. Apparently, the game did such a fabulous job that he couldn't tell the two apart. Then one day, the flesh-and-blood actress somehow got mixed up with her digital clone. When the director went to kiss her, the actress shoved him away. Grant Farmer flew into a rage and viciously attacked the woman. If not for the martial arts she'd learned for a movie role, it's unlikely she would have survived.

Other women weren't quite as lucky. Two were killed when they were confused with their OtherEarth doubles. Their murderers found themselves in Grant Farmer's shoes. They thought OtherEarth was just a game. They never suspected there would be any consequences. Now they had taken lives, and they couldn't explain why without revealing their darkest fantasies to the world. The Company had the videos.

Which brings us to Max Prince. Max wasn't looking for love in OtherEarth. That he could get in real life with a single click. Max wanted an altogether different experience. He had Other-Earth replicate his stepfather.

Every American under age twenty knows exactly how much Max Prince hated his mother's second husband. He talked about it nonstop in his videos. Abigail Prince married Christian Guido shortly after Max turned eleven years old. The three lived together for five years until Max made his own fortune and escaped the family home. According to Max, every day of those five years was hell. The former soccer star delighted in torturing his stepson, mentally and physically. He belittled Max for his baby fat and forced him to work out for hours every day. Max accused his stepfather of trying to kill him. With her son out of the way, Christian Guido would inherit Abigail's fortune.

Nasha believes OtherEarth gave Max the opportunity to finally have his revenge. He'd put on the disk and slip on the glasses. Christian would appear in the room, and Max would murder him. Over and over and over again. Then one day, Max took off his glasses and disk and the corpse on his floor was still there. He'd murdered his mother's flesh-and-blood husband. It wasn't an accident. There was no way Max's stepfather could have shown up in the wrong place at the worst time—unless the Company had sent him.

"You're sure it wasn't an accident?" Kat asks. "The disks are full of bugs. They've killed dozens of people."

"No," Nasha says. "It's not a bug. This is all part of the Company's plan. The people you've heard about on the news are people the Company wanted out of the way for some reason. The ones you haven't heard about are the people it wants to use."

"Use how?"

"We don't know," Nasha admits. "In fact, we don't even know how many there are. We've only identified two of them. One is the vice president of the United States."

"What?" I'm pretty sure I must have heard wrong.

"An agent of ours was working undercover as an aide in the VP's office. One evening he received a text asking him to deliver documents to the vice president's home. We saw him go in the home. He never came out. In the morning, a cleaning crew arrived at the vice president's residence."

"You seriously think the vice president of the United States murdered someone in his own house?" Kat asks.

"We had an asset embedded in the cleaning crew," Nasha replies. "The vice president had dropped his OtherEarth glasses by the body."

"So the Company arranged the murder—and then they cleaned it up?" Busara asks. It's the first time I've heard her voice since her mother came back into the room.

"Yes," Nasha says. "And now they own the vice president of the United States."

A FACE IN THE CROWD

The Company no longer has any use for Max Prince. If they did, they'd have cleaned up his crime scene too. They set him up because they want him out of the way. But even Nasha's employer isn't sure *why*. Like Abigail, they think he may know something he shouldn't. One of the Company engineers he'd befriended was among OtherEarth's earliest victims. The engineer's death and Max's strange crime had to be somehow related.

Nasha's employer is happy to let Abigail's original plan move forward. They'll sponsor our visit to Rikers Island—as long as we share what we learn and accept their technical support.

"We have a lot riding on this mission," Nasha tells us. "In order for it to be a success, you'll have to get past a lot of cameras."

"We know. We've got that covered," her daughter brusquely informs her. Busara nudges Elvis, and he reaches into his knapsack and retrieves the hat he designed to fool facial-recognition software.

Nasha takes the hat from Elvis and turns it over to examine the underside brim. "Cute," she says, and Elvis beams. "But it's not going to work."

"Why not?" Elvis's face blushes bright red. I doubt anyone has ever questioned his genius before.

"You didn't do your homework. Max Prince is being held on Rikers Island. Visitors at Rikers can't wear hats." Nasha flips the hat right-side up and points at the slogan on the front. "And this little joke makes your invention useless everywhere else. Is this the sort of juvenile humor you find amusing?"

Elvis gapes at his girlfriend's mother. For the first time since I've known him, he seems to be at a loss for words. I see him glance over at Busara, who doesn't look back. She's busy staring a hole into her mother's forehead.

Suddenly Nasha's face breaks into a wide smile as she laughs out loud. "Damn, kid, don't look so petrified. I'm only pulling your leg. Your work's brilliant. I know people who are going to wet themselves when they see this. But when you go undercover, you need to blend in and be invisible. The last thing you want to be wearing is something that's gonna make people point and laugh."

It's hard to argue with that logic. I feel the tension begin to ease. Elvis even manages a weak smile.

But there's still one angry person in the room. "So what do you suggest, then?" Busara demands.

"We have professionals waiting in New York. We'll disguise Simon's identity and he'll visit Max Prince on his own."

I'm still not quite sure I heard correctly when Kat jumps in.

"Simon?" Kat says. "Why does it have to be Simon? And why

does he have to go alone? We all work together. We don't make one person take all the risks."

"I understand, but the four of you can't just show up at Rikers and expect to be welcomed inside. We've managed to arrange a visit between Max Prince and his only known relative. Any other guests would appear suspicious. Max's uncle Arnold has been taken to a secure location so there's no chance he'll be spotted in two places at once."

Taken to a secure location. Is that the same thing as kidnapped?

"Why can't I go?" Elvis demands. "I'm a dude, too."

"You're a five-foot-ten *dude* with a Ukrainian accent," Nasha points out. "Uncle Arnold is a six-foot-three American."

Just like me.

"And this?" I ask, pointing to my schnoz. "You really think you can do something to hide this?"

"We aren't going to hide it. If anything, we'll need to make it a little bit bigger," Nasha says. She taps a few words into the computer on her lap. The screen lights up again and she turns it around. "This is Uncle Arnold."

I hear Kat catch her breath. She sees it too.

"Oh my God," Elvis snorts. "I really thought you were kidding."

"That guy's too old to be Abigail Prince's brother," Busara huffs.

"You're right. He's her uncle. Technically he's Max's great-uncle."

I'm looking at a man in his mid to late seventies. He's wearing a slick modern suit and has his hair combed in a crisp part. Other than that, he's a dead ringer for the Kishka. I can feel the blood draining from my face. "Is this some kind of joke?"

Nasha's brow crinkles as she studies my face. If it is a joke, she doesn't seem to be in on it. "Is something wrong with you, Simon?"

"No," I say, trying my best to appear calm. "He just looks like me as an old man. What did you say his last name was?"

"I didn't," Nasha replies. "His name is Arnold Dalton."

I definitely wasn't expecting some fancy British-sounding last name.

"Was his last name always Dalton?"

The question piques Nasha's interest. "I don't know. Why do you ask?"

"I guess he doesn't look like a Dalton to me." Holy. Shit. I don't dare turn my head toward Kat. If Nasha's employer hasn't figured it out, I'm not going to clue them in. The man I'm staring at looks like a Diamond.

We've been belowdeck for so long that I've lost track of time. I assume it's night when we're told to get some rest and the four of us are escorted to separate cabins. Kat protests, but her complaints fall on deaf ears. Either Nasha's employer is deeply religious or they don't want us talking among ourselves.

My cabin isn't much larger than one of the capsules the Company used to store bodies. There's a metal bunk bed with a small desk beneath. The ceiling is too low for a human my size, and when I lie down, my feet dangle off the end of the bed. I close my eyes, but my mind won't turn off. I haven't slept without Kat since we were rescued. I think my sanity might rely on her.

"That Prince kid sure has a handsome uncle."

When my eyes open the room is filled with smoke. I lean over the side of the bunk and find the Kishka sitting below, his wingtips propped up on the desk.

"Who is he?" I ask. "Your brother? Your cousin?"

"Oh come on, he's better looking than *that*," the Kishka scoffs.

"Stop kidding around!" I order. "Something really fucking weird is going on. Is any of this real? Are we in another simulation?"

The Kishka takes a draw on his cigarette. The room is already so hazy that when he exhales I can barely see his face.

"I don't know," he admits. "Does it matter?"

"Of course it matters! There are too many coincidences. Someone made all of this up. I'm living someone else's bad plot."

"Isn't that what fate is?" the Kishka asks. "A story that's already been written? Someone else's bad plot?"

That stops me. "What are you trying to say?" I demand.

"Nothing you don't already know somewhere deep down inside," my grandfather responds, exhaling another cloud of smoke. By the time it begins to clear, he's gone.

The boat arrives in Key West shortly after one in the morning. We're met at the dock by a black SUV and driven to the airport, where we're whisked away on a small private jet. As with the boat, there's nothing to indicate who the plane's owner might be. Nothing has a name on it—not even the box of tissue in the bathroom or the bottles of water that are handed around.

A few hours later, not long before dawn, we touch down at

Teterboro Airport in northern New Jersey. Aside from Nasha, no one has spoken to us throughout the journey. In fact, everyone we've encountered has avoided meeting our eyes. I'm almost enjoying the anonymity when it occurs to me—it might be a long time before I'll be able to show my face in public again.

The sun's rising when we pull up in front of a nondescript building in a part of town I assume is Queens. Along the way we passed bus stops where people were already lined up for the ride to work. Their shoulders were hunched, and you could see the exhaustion on their faces. There's a million-dollar bounty on my head. If someone ends up claiming it, I hope it's someone like them.

Nasha guides us up two flights of stairs to a plain beige door. It opens to reveal a spacious apartment. Everything inside it looks brand-new—from the tasteful pillows on the massive sofa to the dust-free blinds on the windows. It's like a safe house for exiled royalty. Nasha gives us a quick tour. There are two bedrooms with en suite bathrooms and king-size beds. In a third bedroom, four multidirectional treadmills have been assembled. The refrigerator is stocked with everything we might possibly want to eat.

"What? No beer?" Elvis asks.

"Get some more sleep," Nasha orders. "I'll be back in the afternoon. Simon will be visiting Rikers at six this evening."

"Six?" I blurt out. I thought we'd at least have some time to plan.

"We can't afford to lose another day," Nasha informs me. I wonder who she means by *we*. I'd certainly be fine with twenty-four hours of R&R.

Nasha leaves, closing the door behind her. We hear a click as a lock turns. The four of us stand motionless in the center of the room. A day has passed since we've been alone. There's so much we should be talking about. But there's no doubt at all that these walls have ears.

"So!" Elvis breaks the silence. "Turns out Busara's mom is Black Widow. How awesome is that? Like mother, like daughter."

"Stop it," Busara says coldly.

"You know Black Widow is a good guy, right?" Elvis asks awkwardly. "I mean, she wasn't at first, but then—"

"Stop. Now."

Her words take Elvis by surprise. He looks like he's been slapped in the face. I'm pretty surprised myself. I thought my little talk with Busara had done her a world of good. Guess I overestimated my newfound powers. "Sorry, I was just—" Elvis starts.

"I know what you were trying to do," Busara tells him. "You think you can make the situation better if you turn it into a joke. It's what you always do. Usually I laugh along, but—"

"Busara—"

"But there's nothing funny about my mother," she finishes.

Once again, I find myself being dragged into the emotional muck. "Busara, we talked about this. We agreed that coming here was our best option."

"No, we agreed it's our *only* option," she corrects me. "Don't worry. I'm not second-guessing it. But that doesn't mean I've forgiven my mother—or that I ever will. She lied to me and she betrayed my father. I guess I just can't see the humor in any of that."

Elvis steps toward Busara, his arms reaching out to her, but she shies away.

"I'm tired." She heads toward one of the bedrooms. Elvis is starting to follow her when she stops abruptly at the threshold. "I think I need a little time alone," Busara announces before she shuts the door.

The three of us stare at the closed door. "What's going on?" Elvis mutters. "It was a stupid joke, but I was just trying to make her feel better."

I don't really want to look at him. I feel like I've already witnessed something I wasn't meant to see.

"A lot's gone down in the past forty-eight hours," Kat does her best to explain. "It might take Busara a little while to come to terms with it all. She will. You've just got to be patient."

Kat's words of wisdom don't seem to have done much for Elvis. "But aren't I supposed to help her? Wouldn't you two help each other?"

"It's not always that easy," I say. "Everyone gets trapped inside their own head sometimes."

"Why don't you try getting some sleep?" Kat asks.

"Where?" Elvis asks miserably. "I'm not allowed in the bedroom."

"Take ours." I can't believe I'm saying it. In twelve hours I'll be sneaking into a high-security prison to talk to an axe murderer and I'm giving my own bed away. I'm turning into someone I barely recognize.

I'm sitting on a sofa that's beautiful but feels like it's made of rocks. Kat doesn't seem to mind. She's asleep with her legs curled up and her head on my lap. Before she fell asleep, she said Max's uncle Arnold seemed like an interesting character. She knew better than to say any more.

I should be taking this opportunity to rest as well, but I can't. My mind won't turn off. The same thoughts keep cycling through it. Uncle Arnold stars in most of them. There's something weird about all of this. I can feel it.

The television is on with the sound turned low. There are no other electronics in the apartment. As beautiful and luxurious as it may be, the place belongs to another era. They must have searched through every scrap heap in the city to find the television. It gets three channels and the reception is grainy. Sometimes the picture flickers out altogether. But I can see enough to know that Kat and I are the stars of every show. Police are patrolling all the subway stations. Checkpoints have been set up at every bridge and tunnel. There's no way out of the city. That must be why Nasha's employer left the television here for us. They want us to know that we're screwed without them.

The commercial breaks are the strangest part. For thirty seconds at a time, the world returns to normal. Happy kids eat cereal. A man gets rid of his bathtub grime. A senior citizen finds the answer to his chronic constipation. And then New York City appears on the screen. Cop cars race by with sirens blaring. Crime-scene tape blocks off a section of sidewalk outside the building where Scott Winston was gunned down. I'm thinking the news coverage has kicked in again when the camera focuses on a woman standing at the edge of the crowd. She takes a pair of black glasses out of her bag and slides them on. All at once, the world is in black-and-white. The cars are 1940s models and everyone's dressed like they're film noir stars. The woman is now clad in a mobster's pinstriped suit, and she holds a gun in her manicured hand. A pair of old-timey coppers are passing by on the opposite side of the street. One sees her, does a double take and points her out to his partner. As they race through the traffic to reach her, she turns and disappears into the crowd. Then we hear the announcer.

Need an escape?
Experience OtherEarth. Your world—only better.
Available August fifteenth.

I laugh out loud. I gotta hand it to Wayne. It's the ultimate fuck-you. They've taken our manhunt and made it part of the game. Oddly enough, this is exactly what I needed to see right now. Just when I was finding it hard to summon the motivation for the act I'll be playing this evening, Wayne reaches out and gives me all the inspiration I need. I'm going to take that bastard down.

When Nasha returns to the apartment, there's a tiny woman with rhinestone-rimmed glasses and a jet-black bob following her. The lady's wheeling a black suitcase that's large enough for at least one of our bodies, but she doesn't look dangerous. If anything, she seems anxious as hell.

"Lorraine is our makeup artist," Nasha announces.

Lorraine greets us all with a stiff smile, which confirms my hunch—she's a civilian. I watch her eyes widen as they pass over Kat. She must recognize her from all the videos, but she doesn't say a word. Either they're paying the woman extremely well or they have something on her.

Nasha puts a hand on my arm. "This is your subject," she informs the makeup artist.

Lorraine gives me a thorough once-over. "That will need to come off," she says, pointing at the bandage that covers my nose.

When I reach up and pull it off, the woman's eyes widen and she quickly looks away. She knows who I am, too.

Nasha points to one of two chairs in the apartment's dining set. "Sit," she tells me. "The rest of you go hang out somewhere else."

I notice Nasha doesn't acknowledge her daughter. She was listening last night. There's no doubt about it. This family feud is getting ugly.

The makeup artist pulls her bag over to the table where I'm sitting, heaves it up onto the surface before I can offer to help and unzips the case. Inside is the most amazing assortment of putties, paints and hairpieces I've ever seen.

"What happened to you?" the makeup lady says when she finally sees me up close. Her voice is trembling.

"Nose job," I tell her. "Can't you tell?"

The woman brushes her thumb over one of the bruises beneath my eyes. "These are old," she notes. "You've had them a while."

She's smart, this one. She knows the person in the videos wasn't banged up like I am. She knows it wasn't me.

Nasha clears her throat.

"Sorry," Lorraine says. "Just making conversation. Your nose still hurt?"

"Not as much," I tell her.

"Good," the lady says. "'Cause we're gonna have to add some putty, and that will put a bit of weight on it."

"No more chitchat, please," Nasha orders.

Lorraine catches my eye for a moment. Then she gets to work.

Three hours later, there's a knock at the door. Nasha opens it and an arm hands her a black garment bag. When I turn back around, Lorraine is putting her brushes, putty and prosthetic ear hair back into her suitcase.

"I'm done?" I ask her.

She hands me the photo she's been using for reference. "Oh yes, you're done," she says. Then she reaches out and puts her hand gently against my cheek. "Good luck to you."

She knows I'm in deep. Perhaps even deeper than she is.

"Thanks," I tell her. "You too."

When she's gone, I strip down to my underwear. It's time to put on my costume, and I don't see any need to be bashful in front of someone like Nasha. She hands me articles of clothing, one at a time. Each is a work of art. Even the socks must have cost some serious change. But none of them are new, I notice. I suppose that's smart—brand-new clothes might attract attention. But I wonder who broke them all in. When I shove my arms into the shirt, I smell the faint stench of smoke.

"Hey!" Kat calls from the bedroom where she, Busara and Elvis have been waiting. "Can we come out yet?"

I quickly slip on the pants Nasha hands me and zip myself up.

"Yes," Nasha tells them. She steps up to me and threads a tie under my collar. It's a red Hermès tie with little blue diamonds. Then she crafts a perfect double Windsor knot. "Show them," she says when she's finished.

I turn around to a stunned audience. I haven't been near a mirror in hours, but I'm not surprised by their reaction. Lorraine was an artist, and Nasha's employer certainly wouldn't have settled for anything less than the best. But the silence lasts a little too long.

"What?" I ask.

Kat takes a deep breath. "Have you seen yourself yet?" she asks.

"No, why? Is something wrong?" I head straight for the full-length mirror on the back of the bathroom door.

Kat comes after me. "Don't freak out," she whispers in my ear as the mirror comes into view.

I am the Kishka.

PLAY-THROUGH

I am driven to Rikers Island in a Maybach S600 that I'm certain belongs to Max's uncle Arnold. The wallet in my pocket is filled with identification and credit cards that—at least to my untrained eye—don't appear to be fakes. Did Uncle Arnold willingly lend his belongings, I wonder? Or were they stolen? Where the fuck *is* Uncle Arnold? How far is Nasha's employer willing to go for the answers they're after?

I sail past ID check. I ace the frisking. None of the guards gives me a second look. When I get to the visitation room, I'm shown to a cubicle. I can see a reflection in the glass that will separate the visitors from the felons, but the reflection doesn't belong to me. I try to look through it. I do my best to pretend it's not there.

When a kid sits down across from me I almost raise my hand to call the guard over. It's hard to believe this could be the same Max Prince. The guy I'm expecting is a rosy-cheeked cherub who looks like he's been spoon-fed nothing but caviar and pâté de foie gras since birth. But this poor bastard already has one foot in the grave. His face is covered with a nasty rash, clumps of his dull black hair are missing and his body is wasting away. It makes me wonder how bad the food here could be. In Max's emaciated state, his nose dominates the rest of his face. Was it always so big? I wonder.

We sit and stare at each other through the glass, as if daring the other to make the first move.

"Hello, Uncle Arnold," the kid finally says, confirming that I do indeed have the right Max. There's no emotion at all in his voice. He hasn't blinked since he took his seat. "I'm surprised to see you here. You don't usually make public appearances. This must be important."

Clever. The disguise hasn't fooled him. He knows I'm not who I say I am, and this is his way of warning me that he can call my bluff at any moment. If he does, I'll probably be thrown in a cell just like his.

"I'm not here for you," I reply. "I came to see if you've heard from your mother lately."

Max blinks. I think he gets it. I hope like hell he does. "Not for a few days," he says.

"I haven't either," I tell him. "She seems to be missing. I'm trying to find her, and I was hoping you might help me figure out where to look."

The slightly nauseated smile that appears on Max's face can't hide the fact that he's gone sheet white. He knows what I'm trying to tell him—he just doesn't know whether to believe it. "She's probably on an island somewhere, drinking mojitos and ogling the help. She always did have a thing for young studs, as you know."

"Yes well, all the young studs appear to have gone on holiday. I've been calling the island. No one picks up. It's as if the whole island's deserted and no one's there to answer the phone."

That should make things crystal clear if they aren't already.

"Then I'm afraid I can't help you," Max says. "I wish I could offer a clue or two, but it's hard to do much detective work while I'm locked up in here. As I'm sure you know, I'm not allowed to have any devices."

Max is going somewhere with this, I think. He wants me to play along.

"That must be unpleasant for you. Perhaps you'll learn to love reading while you're incarcerated."

"What a funny old man you are." Max isn't laughing. "If you hadn't been born in the Dark Ages, you'd know this shithole was made for Otherworld."

"Otherworld?" I ask as if I've never heard of it, but my heart is pounding inside my chest. We're getting somewhere now.

"Jesus, Uncle Arnold, didn't you ever watch any of my videos?" Max rolls his eyes. "It's a virtual reality game. You put on the headset and you're in a different world. I used to hang out in a place called Albion. You should visit sometime. There's an old bastard there who reminds me of you. Fortunately they don't let *him* leave his cave."

That's the clue I've been waiting for. I'm sure of it. It's time to bail before either of us accidentally says too much.

"Charming," I say, scooting the chair back and rising from my seat. "I see prison hasn't changed you, Maximilian."

Max stands too and leans forward until his forehead is pressed against the window. "Get the hell out of here," he snarls. "And don't come back here again or I'll make what I did to Mama's boy toy look like a fucking paper cut." Then he drops the receiver and leaves it dangling from its cord as he walks away.

The rage is a nice touch. Max is a smart kid. He doesn't want anyone who might be watching to think we're too friendly. Otherwise, they might pay more attention to the little chat we just had. If they did, they might realize—as I do—that Max was suggesting a trip to Albion.

Back at the safe house, Nasha and all three of my friends greet me at the door. I walk straight past them to the bathroom. I don't want to look at myself in the mirror. I don't want to see the Kishka. I peel away the mask and wipe the goop from my skin. When I turn around, the others have formed a blockade outside the bathroom.

"Well?" Kat demands.

"We'll have to go to Otherworld," I tell her. "There's something there we need to find."

"What is it?" Busara asks eagerly.

"No idea," I tell her.

"You have no idea?" Nasha repeats, hands on her hips.

I focus on her. "I'm not telling you a damned thing until I know what you guys did with Uncle Arnold."

"Uncle Arnold is fine," Nasha huffs. I wait until she adds, "You have my word. Now what's this about Otherworld?"

"I think Max left something there. If you want us to find it, we're going to need a computer, an Internet connection and a television that gets more than three channels," I say. "Plus all of the stuff we brought from the island—especially the Otherworld headsets. Now if you'll excuse me, I'd like to get the hell out of these clothes."

Kat follows me into the bedroom and sits while I change. "Tell me," she says. She knows there's got to be more to the story.

"While you were in Otherworld, did you ever visit a place called Albion?"

"No, but I've heard of it," she replies. "It's typical kill quest stuff. Knights and giants and that sort of crap. Is that where we're going?"

"I think Max hid a clue in Albion during his last visit to Otherworld. He said something about an old man who lives in a cave."

"Which old man? Which cave? It's gotta be a pretty big place."

"Dunno," I admit. "But Max recorded his adventures in Otherworld. All we have to do is watch the play-through."

"Really?" Kat groans. "So we're in for an evening of Max Prince's farts and dirty jokes?"

"If you think about it, it's not that different from an evening with Elvis," I say.

"Good point," she laughs. "By the way, it's been hell being stuck here with him and Busara all day. They hardly said two words to each other."

"Look, they're a weird couple. They always were. But I'm sure everyone says the same thing about us, too. Girls like you aren't supposed to end up with head cases like me."

I was trying to make her laugh again, but Kat looks worried.

"Are you okay, Simon?" I know what she's asking—what she can't say out loud.

"I think so," I tell her. I'm not going to lie. I don't know for sure. I pull her toward me and bury my face in her hair. "You saw Uncle Arnold. Remember that picture of the Kishka I found when we were kids? Uncle Arnold looks like an older version of my grandfather. What do you suppose it all means?"

"Do you really want to know?" she whispers, and I nod. "I think it means maybe your friend Gorog was right all along."

Gorog started the *One* bullshit. It's exactly the sort of thing you'd hear from a kid who's watched too many dumb movies. I can't believe Kat's starting to buy into it. I don't need to be put under that kind of pressure. If he were here right now, I'd give Gorog a good kick in the ass. Then I think of the last time I saw him. He'd transformed from an Otherworld ogre into a thirteen-year-old boy named Declan Andrews. I gave him a fortune and sent him away with his parents to hide from the Company. I had to do it to keep him safe, but I wish like hell he was here with me.

"Stop it," I tell Kat. "Or you're going to get a cold shoulder just like Elvis."

"Highly unlikely," she replies, giving me a kiss. "You wouldn't last five minutes."

I'm afraid she knows me all too well.

It doesn't take long to locate the play-through of Max's last visit to Albion. It was the final video he ever shared—posted less than two weeks before he slaughtered his stepfather. I scroll through the comments. Everyone's sharing theories about what drove Max to murder. No one knows Max was testing OtherEarth, of course. Most of the commenters seem to be either stoned or stupid. But a few of them manage to get close to the truth. At some point, Max lost touch with reality. He couldn't tell what was real and what wasn't.

It's just the four of us huddled around the computer, but I'm sure Nasha Ogubu and her buddies are watching remotely. It's so obvious that we're under surveillance that none of us bothered to search for mikes or cameras. Elvis and Busara are seated side by side. Every time Elvis shifts his body, Busara adjusts her position to keep at least six inches between them.

I start the video and settle back on the couch next to Kat. The play-through begins with a close-up of Max speaking to the camera. The guy in the video isn't the walking disaster I visited at Rikers Island, but he's hardly the picture of health, either. This Max has the bloodshot eyes and pasty skin of someone who hasn't slept in days. The stubble on his cheeks has turned into a mangy beard.

"Hey there, I'm back!" he says with forced cheer. "I'd like to thank everyone out there for your thoughts, prayers, death threats and booty calls. As you can see, I have *not* fallen off the face of the earth. I've been testing a new game, and let me tell you, this shit's gonna rock your world. I can't say anything about it right now unless I want a bunch of lawyers up my ass. But I don't want to leave you guys bored and restless. You start sending me pics of your junk when I do. So today we're gonna take another trip to the OG of altered-reality games, Otherworld."

The camera pulls back to show Max on a multidirectional treadmill. He's wearing a custom-made full-body haptic suit that must have set him back hundreds of thousands of dollars. It's a little looser than it should be. Max has already shed some serious weight.

"Hold on, I'm gonna stop the video for a sec," Elvis announces as Max begins to put on his Otherworld headset. He reaches over and hits pause. "This video's dated June fourteenth. Let's see when his previous one was uploaded."

Elvis navigates to Max Prince's YouTube page. "Here it is," he says. "The previous video was uploaded on May twenty-first— over three weeks earlier."

He clicks Play. On the screen is the cute, pudgy Max we've all known for years.

"What the hell happened to him between May and June?" Kat wonders out loud.

"OtherEarth happened to him," Elvis says. "Who knows what else."

Elvis switches back to the last video and starts it up once again. Max has slipped on his headset, and the video has become a split screen. On the left is a kid in a black haptic suit. On the right is a bald, buff avatar with a black mustache and a shag carpet sprouting from his chest. We know what he looks like because he's kneeling over a silvery pool of water so we can see his rugged face on-screen. Then the avatar stands up, and his surroundings are revealed. He's in a forest, walking beneath a canopy of gnarled tree branches without any leaves. No sunlight filters down from above, and a thick mist rises from the forest floor. It's everything you'd want a magical, mystical realm to be. It's weird to be watching Otherworld on a screen, with only two of my senses engaged. I find myself yearning to know what Albion smells like.

The avatar's thunderous baritone is now the only voice we hear. He's making his way toward a horse that's tied to a tree in the distance.

"So today we're in Albion, which has got to be one of the lamest realms, if you ask me. It's basically a virtual Renaissance fair, which is the sort of shit that I'd avoid like herpes in real life. But a lot of you dorks have told me you're into this kind of crap, so today we're going to strap on our codpieces, battle a dragon, ogle some maidens and maybe screw a fairy or two."

Max reaches the horse and hoists himself onto its back. From his vantage point, we can see three small beings cowering behind a bush, desperately trying to stay hidden. They're Children—and if I had to guess, I'd say one parent was an Otherworld chipmunk.

"I don't know what those freaks are supposed to be," Max says to his viewers. He clearly finds them a little unnerving. "They aren't really part of the game—and they don't like players. For a while I thought it was fun to kill them, but they're smart—we're talking some seriously impressive AI—and sometimes they fight back. I lost a few lives that way. If you're here to get shit done, I'd say it's best to avoid them."

He takes the horse's reins and guides it down a path through the forest. Max's voice-over continues as the beast jumps over fallen logs and races past ravenous bears the size of compact cars. Even the deer in this forest look dangerous. I wouldn't be surprised if they are.

"Unless this is the first Otherworld video you've watched,

you know each realm is ruled by a godlike creature called an Elemental. Albion's Elemental takes the form of a wise old hermit who lives in a mountaintop cave. He won't let you leave his realm until you've performed three quests. We've only got time for one quest today, but I'm gonna show you how to reach the realm's big boss—and what happens if you approach him before your three quests are complete."

This time, I'm the one who reaches over to hit Pause. "That's the guy Max mentioned at Rikers—the old man who lives in a cave. Whatever clue we need is going to be somewhere near the Elemental. I'll skip ahead to the end of the video."

"Awwww, come on!" Elvis complains. "Don't skip over *all* of it! Can we at least see a few highlights?"

Busara shoots him the side eye. "You've *got* to be kidding."

"Kidding?" Elvis was definitely not kidding. "Have you never watched a Max Prince video before? His shit is *genius*. There's a reason he's famous, you know. He's seriously funny. He can fart the French national anthem."

Kat nudges me with her elbow.

"Fine," I say with a groan, though to be honest, I'm pretty intrigued by that last part. "I'll play a few seconds here and there along the way. But that's all you get."

I click forward to a random spot in the video. Max's avatar is in the bowels of a castle, fighting an onyx dragon. Everything around the combatants is aflame. Max dodges a timber that crashes down from the ceiling and raises his shield just in time to guard against a blast of the beast's fiery breath. The action is pretty thrilling, and the dragon is terrifying, but Max sounds bored as hell.

"Seriously, if you've fought one dragon you've fought them all. You just gotta look for the weak spot." The beast in front of him rears back on its hind legs, its mouth wide and its wings stretched open. "See what I mean? Look at that patch of unprotected skin just above its junk. It's insulting, really. They didn't even bother to design a real challenge—"

"You can move on," Elvis says, waving his hand in the air like a traffic cop. "Max is right. The Company really phoned it in on that dragon."

I click to another random spot. I don't let three seconds pass before I quickly move on.

"Oh my God!" I hear Busara gasp.

"Were Max and that elf doing what I think they were doing?" Kat sounds completely revolted.

"That was technically a fairy, not an elf," Elvis corrects Kat. "Go back, Simon, so I can show her the difference."

"Are you out of your mind?" I demand. I've had enough. I point at the screen where Max's avatar is now approaching the base of a rocky cliff. "Look—Max just found the Elemental's cave. I'm not going to rewind so you can perv out."

"Perv out?" Elvis repeats indignantly. "Who do you think you are, the pope? I was merely going to point out a few key anatomical differences between elves and fairies. It was meant to be *educational.*"

I ignore him. The video continues, and Max's avatar climbs the steep cliff face. There's an opening far above, not far from the top. We watch in silence as the avatar pulls itself inside. There's not much room to maneuver. The ceiling is so low that Max's avatar is forced to stoop. Against the far wall, a wizened old man sits cross-legged with his eyes closed. Behind him is a small pile of objects—goblets, daggers and golden trinkets—that are covered in a fine layer of dust. Spiders have spun elaborate webs between his body and the walls of the cave. The Elemental of Albion clearly hasn't moved in quite some time. Max's burly avatar sits down across from him. A few seconds pass, and I'm starting to wonder if anything's going to happen when the Elemental's eyes open. They're a pale milky blue with sparks of golden fire that give them the appearance of opals.

"What have you brought for me?" the Elemental inquires in a somber tone.

"This tooth of the Dragon of Castle Le Fay." Max passes an enormous canine to the sage.

The Elemental feels the tooth from top to bottom as if he sees with his fingers instead of his eyes.

"You are the first to complete this dragon quest." He sets the tooth down. "Well done. What else have you brought me?"

"This sacred scroll," Max tells him, handing the sage a rolled sheet of paper.

"Wait, where'd he get that scroll?" Elvis interrupts. "I knew we should have watched the whole video!"

"Shhhh!" Busara orders as she leans in.

The Elemental of Albion unrolls the scroll and passes his fingers over the words written on it. Then he rolls the paper back up again. "This is worthless." He sends the scroll sailing over his shoulder, where it lands atop the pile of junk. "What else do you have?"

I hit Pause. "That's what we need. The clue is on the scroll."

"How can you be sure?" Busara asks.

"Max brought it to the Elemental because he knew the scroll would be safe in his cave," I say.

"Safe?" Kat asks. "What's to keep someone from climbing up there and taking it?"

"I think we're about to find out," Elvis answers. He reaches over and hits Play, and Max's avatar comes back to life.

"I have nothing else to offer you," Max tells the Elemental.

"You came to me without completing three quests?" the Elemental asks.

"Yup," Max admits. "What are you gonna do about it?"

The Elemental's jaw unhinges and his mouth opens wider than any mouth ever should. His entire face disappears, and all that's left is pure darkness—a black hole of rage. Even watching it on YouTube, I shiver as I feel my blood thicken and cool. The noise that emerges from the Elemental's mouth is unlike anything on Earth. The four of us instinctively clutch our ears, but there's no way to filter out the inhuman shriek.

The force of the Elemental's voice sends Max's avatar sailing backward, out the entrance of the cave. We hear the crunch of bones as he hits the cliff wall several times, and the thud as he lands on the ground below. I'm surprised to see the screen go dark and Max's avatar appear at setup. The plunge from the cliff should have counted as a single death—but instead it's taken all three of Max's lives.

The split screen disappears and real-life Max takes over full screen. When he pulls off his Otherworld helmet, his hair is sopping wet with sweat and his skin is the color of raw squid. It looks like the exertion came close to killing him.

"So there you go, guys." He's making an effort not to pant, but his body's not cooperating. His hand is clutching the railing of his multidirectional treadmill as though to keep him from falling. "If you're the kind of dork who likes a good joust, Albion may be the realm for you. But take it from me, don't fuck with the Elemental."

The video ends abruptly, and the four of us continue to stare at the screen.

"So," says Busara. "If we want Max's little clue, we'll have to complete three whole quests and then ask the Elemental if we can root around in his discard pile?"

"If it's really a clue Max wanted someone to find, why didn't he leave it someplace a bit more accessible?" Kat wonders. "Who the hell did he think was going to be able to get to it?"

"I dunno. Maybe he had someone *special* in mind," Elvis says coyly.

"Don't," I warn him.

"You mean like *the One*?" Busara teases. Whatever is going on between her and Elvis, it hasn't prevented them from ganging up on me.

All three of them are suddenly looking at me. "Stop it!" I order. "This shit isn't funny anymore."

ALBION

Kat insisted we all get a full night's sleep. After we scarf down some breakfast, we hop on the treadmills. I'm the first one back in Otherworld. James Ogubu is sitting right where we left him—in the same spot on the same couch, in the same pair of dad jeans and slip-on shoes he's been wearing since he got here. He says hello, but I don't reply. I'm struck dumb by what's happening outside in the White City.

The sky is thick with smog, and buildings have risen like a forest around us. The city's driverless cars are now airborne. They zip past the surrounding apartment buildings, where every room I can see is filled with Children, all lounging on the floor with black masks over their eyes.

"How long has it been since our last visit?" I hear Kat ask.

"Almost fifty years," Ogubu says as he stares out the window. "I've tried to warn them. I told them what technology has done to our world. Some of them have listened. Most have chosen to move on regardless."

"Dad." Busara's avatar suddenly springs to life. "Did you know—" She stops. "Oh my God. What the hell is going on out there?"

"The Children have evolved," I say.

"No," James corrects me. "Their technology has advanced—well past our own, as a matter of fact. The Children, however, have remained the same."

Busara joins me at the window. "The masks some of the Children are wearing—they're virtual reality?"

"Something akin to it," her father says.

"That's not good," Busara mumbles.

I suddenly feel Kat's hand on my shoulder. "We need to go," she tells me. "It's going to take us a while to reach Albion."

"Albion?" James Ogubu says. "Are you certain that's where you want to go?"

"Oh, believe me, I don't *want* to go there, but we don't have much choice. Kat's right. We need to start walking."

"You can't walk to Albion," Ogubu tells us. "You must hire a guide to take you."

"I think we'll be okay," I assure him. The truth is I'm eager to be alone with Kat. Our walks on the island seem like a long time ago. "We're wearing headsets, and we're pretty good at taking care of ourselves."

"I don't doubt it," says James. "But I'm afraid it's no longer possible to reach most of the realms by foot."

I don't want to ask the question, so I'm relieved when Kat chimes in. "Why not?"

"I know only what others have told me. But you two will soon have an opportunity to see for yourselves. There's a Child by the name of Bird in the city. She visits me from time to time. She's one of the few who will listen. I believe she has a business a short distance from here."

"Her name is Bird?" I snicker.

"Many Children these days are named after things that no longer exist."

"There are no birds left in Otherworld?" The first creature I encountered here in the White City was a beautiful bird with iridescent green feathers. It's hard to imagine a world where only machines fill the skies.

"Perhaps you could find a bird in one of the far-distant realms," James says. "The last one I encountered was a corpse on the balcony. I haven't seen a live bird here in decades."

I have a very bad feeling about all of this. All I need is a glance at Kat to know she shares it.

"Let's get a move on," she tells me. "I guess we need to find Bird." I follow her reluctantly.

"Where is Elvis?" I hear James ask his daughter before we make it to the door.

"He wasn't invited," Busara responds. "I need to talk to you alone." She turns to us. "Would you mind?"

"Of course not," Kat says. She opens the door to leave but hesitates before stepping out into the hall. Time has stood still inside James Ogubu's apartment, but the rest of the building hasn't been spared. A thick layer of dirt and grime covers the floors, and strange graffiti has been scrawled on the walls. When we reach the atrium, we see that the glass elevator that once glided between the floors has stopped in the middle. Inside, two mummified corpses are slumped against the wall, their mouths stretched open in silent screams. I shudder to think how long they've been sitting there, waiting for rescuers who'll never arrive.

"How did it get to this point?" Kat asks. "Even if the Children have let everything go, where are the NPCs who used to work here?"

"No idea," I say. Given the fate that's befallen the Children, I'm not sure I want to find out, either.

After a frustrating search, Kat and I find a set of stairs and make our way outside, where it's already as dark as night. Flashing signs paint the city a rainbow of colors. The street itself is hidden beneath trash that's been tossed from the apartment balconies above. I glance up just in time to spot a cascade of garbage raining from a building nearby. After it crashes to the ground, the city is eerily silent once again. I see no signs of life other than two giant rodents wading through the refuse. I'm getting the sense that we're not in the best part of town.

"Look." Kat points to a sign down the street.

OTHERWORLD TOURS, shouts the video billboard. SEE THE REALMS WITH YOUR OWN EYES! A picture of a luxury boat on a bright blue lake appears. The deck is crowded with Children looking over the side at the tentacles of an enormous sea creature that are reaching up from below. VISIT NEMI AND ENCOUNTER THE BEAST! I encountered the beast once. I knew her son. It's tragic that she's become a tourist attraction.

I press the button on the wall and take a step back.

"What?" a feminine voice rudely demands.

I'm not quite sure how to answer. "Hi, my name is Simon and

my friend is Kat. We're looking for Bird. We were told she might be able to take us to Albion."

"Albion?" the voice responds. "No one offers tours of Albion. You can visit cities or vacation realms. The rest of the realms are too dangerous for tourists."

"We aren't looking for a tour. Just a ride."

"To *Albion*?" She can't seem to wrap her mind around it.

I glance over at Kat and she shrugs. "Yes, to Albion."

There's a long pause. "I don't do body disposal or transport illegal substances."

"Excellent. Neither do we," I assure her.

"Just drop-off. No waiting, no pickup."

"Sure," I respond with a sigh. The door pops open in front of us.

Inside, the shop looks abandoned, but there's a Child behind the counter. I don't know if she's aware of it, but she's definitely a descendant of Magna, Milo Yolkin's old avatar. When we first enter, her skin is a pale, silvery blue. The moment she sees us, she flushes a bright, pulsating red. I'm standing twenty feet from her, and I can feel the heat radiating off her body. Something's triggered the reaction—she seems strangely disturbed by our appearance. I don't recognize the device she pulls from under the counter and aims in our direction. But it's safe to assume that it's some kind of weapon.

"What are you?" she demands. "Where did you come from?"

I guess it's been so long since humans visited Otherworld that no one knows what we are.

"We're avatars," Kat tells her.

"The Children once called us guests," I add. My explanation

doesn't help at all. If anything, she looks much more eager to pull the trigger.

"My grandmother told me the guests were evil."

"Most, but not all of them." As always, Kat's kept her cool. "The man who lives in the tower was a guest once, too. He's the one who told us about you. He said you could take us wherever we needed to go."

I breathe a sigh of relief when the weapon is lowered. "You know the Ancient?"

"The Ancient?" I ask.

"They call him that because he has been here for as long as anyone can remember. He tells us what the world was like after the guests left and before the Children discovered machines. My parents knew him when they were children. He never leaves his house and he never grows any older. He insists he is not a god, so we call him the Ancient. He's sent you here?"

"Yes," Kat confirms.

"Then I will gladly help you. The Ancient has always been kind to me."

Bird's skin began to cool as she spoke. By the time she's finished, it's returned to its original silvery blue. Her tone has changed just as dramatically. Once hostile, it's now almost reverent. Nothing beats having good connections, I suppose.

"Thank you," Kat says.

"Albion is dangerous," Bird warns her. "It's not what it once was."

"We're ready." Kat reaches back and shows Bird an arrow from her ever-present quiver. "In fact, we're in a bit of a rush. When will you be able to leave?"

"I can go now if you like," says the Child.

I glance around at the shop. There's nothing here that would suggest that Bird's operation is prepared for anything other than a good mopping.

"You're sure about that?" I ask. "How are you going to get us there?"

"In my vehicle," she replies, pulling a small device out of her pocket. She clicks a single button and the wall behind her lowers into the ground. Behind it is a slick black machine that's the shape of a skipping stone. "Open," Bird orders, and doors rise on either side, exposing an interior with two rows of plush seats and a control panel fit for a spaceship.

"Wow," Kat marvels.

"I inherited it from my father," Bird says bashfully. "I know it's old, but I do all the maintenance myself. I promise it will get us there alive."

The smog starts to thin as we fly out over the Wastelands. I had my first brush with death down there in the rocky red desert. Unlike in the White City, little seems to have changed here since then, and I gotta admit I'm feeling a little nostalgic. Dust devils spin the scorched red soil into frail tornados that sweep across the plain. I scan each rocky outcropping we pass, searching for the goats that almost made a meal out of me. I can't see any signs of life, though. Even the weeds that once grew between the rocks are gone.

I spot a cloud of dust on the horizon and nudge Kat with my elbow. "Look, it's the buffalo," I say.

"Buffalo?" scoffs the Child. "That's a water transport vehicle. Most realms would die without them. The buffalo are just a story parents tell to keep their offspring from wandering into the Wastelands."

I don't bother to correct her. I watch the vehicle take shape. At least two dozen pods are linked together by a flexible cable, a design that allows it to curve around obstacles without changing course. Though the vehicle can move like a snake when it needs to, it looks more like a human spine. It appears to be heading for a massive wall that's come into view up ahead. Made of a lusterless metal, it rises so high that only the tip of the volcano it surrounds can be seen.

"Is that Imra?" Kat asks.

"No one calls it that anymore," the Child tells her. "It's home to the Scoria, the third-wealthiest family in Otherworld."

"The entire realm belongs to a single family?" I ask. "How many of them are there?"

"Six," says the Child as the car swings to the left. "If you don't count their army of slaves."

"Slaves?" Kat asks.

"I think she's talking about NPCs," I explain.

"Call them what you like," Bird says. "They'll shoot us down if we try to fly over. That's why we're skimming the periphery."

"And all the walls and guns are okay with Pomba Gira?" Kat inquires.

"The old Elemental of Imra? The Scoria claim to be her descendants, though most of us doubt it's true. They had Pomba Gira locked up as soon as their machines could rival her magic. They say she's still down there. The Scoria use the energy from her volcano to power the city."

"And Gimmelwald?" I see no sign of the tiny realm that once

bordered Imra. The last time I visited, the Elemental there had turned what had once been a play area for underage guests into a magnificent garden teeming with tiny green Children.

"Gimmelwald? Wow, how old are you guys?" Bird asks. "That place burned to the ground a long time ago."

I watch in horrified silence as our journey continues. Imra isn't the last walled realm we pass on the way to Albion. We fly over the Wastelands, careful to avoid the airspace over each realm. Glittering realms like Mammon are protected by walls. The vacation lands are easy to spot—they're the only vibrant patches of blue and green. Most of the realms are disaster zones. Some are massive slums with tiny dwellings stacked atop one another. Others look as though they've been destroyed by war. The Children have already built bombs to rival those found on Earth. We fly over one realm that's nothing more than a giant crater. Technology has destroyed this world.

The only realm that seems to be flourishing is Imperium. Bird won't get close enough to allow us to see it properly, but from a distance, there appear to be new patches of lush vegetation growing up the sides of the city's stark glass skyscrapers.

"The Empress has a green thumb," Bird explains. "But I've heard rumors that her heart is black."

"Empress?" I ask. Imperium must have a new ruler. "Who is she?"

"One of you, they say," Bird answers. "I have no interest in getting close enough to confirm it."

We're far past Imperium when I feel the car beginning to descend. I can't figure out why we'd be landing. There's nothing around as far as I can see.

"We're here," Bird announces.

This can't be it. There's no sinister forest. No dragons or lairs. The entire realm is a junkyard, with towers of twisted metal and discarded electronics that rise up toward the smoke-filled sky. The sun overhead casts a dim glow, its rays unable to penetrate the smog.

The vehicle lands and the doors open.

"Is this the right place?" Kat whispers to me as we exit the vehicle. "This doesn't look like the realm we saw in Max's video."

"Are you sure this is Albion?" I ask Bird once we're outside. "Aren't there supposed to be castles and villages?"

"There were once," Bird says. "They were built for the amusement of the guests. But most Children these days don't want to live in a castle or a village. The realm was abandoned shortly after the liberation. Nearby cities now use it to dump their refuse."

"What happened to the Elemental?" Kat asks. I hold my breath as I wait for the answer. If he's gone, this entire visit is a giant waste of time.

"He's still here, but he does nothing to stop it," the Child tells her. "I've never seen him myself. I don't think he leaves his cave." Bird points to a spot in the distance that I assumed was just another pile of trash. Now I can see it's the cliff from Max's video.

"How are we going to speak to him?" Kat asks me. "There are no quests left to complete. If we don't bring him three prizes, he'll toss us both out."

It keeps getting worse and worse. I have no idea how we're going to pull this one off.

"I think I can help you with that," Bird tells her. "Come with me." She gestures for us to follow her as she sets off toward the cave.

"Didn't you say you weren't going to stay?" Kat calls after Bird.

"I guess I changed my mind," Bird replies over her shoulder. "Maybe you've grown on me."

The smile Kat gives me is filled with relief. I don't think either of us was looking forward to being in Albion on our own.

"How do you know your way around?" I ask when Kat and I catch back up with her.

"I make a point of visiting all the realms," she says. "You could say it's my hobby."

"What are you looking for?" I ask.

Bird shrugs. "Hope, I guess."

There's a path that winds through the mountains of garbage. I'm glad I'm not wearing a disk. The smell of the place must be nauseating—and the trash towers are unstable. Every few minutes, we hear the rumble of avalanches and the crash of falling debris. Plumes of dust rise into the sky, then disperse and join the clouds around them.

We walk for miles before we reach the ruins of one of the realm's many castles. Everything useful has been stripped away. The roof has collapsed and only a single turret remains standing. It's hard to believe all of this destruction has taken place over a few days on Earth.

"The Dragon of Castle Carlisle waits inside," Bird says. "The Elemental will accept one of its teeth as a prize."

Kat reaches over her shoulder and pulls an arrow from her quiver.

"That's not going to be necessary," the Child assures her.

Still, Kat keeps her bow ready as she makes her way to the castle's entrance. I follow. The realm is quiet aside from the crunch of broken glass beneath our feet and the occasional crash in the distance.

Kat stops at the threshold and puts her weapon away. When I join her, I see why there's no need for caution. Inside, in what would once have been the castle's great hall, lies an enormous skeleton. A city bus could have fit inside the creature's rib cage. The wings, when outstretched, must have cast a remarkable shadow, and the long skull with its sharp teeth was large enough to swallow an avatar whole. Yet there's nothing fierce about the dragon now. It died curled up by the hall's massive fireplace, its head tucked beneath its wing.

I hear Bird coming our way. "The creatures here can't leave the realm unless the Elemental releases them. Eventually there was nothing left here to sustain the dragon and she wasted away."

I can't believe I'm getting all weepy over a dragon, but the whole scene is pathetic. In less than an Otherworld century, a once-magnificent realm has been utterly destroyed.

"Is this what happened to all of the creatures who inhabited Albion?" Kat asks, her voice cracking.

"No," says Bird. "The dragon was lucky. It's been far worse for the others. Go ahead—take a tooth as a prize."

Before we leave, I wrench a giant tooth from the dragon's jaw. I try to be as gentle as I can, but the moment the tooth comes free in my hand, the entire skeleton collapses into a pile of bones. A cloud of dust envelops me. I let my chin fall to my chest as I wait for it to dissipate. I'm too overcome with sadness to move.

"We'll visit the giant next," Bird announces. "His belt is another one of the realm's prizes. But he'll eat you unless you can promise to set him free from this realm."

"Fabulous," I mutter. "I can't wait to meet him."

Not far from the castle, a river snakes across the realm. Trash drifts along on the surface, and the banks on either side are pitch-black. Nothing could possibly live in these waters and yet there's something flesh-colored floating midstream. As we draw closer, I can see it's a head. Someone's left a pair of ragged trousers and a threadbare shirt by the side of the river. Their size tells me the head is that of Albion's giant, who must be out for a swim.

Lying among the discarded clothing is a leather belt with a large golden buckle. I give Kat a look and she shrugs. She knows what I'm asking, and she's not sure how to respond. I'm not going to let the opportunity pass. I'm reaching down to snatch the belt when the giant turns back toward the shore.

"Shit, Simon," I hear Kat groan behind me. "Now I'm gonna have to shoot him."

"Not yet," I tell her. "Give it a second."

The giant is hideous for sure, with a snout for a nose and a single bloodshot eye in the center of his forehead. But for some reason he hasn't struck any fear in my heart. He seems to be struggling. As he emerges from the water, his chest and arms come into view. The skin sags off his bones. The flesh that once covered them has wasted away.

"You dare touch my belt?" he manages to boom in a classic giant voice. Then he stops, still waist-deep in the water, to catch his breath. He's clearly famished. I see him begin to teeter on his legs, and then he topples over with a splash and disappears under the water.

You face some weird ethical dilemmas here in Otherworld, that's for sure. You can take a belt and let a starving giant drown—or save a bloodthirsty monster who's probably eaten hundreds of players and would do just about anything for a taste of you. Fortunately I have Kat to make these decisions for me. She almost shot the guy a few seconds earlier and suddenly she's sprinting down to the river to save him. I love her like crazy, but I swear I don't understand half the shit she does.

I jump into the water after her, and together we manage to drag the giant to the riverbank. He's so frail that I doubt he weighs much more than I do. The loincloth he's wearing looks like it could slip off his hips at any moment. Once again, I thank whoever's listening that I'm not wearing a disk. The foul soup I just swallowed would have killed me, I'm sure. Even with a headset on, the experience of swimming in water with the texture of vomit was extremely unpleasant.

Kat and I get the giant laid out on the ground. He's still not moving, and it's starting to seem like one of us is going to have to administer CPR. I'd rather not watch Kat lock lips with a cyclops whose mouth is crammed full of rotten teeth, so I decide to take one for the team. I'm leaning over the giant when a fountain of water gushes up from his throat and hits me square in the face.

"FEE FIE FO—" he sputters.

"Oh for God's sake, would you stop with that tired old crap?" I shout. I'm still dripping with the water that just shot out of his lungs and I'm in no mood for this bullshit. "You're not going to eat anyone right now."

And with that, the giant breaks down in tears. Snot streams from both nostrils, flows across his emaciated cheeks and trickles down to the ground beneath him. It's an absolutely hideous sight.

"Geez, Simon, was that really necessary?" Kat asks me.

"What?" I demand. "He wants to eat me!"

"He's starving!" Kat shoots back. "Tell him you're sorry."

"No way," I respond.

Kat shakes her head and kneels down beside the giant. "We apologize for stealing your belt. We need to speak with the Elemental of Albion, but before we can, we have to gather three prizes to give him. We're hoping we can convince him to release you and any other creatures from the realm."

"I'll be free to go?" the giant asks, snorting some of the snot back into his skull.

"Hopefully," Kat says.

"But no more eating Children or avatars," I add. "Stick with beasts from now on."

"Most realms no longer have beasts," Bird says.

"Then he'll just have to learn to love salad," I snap. "You get the point, right?" I ask the giant.

He grunts in response, reaches over for his pants and digs into a pocket. When he stands up again, he's holding an iridescent gold feather.

Beside me Bird gasps, snatches the feather and proceeds to examine it. "Is this from the Phoenix of Fife?" she demands.

The giant nods bashfully.

"You *ate* it?" the Child asks. The giant's head sinks even farther. Disgusted, Bird holds the feather out to me. "They said it was the last bird in Otherworld. It had wings the color of fairy gold. It never hurt anyone unless they tried to steal a feather. Then it would pluck their eyes out with its beak."

"Don't give it to me," I say with a grimace. I want no part in the eating of magical creatures.

"You have to take it," Bird demands. "It was one of the realm's most difficult prizes. You have three of them now—tooth, belt and feather. You may visit the Elemental of Albion."

I should feel relieved, I suppose. Instead all I feel is nauseous.

It appears that the Elemental of Albion is the only thing in Other-world that hasn't changed over the decades. We find him sitting cross-legged on the floor of his cave, eyes closed as if in a trance. The spiderwebs that surround the Elemental make him look hazy, like he's only half there. Nothing seems to have been touched since Max Prince visited the cave. A thick layer of dust covers the pile of discarded offerings behind the Elemental, but I can see the scroll that Max left behind.

The Elemental doesn't budge as we approach him. One of the spiders that's built its home here emerges from the Elemental's beard to see who's come to visit. It's a giant specimen, and it seems eager to welcome us to its web. We steer clear of its silky strands as we take our seats before the ruler of Albion. The moment our legs are crossed in front of us, his eyelids open, revealing his strange opalescent eyes.

"What have you brought for me?" the Elemental drones.

"A tooth from the dragon that lived in Castle Carlisle," I reply, laying the first of our prizes out in front of him.

The Elemental examines the tooth with his fingers, just as he did when Max paid his visit. "Well done," he says at last. "The dragon is a fearsome monster. Her sister was defeated years ago, but no one has managed to conquer this beast. What else have you brought for me?"

"We have brought you the giant's golden belt buckle and a plume from the Phoenix of Fife," Kat says, passing him the belt and golden feather.

The Elemental takes both and examines them thoroughly. Once they pass the test, he gently sets each one aside. Kat must sense how nervous I am. She grabs my hand and squeezes as we wait for the show to begin. His eyes spin in their sockets until ordinary irises and pupils appear. As if he's just woken up from a long sleep, the Elemental takes in his surroundings and sweeps the spiderwebs away from his face.

"You are the first guests in Albion to complete three quests. You are formidable knights and you have earned a wish. What is it you desire? Wealth? Power? I can make your fondest dreams come true for as long as you remain in Albion."

"You have been asleep for a very long time," Kat tells him. "The guests are gone. We want you to leave this cave and see what's happened to your realm."

"That is your greatest desire?" the Elemental inquires skeptically. He turns to me. "Do you concur?" he asks.

I hesitate for a moment. If it were up to me, I'd have asked for the scroll and figured the rest out later. Then Kat pinches my side. "Yeah," I grunt. "What she said."

I hear the cracking and creaking of old bones as the Elemental rises from the spot where he's been sitting since time in Otherworld began. Slowly he walks to the mouth of the cave. There he stands silently, looking out over his realm for what feels like another hundred years. At last he turns around. The grief on his face is too terrible to witness, and my eyes drop down to my feet.

"What have I done to offend the Creator?" he asks. "Why has he visited such ruin upon me?"

Kat rises to join the Elemental, and I follow. "The Creator is gone," Kat tells him. "Otherworld is now ruled by the Children of Elementals and beasts."

The Elemental blinks. None of it makes any sense to him. I'm guessing he never left his cave long enough to make any Children himself.

"Your realm can be restored," I assure him. "It won't return to the way it was, but the land can heal. I've seen it happen before. Volla, the Elemental of Gimmelwald, brought her realm back to life once." I don't mention that Gimmelwald is gone now, and Volla herself is missing, presumed dead.

"The forests will grow again? The river will be blue?" the Elemental asks. It would be so much easier to say what he wants to hear. But I know that Kat never lies. She won't even exaggerate.

"We don't know," Kat tells him. "All we know is that you must release Albion's creatures from your realm. There's no longer enough food here to support them. They've been forced to eat one another."

I see the horror on the old man's face turn into a steely determination.

"I will grant your request," he informs us. "And I will make you a promise as well. I will not sleep until my realm is restored. This cave and its contents are yours if you'll have them. I shall not return here again."

He steps off the edge and vanishes. I look over the side, expecting to see his body splayed out below. But before he could plunge to the base of the cliff, the spiders that live inside his beard and clothes shot webs at the cliff walls. I watch as the silken strands lower the Elemental of Albion safely down to the ground. When he lands, he gently wipes the webs from his robes and sets off across his land.

I will never question Kat's genius again. She got everything we needed while doing the right thing. I grab the scroll Max left behind, blow off the dust that's collected on one side and carefully unroll the paper. It's so old at this point that the edges crumble as they brush against my fingers.

The ink has faded over the years, but the handwriting remains legible.

If someone told me a week ago that I'd be writing this letter, I would have said they were fucking insane. I still think it's crazy. Then again, I've seen some shit lately that makes this seem totally normal.

I was warned to stay away from the Company. I was told

they were making things that could destroy the whole world. I should have listened, but I didn't.

The Company has a secret lab in Manhattan. I got in good with one of the engineers, and he gave me a tour. (I don't remember the exact address. It's a white building on Franklin Street in Tribeca.) I saw some seriously sinister shit in there. If they know I saw it, I'll be dead soon. If I say what it was, you'll think I'm nuts.

My family knows something's wrong. I can't tell them what I've seen or they won't last long either. They already suspect it has something to do with the Company. They say there's someone out there who might be able to help me. I find it hard to believe such a person exists, but I'm leaving this letter here just in case. Maybe he or she will be able to find it. If not, this letter will stay here with this crazy old geezer until the end of time.

I look up from the scroll. We're standing at the edge of another rabbit hole, and there's no telling what we'll find at the bottom.

"So there's another secret lab. What do you suppose he saw?" Kat asks. "Do you think they have more people trapped in capsules?"

"No clue, but if it shocked Max it must have been pretty bad," I say. "We've got to get back to New York." I reach up to remove my headset. We can't waste another moment.

"Not yet," Kat says, reaching out to stop me. "We have plenty of time. I bet barely a minute has passed in our world. Let's take the letter back to James Ogubu and see what he thinks it could mean."

I shove the scroll into my pocket and we climb back down

the cliff. Bird said she'd wait for us while we paid a visit to the Elemental, but when we reach her vehicle, she's nowhere to be seen.

"Maybe we shouldn't have left her alone," Kat says.

"Do you think something could have eaten her?" I ask. Who
knows how many starving creatures were still in the realm?

We get our answer when five human-shaped figures appear
from behind a trash tower. One of them has Bird in a choke hold
with a weapon aimed at her temple. It's been so long since I've
seen NPCs that I almost mistake them for guests. But no five
players would ever choose to sport identical outfits—particularly
ones that make them look like a fascist boy band.

"Come with us," one grunts.

They aren't pointing their guns at us—only at Bird. The NPCs
seem to know we can't be injured. That means they know we're
humans wearing headsets.

"How could we turn down such a charming invitation?" Kat
says. "But would you mind telling us where we're going?" I think
Kat's trying to buy time, hoping I'll figure out what to do. But my
brain isn't cooperating. Every plan I can think of ends up with
Bird dead.

"You have five seconds to come with us or the Child will be
killed." The lead NPC won't be stalled.

"If you kill the Child, you won't have anything left to bargain
with," I point out. I think it's a very smart observation, but Kat
clearly doesn't.

"Stop," she hisses at me. "We'll come with you," she tells the
NPCs.

That's not an option either, I'm afraid. It doesn't matter who
they're taking us to see, I have no intention of sharing the scroll in

my pocket with anyone. I wonder what they'll do if I make a break for it now. I know Kat will be fine—she's wearing a headset. The worst-case scenario is that she ends up back at setup. But what will happen to Bird if I manage to escape?

Kat knows what I'm thinking. She's shaking her head. She does not approve at all. And she's right. If the scroll falls into the wrong hands, it could put our entire world at risk. But it's still not worth the sacrifice of a single sentient creature. I'll have to figure something else out.

"Fine," I say. Just as I take a step toward them, the NPC holding Bird lets go of her and flies backward into one of the towers. The structure immediately collapses, burying him in a mountain of garbage. Bird bolts in our direction, and the other NPCs watch her go, too stunned to follow.

For a brief moment, I start to wonder if I've acquired superpowers. Then a skeletal old man appears. His back is bent and his robes faded, but he's still a force to be reckoned with.

"Have the old laws been completely forgotten?" The Elemental's booming voice makes the trash towers quiver. "Your kind is bound to the realm in which you were conceived. Why are you in Albion when you belong to Imperium?"

Imperium. I should have known. I'm starting to think that the rumors Bird heard about the Empress were true. I have a hunch she's a human like us.

"Speak!" the Elemental shrieks, but the NPCs remain silent. They refuse to follow his orders. "Then perish," he says. His mouth opens into the gaping black hole we saw on Max's video. The force of his scream shatters the soldiers. All that's left of them is a fine black dust, which falls out of the air and collects in small piles where their feet once stood.

The Elemental's mouth closes and when his face reappears, his eyes immediately lock on Bird.

"You don't belong here either." He shuffles toward her. "What kind of creature are you? Are you one of those who've brought destruction to my realm?"

Bird glances over at Kat as if hoping she might have the answer.

"Her name is Bird, and she is the one who brought us to Albion," Kat tells the Elemental. "She showed us where to find the prizes we brought to your cave. Without her assistance, we couldn't have helped you."

The Elemental's tone instantly softens. "Then I am in her debt. What can I give you in return?" he asks Bird. "I offer you the same reward your companions turned down. You may have whatever your heart desires, as long as you remain in Albion."

"Is this guy serious?" Bird asks us.

I have to laugh. "I doubt he's ever told a joke in his life," I say.

Bird turns back to the Elemental. "May I have a few minutes to think about it?"

"Yes. A few minutes, but no longer," he replies. "There is work to be done here, and I can't put it off any longer."

Bird nods thoughtfully. "Then I will have to turn down your offer. I need to fly these two back to the White City. It's my responsibility."

"We're not returning to the White City now," Kat tells Bird.

I lift my eyebrows. That's news to me.

"The Empress sent those soldiers to find us. If she's watching, the last thing we want to do is lead her to James Ogubu. We have to get out of Otherworld."

She's right, as always.

"Time moves more slowly in our world," Kat tells Bird. "We may not return to Otherworld in your lifetime. Thank you for everything that you've done. May the wish you've been given offer the hope you've been searching for."

Bird's pale blue skin flushes a lovely red, and a wave of heat passes over me. I think she may have just figured out what she wants.

"Hey, what are we going to do with our avatars?" I ask Kat. "We need to leave them somewhere safe."

"I was thinking we could have them sent back to setup," Kat tells me.

"We'll have to die three times," I say. "You really want me to stab you? Or were you looking forward to shooting me first?"

"Not too keen on murder-suicide," says Kat. "I'm hoping our new Elemental friend will save us the trouble and do the honors."

"You're kidding." I can't imagine a worse way to go.

"Nope," Kat says. "Don't you want to see what it's like?"

"Absolutely not," I tell her. But I know I'm going to find out anyway.

DEATH WISH

With the Elemental's inhuman shriek still echoing in my skull, I pull off my headset. I plan to thank Kat for one of the most horrible experiences I've ever endured. But the first person I see is Nasha Ogubu. I have no idea how long she's been standing there, waiting for us to emerge. It makes me feel a little self-conscious. I don't like being watched—especially when I'm wearing these ridiculous haptic booties.

"Okay, I'm pissed," I hear Busara announce. Her headset must be off as well. "Dad knows who you work for, but all he'd say is you'd tell me when it's time."

"What's going on?" Kat's back now too.

I'm expecting a family brawl to break out at any moment, but Nasha isn't paying her daughter any mind. She's heading across the room toward me.

"Mom! Are you listening?" Busara shouts. "It better be time for you to tell me who you work for or I'm out of here!"

Nasha wheels around. "I can't tell you for the same reason your father can't. The information could fall into the wrong hands."

"Do you guys really need to do this now?" I groan. "My head is literally about to explode."

Nasha stops in front of me and grips the railing of my treadmill. "Simon, who was in the room at Rikers when you spoke to Max Prince?"

She's not asking out of curiosity. My brain may be scrambled, but I can tell the answer is going to be important. I try to think back to my visit. "No one as far as I can remember—aside from the guard."

"He was one of ours. Do you think anyone else could have overheard your conversation?" Nasha demands.

"I have no idea." I step off the treadmill and remove my haptic gloves. I spot Elvis lurking in the doorway. He must have come in behind Nasha. "I doubt anyone would be able to make sense of our conversation anyway. What's this all about?"

"Max is dead," Nasha says.

"No." The news feels like a kick in the gut. "I just saw him! He can't be dead!"

"It's true," Elvis says.

"Oh my God. What happened?" Kat asks.

"We don't have final confirmation yet." Nasha keeps her eyes on me as if my face might hold the clue she's been looking for. "But our people inside Rikers say it might have been a suicide."

"How can you be sure that he's dead?" Busara asks.

"Come with me," Nasha orders. "There's something all of you should see."

She leads the four of us out to the living room, where a laptop sits open on the coffee table. A video is paused on the screen. We gather behind Nasha as she takes a seat in front of the computer and hits Play.

A title slide instantly appears—the type is simple black on white.

Max Prince is dead.

The slide vanishes and is quickly replaced by another.

A chip embedded in his body was monitoring his vitals.

He arranged for the following video to be posted to his social media accounts when his heart stopped.

Max Prince died at 6:42 this morning.

Anyone claiming to be him is an impostor.

The video that follows starts with Max, though it takes me a second to identify him. His entire face is covered in blood. Then he takes off a pair of glasses that have shielded his eyes from the splatter. From the little we can see of his surroundings, it appears he's in a luxurious bathroom that's drenched in gore. Something is lying on the floor behind him. One of my friends retches when they realize it's a chunk of flesh. Max must have filmed the video on his smartphone shortly after he murdered his stepfather.

Max appears oddly emotionless. He must be in shock. "This is the future," he announces to the camera. "From this moment forward, you won't be able to trust your eyes. You won't be able to tell the difference between real and unreal."

He holds up the glasses. They're dripping with his stepfather's blood.

"The Company gave me these. They said I'd be able to indulge all my fantasies. They told me no one would ever get hurt. The Company lied. They've been lying to all of us. They call these things games, but that's not what they are. They're weapons that are being used to destroy humanity."

Max's eyes disappear as he puts the bloody glasses back on. The video ends. None of us moves.

"So he really is dead?" Kat asks.

"We think so," Nasha says. "We know the chip was real. He had it implanted himself."

"The Company could have gotten to him in prison," Elvis says, stating the obvious. He glances at me as if expecting me to have some wisdom to share. It will be better for everyone if I keep my thoughts to myself.

I promised Abigail Prince we would do our best to save her son. We failed miserably. Max was told there might be someone who could save the world. We now have definitive proof that I am not that person.

"Put on the news," Busara orders. "The Company must have responded by now. Let's find out what they said."

I'm expecting to see one of the Company's well-groomed spokesmen. But when the screen comes to life, Abigail Prince's sculpted face is in its center.

"Holy shit," I mutter, breaking out of my shame spiral. I can't put a finger on what it is, but there's something off about her appearance. If I didn't know who's been keeping her company over the past few days, I'd assume she'd had another nip and tuck.

"It's a fake video," Kat says. "Just like the one they made of us." Then the camera pulls back to show Abigail outside her apartment building. A well-known television reporter stands beside her, a microphone in his hand.

"It's not a fake." Elvis steps up to the television. "The reporter is real." That means the Abigail Prince we're seeing is real, too.

"Thank you for stopping to talk to us," the reporter says. "I know this must be a terrible time for you."

Abigail lifts a hand holding a handkerchief and dabs her left eye, but I don't see any tears. "My son is dead."

"I'm very sorry, Ms. Prince. Has it been confirmed that he took his own life?"

"It was suicide," she says.

"And what do you make of the video that was released earlier today? Your son made some fairly startling accusations regarding the Company and what appears to be their latest offering, the augmented-reality game known as OtherEarth."

"I loved my son very much." The camera moves in on Abigail's face. There's something not quite right about it. "But my little Max grew up to be a disturbed young man."

What? This is all very wrong. Abigail Prince adored her son.

"You don't think the Company played any role in the murder of your late husband, Christian Guido?"

"Absolutely not," Abigail says. "Max was mentally ill."

There is no way in hell Abigail Prince would willingly say that. What has the Company done to her?

"Thank you for your time, Ms. Prince," says the anchor.

Abigail has her face in her hands as the camera pulls back from the pair, revealing two bodyguards standing nearby. Busara and I both lunge for the remote at the same time. She reaches it before I do and hits Rewind and then Pause.

We meet in front of the screen. The face we're looking at is in profile, and most of it is hidden behind the guy standing next to him.

"What do you think?" I ask, tapping the face with my finger. "Is it him?"

"Oh, it's him," Busara confirms. "No doubt about it."

"Who?" Elvis asks. He and Kat don't recognize the bodyguard. They've never seen him in real life. They only know him from Otherworld.

"*Todd*," I sneer.

"The engineer from the Company? The one who controlled Moloch?" Kat rushes over to join Busara and me in front of the television. "*That's* the monster who massacred the Children and murdered Marlow? He looks like a malnourished frat boy."

She's right. It's hard to believe the debonair Moloch was an avatar controlled by this sad sack masquerading as a bodyguard. Judging by his appearance, Todd hasn't eaten a fruit or vegetable in ages. I hope he's developed a debilitating case of scurvy.

"Are you talking about Todd *Bolton*? That kid who used to work for your father?" Nasha sounds skeptical. "James always thought he was harmless."

"Yeah, Dad wasn't a very good judge of character," Busara says. "He never could spot the sociopaths."

"Think you can find out where Todd lives?" I ask Nasha. "I want to pay him a visit this evening."

"You mean *we're* going to pay him a visit," Elvis corrects me. "I'm tired of everyone else getting to have all the fun."

"Fun?" Kat scoffs. "Do you have any idea how much our last trip to Otherworld sucked?"

"At least you haven't been cooped up for days!" Elvis says. "I need some guy time! I want to go visit Todd!"

"None of you are going anywhere tonight," Nasha announces. "I'm sorry, but I can't authorize it."

Now the truth is going to come out. Nasha's been pretending we're all partners in this, but I have a feeling the situation's not quite so simple.

"I wasn't aware that we need your permission to leave the apartment," Busara snaps.

"You don't," Nasha replies curtly. "I'm not the final authority on these matters."

"If you're not in charge, who is?" Kat demands. "Can we talk to them?"

"No," Nasha says.

The five of us stand in the living room, waiting for someone to make the next move. Once again, it's Busara. "So we're being held prisoner? Is that what you're telling us?"

"Don't be ridiculous. I'm saying no because it's too dangerous. We haven't performed any reconnaissance. Someone from our organization would need to accompany you, and we don't even—"

She stops abruptly. In the silence, I can hear a soft buzzing. Nasha's face is stony as she pulls a phone from her pocket and clears her throat nervously before answering.

"This is Nasha." Then she listens. Her eyes stay on me the

entire time. "Yes, sir," she says. The call ends immediately and she puts the phone away.

"The operation has been approved," she tells us. "Simon and Elvis, you're on your own. Todd Bolton lives at 428 Henry Street in Brooklyn."

"Who approved it?" Busara demands.

"The orders came all the way from the top," Nasha says. She turns her eyes to me. "Someone believes in you. Try not to get yourself killed."

"Don't you worry, Ms. Ogubu. He'll be fine," Elvis says in his superhero voice. "I'll be there to protect him."

Nasha snorts and shakes her head. "Girl, you sure know how to pick them," she says to her daughter.

KILLER EXPERIENCE

The only thing I didn't factor into my brilliant plan was being stuck in a car with Elvis on our way from Queens to Brooklyn. Despite everything that's been going on, the one subject he's eager to discuss is the one subject I'd rather avoid—the Ogubus.

"Nasha knew I was joking about protecting you, didn't she?"

I glance over at Elvis and find his handsome face ashen with worry.

"How the hell would I know?" I tell him. "The woman's a mystery. Her own daughter doesn't even know if she's a good guy or not."

"What? That's ridiculous. She's definitely a good guy." It doesn't sound like there's a single doubt in Elvis's mind.

"Do you know something I don't?" I ask.

"I know *lots* of things you don't," Elvis assures me. "But I assume you're talking about Nasha."

"Of course," I say. I expect him to keep going, but I have to give him a prod. "Care to enlighten me?"

"I don't know if it's a secret. I mean she didn't *ask* me not to say anything."

"What!" I demand.

"She cried."

I find that very hard to believe. "When?"

"Today, while you guys were in Otherworld. I found the video Max released. I showed it to her and she cried. Not a lot. I could tell she was trying to keep it together. But there was a tear. I saw it."

I have no idea what that means. Did Nasha know Max—or is she just the sort of tenderhearted spy who breaks down in tears at the tragic loss of a YouTube star?

"That's what makes you think she's a good guy?" It seems like fairly flimsy evidence to me.

"Well, that and the fact that she was married to James Ogubu," Elvis says. "The man's a genius. He knew Nasha was keeping tabs on his work. He *let* her. They were in on it together. I'd bet you anything."

It's an interesting theory. "Who do you think Nasha works for?"

Elvis shrugs. "Dunno. Don't think it's a government. Probably not another tech company either. If I had to guess, I'd say there's some secret society bankrolling the whole thing."

"A secret society?" I laugh. "You mean like Skull and Bones or the Illuminati?"

Elvis laughs too, but I get the impression he's laughing *at* me. "After everything we've been through, you find the idea of a secret society hard to believe? Is it any weirder than a pair of glasses that can turn people into murderers?"

He does have a point. "Have you shared this brilliant theory with your girlfriend?" I ask.

"I haven't had a chance." Elvis suddenly looks like he might break into tears too. "As you've probably noticed, Busara's been giving me the cold shoulder since we left the island. To be honest, I'm not even sure if she's still my girlfriend."

I really don't know why people come to me with these problems. I think maybe they just enjoy seeing me squirm. "Look, Busara just found out that she never really knew her mom. I'm sure it's messing with her head. Maybe she's worried that you'll turn out to be someone different too."

Elvis throws his hands up in frustration. "That doesn't make any sense. Who else could I be? And if I were someone else, and I could *act* like me, why wouldn't I just *be* me? I'm awesome!"

"And humble."

"That too!"

"You're making my head hurt," I tell him.

"Imagine how mine feels!" Elvis shouts in frustration.

"You're probably right," I agree, eager to leave the subject behind. "I'm sure Busara knows you're too awesome to be anyone but yourself."

"So why do you think she's avoiding me?"

And on and on and on it goes. By the time we get close to Todd's house, I'm wondering if Elvis is prepared to take our mission seriously. I'm ready to call the whole thing off when he suddenly snaps into professional mode.

"Let me fix this," he says, leaning over to adjust the brim of my hat. "As we approach the house, keep your eyes straight ahead. Don't look for cameras, just assume there are ones we don't know about. Even doorbell cams use facial recognition software these days. And by the way, thanks for letting me come along. As you can probably tell, I really needed to get out of that fucking apartment."

The car comes to a stop on a tree-lined Brooklyn street. The address Nasha gave us belongs to a brownstone that looks like something you'd see on a Christmas card. Elvis studies the building through the car window.

"Weird," he says. "Looks like he's got a couple of deadbolts and a doorbell camera. I don't see any fancy security."

"Doesn't mean it's not there," I point out, hoping I haven't led the two of us into a trap.

Our driver gets out, deactivates the doorbell camera and picks the locks on the front door. When he returns to the car, it's Elvis's and my turn. I'm worried about what we'll find inside, but there are no laser beams or deafening alarms. By Company standards, Todd's practically living off the grid. The interior of the house is tastefully decorated in muted grays. There must be ten pairs of sneakers piled up in the foyer, but it doesn't look like anyone's ever entered the living room. There's a giant picture of a cowboy hanging on one wall.

"Evil pays well," I whisper.

"I've seen that picture, it's an old Marlboro ad, isn't it?" Elvis asks.

"Yeah, the artist steals old ads and calls them art. That piece right there is worth millions of dollars."

"How does *that* work?" Elvis asks.

"No idea," I tell him.

We head up the stairs toward the bedrooms. Todd's snoring makes it easy to locate him. His room is as beautifully hip as the rest of the house. I suspect the only things Todd added to the décor were the empty Doritos bags strewn across the floor and the orange fingerprints on the white duvet cover.

I look down at the man who murdered Marlow Holm and did his best to kill Gorog. Not to mention the man who tried to exterminate the Children. I would like nothing more than to take one of his fluffy down pillows and smother him to death. I think Elvis knows what I have in mind, because he shakes his head and mouths the word *NO*.

So I rein in my impulses and sit down on the side of the bed. "Wake up, sleepyhead," I sing in Todd's ear.

Todd lurches forward into a sitting position. "What the actual fuck?" he mutters. Elvis makes sure Todd sees the gun he brought with him. Then I put my hand on Todd's forehead and roughly shove him back down on the bed.

"Just relax," I coo as I tenderly brush the hair back from his face. I am so itching to kill him right now.

"Who the hell are you?"

"Oh, come on, Todd, you don't remember me?" I switch on a bedside light. "We used to be such good friends."

Todd blinks furiously as his eyes adjust to the light. "Shit," he groans. "Did I do something wrong, Mr. Gibson?"

"Gibson?" He must still be half asleep if he's mistaken me for Wayne. "Do I look like that sadistic old douchebag to you?"

Todd rubs his eyes. "Simon? For real?" he asks as if he can't quite believe it. Elvis steps forward and Todd gazes up at him in wonder. "Who's this?"

Elvis takes a seat beside him on the bed. "Just your biggest fan. I saw you on television today, and I thought it might be fun to drop by to say hi."

"On television?" Todd repeats. This isn't the cocky smartass I've come to know and despise. He seems uncertain whether any of this is real.

"You were there when Abigail Prince gave her first interview following her son's tragic death. How'd you guys arrange that one, anyway?"

"I don't know what you're talking about," Todd says. "Is this some kind of test?"

"Get up," I order.

"What are you going to do to me?" he asks.

"We won't hurt you as long as you agree to help us with a few things," Elvis says. "Now do what he says and get your ass out of bed."

Todd looks at Elvis, his head tilted quizzically to one side. A smile begins to spread across his face. "Okay, I know who you are now. Elvis Karaszkewycz—the only kid on Earth without a social media presence. We don't have any footage of you. You're so good at avoiding surveillance cameras that some of my colleagues don't even think you exist."

"It's probably difficult for a bunch of Company assholes to ac-knowledge the existence of superior intelligence."

Todd laughs as he slides out from beneath the covers. He's wearing a pair of boxers with a TARDIS on the crotch.

"Adorable," I say.

"Thanks," he snaps back. Something about him has changed in the past sixty seconds. He's no longer terrified. "Nice hat. *Master Baiter.* I'm sure it suits you." Now, there's the Todd I know and despise.

"Put this on." Elvis keeps his gun trained on Todd as he pulls a gray sweat suit out of a knapsack we brought with us. "The three of us need to leave."

"Are you guys asking me out on a date?" Todd jests.

"Oh, we're going to have a lot of fun together," I tell him. "There's a place on Franklin Street that Elvis and I have been dying to check out."

Suddenly Todd's not laughing anymore.

"How the fuck do you know about that?" he blurts out.

"Guess you Company guys aren't quite as smart as you think you are," Elvis sings as he toys with a small device that's been left on Todd's dresser. "This is pretty cool. D'you make this? Mind if I borrow it?"

"I asked you a fucking question!" Todd snarls.

"I'll take that as a no," Elvis says, dropping the gadget into his pocket.

I'm going to answer Todd's rudely posed question. Not because I feel any need to confess. The truth's going to hurt, and I really want to rub it in. "Max Prince told us," I inform Todd. "He said he saw something on Franklin Street that blew his mind. Elvis and I are keen to have a look too."

"Max Prince is dead," Todd snaps. "Before that he was in prison. He didn't tell you anything."

I throw my hands up in the air in fake exasperation. "Okay,

you got me. Max didn't visit your hidden lab with one of your fellow engineers. And he didn't see anything there that fucked him up for good. And he *certainly* didn't write it all down on a scroll and hide it in the Elemental of Albion's cave. Nope, you're right, Todd. None of that ever happened."

Todd takes it all in. He knows it's true. "Max didn't tell you what he saw, did he?" he asks.

"Maybe, maybe not," Elvis says with a shrug.

"You know what happened to Max, right?" Todd asks.

"He died," I say. "The official story is that he killed himself, but I'd say there's a good chance he had some help."

"Either way, do you have any idea how lucky Max was?" Todd asks. He really does not look well. "Do you know what happened to Rory?"

"Rory?" I ask. "Who's that?"

"He was the fanboy engineer who gave Max the tour of the lab you're so *keen* to see."

I don't think I ever knew the engineer's name, but I remember his story. It made the news. It's not every day that a young engineer with no history of heart disease dies of a massive coronary on the job. "Death by OtherEarth?"

Todd nods. "Wayne's brought in a guy to design what he likes to call 'killer experiences.' The dude's a Saudi. I've heard he worked for the police there. Wouldn't be surprised if he still does. No one but Gibson knows what he builds. But we've all seen his work in action. Gibson made sure there were lots of witnesses the day Rory got to test-drive OtherEarth."

He stops and rubs his lips together nervously.

"And?" Elvis asks.

"We all watched Rory die," Todd says. "It was the worst thing I've ever seen. And believe me, I've seen some terrible shit."

I find it extremely hard to believe that Todd's sensitive side isn't one big act. "Give me a break. How many Children did you murder?" I demand angrily. "How many people did you help send to their deaths? Suddenly one of your kind dies and you grow a conscience? I don't buy it for a second. You're a fucking psychopath, just like Wayne."

"Give me a break, Eaton," Todd says. "The Children aren't flesh and blood. And the patients we sent to Otherworld at least had a chance to survive. Rory put on the OtherEarth glasses and disk and started screaming. He didn't stop for a full ten minutes. Then his heart must have exploded inside his chest and he dropped to the ground. I don't know what he saw in those glasses, but I do know it was worse than anything you've come across in Otherworld."

"Then why didn't he just take off the disk and the glasses?"

"I don't know. Like I said, I didn't design the experience. I only witnessed the effects. Gibson had us watch for a reason." Todd takes in a breath so deep you'd think it might be his last. "It was a warning not to step out of line. He can kill any of us in the worst way imaginable—without leaving a single mark. That's why I won't be going to the lab with you dickheads."

"Oh, I think you will," Elvis says, pointing his gun at Todd's temple. "Otherwise I'm going to kill you in real life, right now."

THE LAB

Lucky for us, there's only one white building on Franklin Street. From the outside, the place doesn't exactly scream "secret lab." It's one of the beautiful old cast-iron warehouses that make the Tribeca neighborhood unique. Most have been turned into spas, shops and apartment buildings that draw rich and famous tenants from all over the world. There's no name on the door of this particular building—and no sign of security. I'd worry that we were at the wrong place if it weren't for Todd. He didn't say a word the entire way here. Now he finally comes out with it.

"You really are going to get us all killed."

"Shut up and get us inside," I reply.

"Just warning you." He sounds resigned to his fate.

Todd ambles up to the front door, reluctantly pulls a set of keys from his pocket and inserts one into the lock above the handle. Elvis and I stand back until the door is open. When Todd gestures for us to follow him, we check both sides of the deserted street before we duck inside.

"That's it?" Elvis asks as he takes in the bare white walls of the building's small foyer. "Where's the security?"

"Upstairs," Todd says.

He unlocks another door and holds it open for us like a doorman. Beyond the empty foyer is a luxurious waiting room. Sleek leather armchairs are grouped around Persian carpets. Every piece of furniture is pristine. I doubt a single ass has ever dented the chair cushions. The decorator did a great job, but something about the space feels wrong. It takes me a second to figure out what it is. There are no windows anywhere in the room. At the far end, identical staircases on either side lead up to a mezzanine, where glass walls enclose a conference room.

Todd must be watching as my eyes land on the glass box above us. "That's where we have our client consultations and they tell us what custom experiences they'd like us to develop. When we first started, I figured most people would be after disgusting sex of some sort. But you'd be surprised how many of these guys prefer murder. Some ask for a bit of both. If Otherworld didn't make you lose faith in our species, this shit sure will. We've had some of the most famous people in the world up there, and you wouldn't believe what they ask for."

"Doesn't seem like the most private place to go confessing your darkest desires," Elvis remarks. "It looks like a big aquarium."

"The room is perfectly soundproof. The clients often send their own tech guys over to check it out first. They want total assurance that whatever's said in that room will only be heard by the people inside it. All visitors are checked for recording devices. There's also a switch that turns the glass completely opaque. Gibson likes to joke that he built the first perfect black box."

I stare at Todd for a moment. I'd have never guessed the room's true purpose if he hadn't volunteered it. Why did he want us to know?

"That's where Rory died," Todd says. "Gibson left the glass clear the day he was killed. I stood right here with the others. All ten of us were forced to watch. Rory was screaming and banging on the walls, but you couldn't hear a sound. Toward the end he stopped thrashing around and just stood up there with his palms pressed against the glass, pissing all over himself. A giant stain spread across his crotch, and then he dropped dead."

"Holy shit," Elvis mutters.

"Yeah," Todd agrees almost wistfully. Then he snaps out of his reverie. "So I guess I have that to look forward to."

There are few people on Earth I hate more than Todd Bolton. But I wouldn't wish Rory's fate on anyone.

"Come on," Todd says with fake cheer. "Since we're here, I might as well give you a tour! As I mentioned, all the good stuff is upstairs."

Todd places his palm against a glass panel on the wall, and a set of perfectly camouflaged elevator doors open. "Stay quiet while we're inside," he orders. "If you say the wrong thing, you could set off alarms."

The elevator car is unusually deep. As I recall, the elevators at the Facility were built the same way—because they were meant for transporting bodies on gurneys. Todd places his palm against another scanner to the right of the doors.

"Hello, Todd," says a disembodied female voice that's emanating from a small black circle on the wall above the scanner. "Working late again tonight?"

"Hello, Dot," Todd replies casually. "Just trying to keep the boss happy."

"I can sense an additional three hundred and thirty-two pounds in the car."

"Yep," says Todd. "I'm bringing in two for downloads and storage."

"Wonderful," says the voice. "Please choose your floor."

Todd reaches over and hits the number two button. A buzzer sounds angrily. "You do not have access to that floor, Todd."

"Sorry, Dot," he says. "I meant to press three."

Todd punches the button, which lights up. The elevator doors close and we start to rise. When the doors open once again, we step out into the dark.

"Why wouldn't she take you to the second floor?" I ask Todd.

"That's AJ's floor. He's got two guys who work for him, and they give the clients what they ask for. AJ develops Gibson's killer experiences himself. Only the two of them know what they are. AJ doesn't like me very much, so I'm banned from his lab. But don't worry, Max Prince never made it onto the second floor either. Let's have a quick look at three."

He switches on the lights and we find ourselves staring into a massive room that looks like a cross between an orthodontist's office and a morgue. Every surface is white and all the equipment is chrome. In the center of the room are two white leather dentist chairs with hydraulic lift systems.

"What is this place?" I ask.

"This is where I work. Floor three is where we perform the extractions," Todd replies. "We've only done a few so far. That stage of the operation is only just beginning."

"Extractions?" Elvis says. "What are you removing?"

I already know. There are six white helmets without visors resting on a rolling operating tray near the dentist chairs. They're all identical to the helmet that was placed on my head after Kat and I were kidnapped at the Waldorf Astoria. I'll never forget the experience. Back then, there was no reason to believe we'd survive with fully functional brains.

"We're extracting memories." Todd confirms it.

"In order to create more simulations?" Elvis asks.

That's what the Company did with the memories they stole from me and Kat. They turned them into a game. The thought makes me want to rip the whole room apart.

"No," Todd tells him. "That was a one-off. Didn't go as well as we'd hoped. Wayne's got other plans for the downloads we're doing now."

I wait for the rest. "And what are those plans?" I finally have to ask.

"The answer to that is on the fourth floor."

We ride the elevator one more stop. The doors open onto another floor of the old warehouse. The walls here are bare, and the wooden floorboards have been painted black. Before us are four long rows of capsules stacked three high. I wasn't expecting to see them. I feel like I've stepped back into a terrible dream.

"Are these what I think they are?" Elvis gets out to investigate. He's heard all about the Facility. He knows how the Company stored the bodies of the people they forced to beta test

Otherworld. But until now, he's never seen a capsule up close. I join him as he walks to the nearest hexagonal window and peers into it. The interior is only slightly more spacious than your average coffin. If there were a body inside, it would be resting on a rolling, stainless steel shelf. An IV inserted into its arm would deliver sustenance as well as the drugs needed to keep the body in a comatose state. Other tubes and wires would monitor the body's pulse and eliminate its waste.

The Company's beta test of the Otherworld disk is over and the Facility was closed. I should have known they'd find another use for the capsules.

"I'm pretty sure this is the floor that Rory brought Max Prince to see." Todd seems as uncomfortable as I feel. "Rory probably didn't think it would be such a big deal. I mean, the capsules had all been empty since we opened the place. He didn't realize that Wayne had filled one of them."

I find myself staring at Todd. With his hoodie up and his hands shoved into the pockets of the gray sweat suit, he looks like a lost little kid. I wonder how old Todd actually is. Probably not even thirty. It occurs to me that he hasn't cracked a single joke since we arrived at the lab. I have the impression he can't stand being here. Rory's death obviously got to him, but I don't think that's the whole story. Something else about this place has Todd totally spooked.

"Who was in the capsule that had been filled?" I ask.

Todd doesn't answer for a moment. "Have a look for yourself." He holds out an arm like an usher. "Row two. Sixth column. Middle capsule."

I feel like a character in a horror movie. A serial killer has invited me into his dungeon. Everyone in the theater is screaming out warnings. But I can't help myself. I step inside.

As I start to walk down the first row of capsules, I spot a small seating area at the far end. Three upholstered chairs circle a wooden coffee table. One of the chairs isn't empty. I catch a glimpse of the back of a blond head before I quickly step back out of sight.

"There's someone sitting at the back of the room," I whisper. "I think it's a woman."

"Anyone you recognize?" Todd doesn't bother to lower his voice. He doesn't seem to care if the person hears him.

For a moment I'm convinced this is some kind of setup. Or maybe Todd triggered an alarm. But if that's the case, why have we gotten so far?

"What are you waiting for?" Todd asks flatly. "Why don't you guys go over and say hi?"

I glance over at Elvis and find he's already looking at me. He seems terrified but game, so I give him a nod. I know in my heart there's no chance this will turn out well, but I'm not sure we have any alternatives. I start down the first row, heading toward the figure on the chair at the end. Along the way, I see bare feet at the ends of some of the capsules. Since Max was here, at least five more have been filled. But I don't stop to look inside. I keep my eyes glued to the woman's blond head. By the time I've reached the end of the row, I've picked up speed. I know who she is.

"Abigail?" Before I even get the name out, I've confirmed my hunch. I'm in front of her now, and there's no mistaking that care-fully sculpted face. She's staring straight ahead at the wall in front of her. I recognize her outfit—it's the same Chanel suit she was wearing this morning.

"Are you okay, Ms. Prince?" Elvis asks her when he arrives at my side.

Abigail blinks and her eyes roll in our direction. I don't know what kind of drugs they have her on, but she doesn't seem to share our panic. "Hello," she says coolly. "What are you two doing here?"

Whatever they've done to her, at least she still seems to recognize us.

"We're trying to finish what we set out to do. What are *you* doing here?" I ask. "Have they been holding you here since you left the island?"

"Holding me?" One of Abigail's eyebrows lifts, rippling the pale skin above it. The wrinkles catch my eye. Back on the island, Abigail's forehead was too Botoxed to budge. "I'm waiting for my next assignment."

That last word prompts a million questions, but it doesn't seem like Todd's going to let me ask any of them. "Now, now, Abigail," he says, as if lecturing a naughty child. "You aren't supposed to speak about your assignments with anyone other than me or Mr. Gibson."

"My apologies, your holiness," she replies. "It won't happen again."

"What the fuck? Your *holiness*?" Elvis grimaces. "Even I know that's in bad taste, dude."

"I hoped it would be funnier," Todd replies humorlessly. "Like my grandmother used to say, you either look for ways to laugh or you spend your life crying. But just so you know, I've been meaning to change it. I don't find it very amusing anymore."

"I don't get it." My eyes flick back and forth between Abigail and Todd. "What's going on?"

"She's a robot," Elvis explains. "These assholes made a copy of Abigail."

I instinctively take a step back from the woman on the chair. I don't know why. Abigail's watching me with the same haughty, bemused expression I got to know on the island. Now that I realize what she is, I can spot a few minor imperfections. But whoever made Abigail's clone must have studied her well.

"What did you do with the real Abigail Prince?" I ask Todd.

"How dare you? I *am* the real Abigail Prince," the robot answers angrily.

"Thank you, Abigail. We're done with you now." Todd puts a hand on her shoulder. "I was sweating bullets when Abigail's clone spoke to the press this afternoon. The bots look good, but the tech isn't really ready for prime time yet. We could have done a lot better if we'd designed them in-house, but the Company was never interested in developing anthropomorphic robots. Milo thought they were creepy."

Milo—the guy who invented a virtual reality game where he could satisfy every disgusting fantasy—thought the idea of anthropomorphic robots was creepy. I'd laugh at the irony if the human race weren't so royally screwed.

"Then where did the tech come from?" Elvis asks.

"When Milo started spending all his time in Otherworld, Wayne bought a robotics company on the sly."

Abigail's clone is now facing the wall. Her silk blouse continues to flutter with each breath, and her fake eyelashes lower and rise at a regular pace.

"Where's the real Abigail?" I demand again.

"Here, of course." Todd walks over to one of the capsules and taps the glass on its hexagonal window. He glances over his shoulder to where Elvis and I are still standing several feet back and waves to us over to join him. "Come on, take a look. Don't worry. You're not going to see anything you don't want to see. I've got her all covered up."

Inside the capsule, the naked body of a middle-aged woman lies with a sheet covering the space between her shins and collarbones. Without makeup to color her lips and outline her eyes, Abigail's features are a beige blur. Life-support machines monitor her pulse and respiration. There are beige half-moons at the top of her bloodred nails where her manicure has begun to grow out. I was never Abigail's biggest fan. I'm sure she'd say the same of me. But the indignity of her current situation is sickening. Even discount-store heiresses with questionable morals deserve far better fates than this.

"After the download, Gibson wanted to dispose of Abigail Prince's body. The artist who designs the robots was the one who convinced him to keep it. As Abigail ages, they can modify the copy. The artist said it would be the best way to achieve verisimilitude."

I'm sure this isn't where Abigail Prince imagined herself growing old.

"So they're going to keep her here? Like *that*. Forever?" I've never heard Elvis sound so horrified. "And you're okay with it?"

"Don't try appealing to his conscience," I warn. "Todd

doesn't have one. Back at the Facility, he managed a whole body farm. We're talking hundreds of people locked up in capsules just like Abigail. He claimed their sacrifice would be worthwhile when he eventually won his Nobel Prize. Isn't that right, Todd?"

"That must have been Martin who told you that." Todd bristles at the thought of his old partner. I wonder if he still blames me for his death. "He was convinced our tech would end up saving the world. But nobody's going to win a Nobel Prize for this shit."

"Yeah, they usually avoid giving Nobels to monsters," Elvis notes. "Watson was the exception, not the rule."

Something's brewing inside Todd. I watch as it bubbles up to the surface. Red splotches spread across his cheeks as words begin to spew from his lips.

"Don't be naive," he sneers. "You seriously think other scientists haven't done worse? The reason nobody's going to win any awards is because this tech won't ever go public."

I still don't understand why he's furious. "What do you mean?"

"I've spent years slaving away at this place. I haven't had a girlfriend since college. I've given everything to the Company. Everything! Fuck, I've watched people get killed for it! Martin, Rory, those people in Otherworld—I don't even know how many. And they all died for *nothing*. Nothing! What really gets to me, though, is that it took this goddamned long for me to figure it out. I don't know what Gibson's got planned, but I know one thing for sure, fame and glory aren't going to be part of it."

Elvis looks as stunned as I feel by the outburst. Todd shakes his head. We don't get it, and he's disappointed in both of us. "Two capsules down from this one. That was the first one that was filled. That's who Max Prince saw when he came here. After you see who it is, you'll know what I'm talking about."

I can see a pair of feet at the end of the capsule. The occupant is male. I catch Elvis's eye and we walk the few steps together. He bends down first and immediately straightens back up.

"What the fuck?" he gasps. His face is powder white.

I pull in a breath and go down for a look. There's a man lying in there on the stainless steel roll-out tray, naked aside from a strip of cloth that's been tastefully placed over his groin. I recognize him in an instant. Any American would. "Holy shit, you've got the vice president of the United States in here."

"It's a copy," Todd tells me. "Look closer. The body's not hooked up to life support."

"You're sure about that?" Inside the capsule, the man's chest is rising and falling. The hair on his chest flutters each time his nose expels air. "That's a pretty impressive copy."

"I'm ninety percent sure," Todd says. "But I can't open the capsule to check. See the door? They added a special lock. Only Gibson can access that particular capsule. Which means only Gibson really knows who's in there—and who's in Washington as we speak."

I can think of a million terrifying reasons to clone the vice president of the United States. Which was the one that inspired Wayne?

"Now—do you understand why Max Prince had to die? Do

you understand why Gibson murdered Rory in front of us? Do you understand why there's no fame or glory in any of this for me?"

As I stand up, I scan the capsules all around me. They suddenly seem more menacing than ever. "Who else does Wayne have locked up in here?"

This time, Todd doesn't answer. His eyes dart toward the exit as he lifts a finger to his lips. In the silence, I can hear the soft hum of a motor.

"It's the elevator." Todd doesn't seem surprised. He opens one of the capsules on the bottom row and grabs Elvis's arm. "Get in," he orders. "Quickly."

"What?" Elvis recoils, wrenching his arm out of Todd's grasp.

"Trust me. There's no way out."

"You want him to trust you?" I can hear the elevator rising. "Are you out of your mind?"

"Don't be stupid," Todd snaps. "If I wanted to have you both killed, I could have sounded an alarm the second we got here. There are panic buttons all over this place. I brought you up here because I *wanted* you two to see this."

I could fucking kick myself. I can't believe I've gotten Elvis and myself into a situation where our lives depend on a man who fits the dictionary definition of a serial killer to a T.

"You have to get in," I tell Elvis. "I'll find one too."

"No, don't," Todd tells me. "Just play along and everything will be fine. If I ask you a question, answer it simply and honestly."

I've watched Todd slaughter Children in Otherworld. I've seen him try to kill one of my own best friends. There were quite a few times he would happily have murdered me. And now I'm utterly at his mercy.

I hear the swoosh of the elevator doors opening. It's followed by footsteps and the sound of wheels on wood. Elvis scrambles into the open capsule, and Todd gently closes the door behind him.

"Come with me," Todd orders. We're going to greet our guests.

DOPPELGÄNGERS

A man in black military garb wheels a gurney out of the elevator while an older man watches, his back to us. The body on top of the gurney is covered from ankles to ears. I can't see its face. All I can tell is that it's a male with sandy blond hair.

"Go get him ready," the older man orders the man in black. "Be careful. This one's near and dear to my heart." The voice is commanding and brusque, with just a hint of an accent. There's nowhere to hide anymore, so I prepare to attack. Todd elbows me and points at my hands, which are clenched into fists. I reluctantly shake them out.

"Another guest, Mr. Gibson?" Todd asks casually.

Wayne Gibson glances over his shoulder and gives us a nod. He's not surprised to see Todd, and he's not at all disturbed by my presence. It's almost as if I'm completely invisible. "Morning, Bolton," he says. "The system told me you were here. When's the last time you slept, son?"

"Sleep's for pussies, sir," Todd responds. "I can sleep when I'm dead."

Wayne cracks a grin as the gurney is wheeled away. He must have liked what he heard. "I appreciate the dedication, Bolton. But at some point, you're going to start delivering diminishing returns." Wayne ambles over to us. I don't know how I'm supposed to behave. Should I look at him? I let my eyes settle on his face, but I keep my expression blank.

Todd and I both tower over Wayne. He may not be a tall man, but he's built like a pit bull. Everything about him screams former military—from his perfect posture to the shine on his shoes. I've never had a chance to really study him like this before. Up close his skin appears weathered, like an old baseball glove. The eyes behind his wire-frame glasses are a vivid blue.

"I'll make sure to get some sleep soon, sir," Todd assures him.

"Glad to hear it." Wayne pauses to give me a once-over. "That a new outfit?"

I have no idea how to respond, so I let Todd do the talking.

"I brought it from home," Todd explains. "It feels strange dealing with them when they're naked. It's getting hard not to see them as human."

My blood runs completely cold. Wayne laughs and gives Todd a hearty slap on the back. "That's when you know you're making real progress," he says. "Show me what our boy can do."

Todd faces me. "Simon, how do you feel about the Company?"

Answer honestly, he told me, so I do. "It's an evil organization that values nothing but power and money. It will do whatever it takes to accumulate both, even if it means destroying the world."

Wayne screws up his mouth and strokes his chin as he

ponders my response. "I don't know," he announces. "Something still sounds a bit off with the voice. And the answer was a little too fancy. Our boy's not that bright. Let's hear some more."

"Simon, if you found yourself alone in a room with the man who runs the Company, what would you do to him?"

That one's easy. "I'd rip his head off with my bare hands and piss down his throat."

Wayne lets out a howl of laughter and slaps his thigh. "You got it! That sounded just like the little bastard. God, I hate that kid. Nice work, Bolton. You never cease to amaze me. Now do me a favor. Hook up our new guest. Then put the kid back in his box and go get some sleep."

"Sure thing, sir." Todd starts toward the capsule where the new body is to be stored. I don't know what else to do, so I head after him.

"Why's your buddy going with you?" Wayne calls out from behind us. There's a note of suspicion in his voice. Todd stops and I do too. I think I may have just screwed everything up.

"It's just the setting I have him on," Todd replies. "The bots need practice walking around, so I programmed this one to fol-low me."

"He keep you company in the bathroom, too?" Wayne asks. Todd seems to be searching for a reply when Wayne chuckles. "Just joshing, son. Make sure you get enough rest. We need to get started on our new guest tomorrow."

"Will do, sir," Todd responds.

"Hey, you!" Wayne calls out to the man in black, who's just finished loading the new body onto one of the sliding stainless steel trays. "Come give me a ride home. I'm too pooped to drive."

The man immediately drops the life-support wires and tubes and marches to join Wayne in the elevator. He reminds me of an NPC soldier in Otherworld.

Just before the doors slide shut, Wayne shoves a hand between them. The doors open once again, and this time I'm sure we're fucked. Wayne's pointing right at me.

"You know what, Bolton? Give that little shit a kick in the ass before you go home," Wayne says. "Just for me."

"Will do, sir." Todd smirks.

Once we hear the elevator begin to descend, I finally face Todd. I'll admit, I was slow to catch on, but now I know. Wayne thought I was one of his robot clones. That means there must be an identical version of me inside one of these capsules. Wayne had them copy me while I was in their custody. As bad as that is, there's another thought that bothers me far more: they must have done the same thing to Kat as well.

"When were you planning to tell me?" I growl at Todd.

He sighs. "To be honest, I hadn't made up my mind if I should. I didn't know how much it would screw with your head."

"What do you say we find out? Show me," I order.

As we pass the gurney that's still waiting in the aisle, I hear faint thumps coming from somewhere below. Elvis must be banging on the inside of his capsule. I should have warned him he'd be temporarily trapped. I forgot that the capsules can't be opened from the inside. I squat down, open the door and roll Elvis out. He's only been inside for a few minutes, but his face has turned magenta and his hair is dripping with sweat.

"Guess what? I just discovered I'm claustrophobic," he manages to say as he gulps in huge breaths of air.

"Then it's a day of self-discovery for both of us," I tell him. "I just found out that I have a twin."

Elvis's eyes widen comically. He's no longer hyperventilating, but he looks like he might spontaneously combust. "No!"

"Yep." I point to Todd, who's already standing in front of a capsule at the end of the row. "I'm going to meet him now."

I move toward Todd while Elvis scrambles to his feet. When I reach the capsule, I have to force myself to look through the window. When I do, I see my own body lying motionless in front of me. I glance inside the neighboring capsule. Kat's copy is in there, completely nude. I avert my eyes, ashamed I looked in the first place. It seems robots don't even get the benefit of the metallic Speedos the humans use.

"Don't worry, I didn't see Kat," Elvis assures me as he shields his eyes. I don't call him on it, but there's no way he could have known it was Kat in the capsule unless he had taken a look.

I study my own double. Everything about the body is perfect. They've even re-created a small birthmark on my right thigh.

"Wow, this is much more awkward than I thought it would be," Elvis says. "I'm not sure I want to know you this well, Simon."

I don't know how to describe what I'm feeling, but I'm definitely not in the mood for Elvis's jokes. I was still trying to get used to the fact that the Company's been inside my head. Now I know the rest of me has been violated too. The thought makes me cringe. But the idea that they did the same to Kat? That makes me want to kill.

"Did you do this?" I ask Todd, surprised to hear how calm and steady my voice sounds.

Todd catches on and backs away until he runs up against the

capsules on the other side of the aisle. "No," he swears as I take a step toward him. "I downloaded your memories into the clones. That's all! The rest of the work was done upstairs on five. That's where the artist makes the bodies."

"Can we see what's on the fifth floor?" Elvis asks eagerly.

"Yes, I think it's time to pay a visit to the artist's studio," I agree. I have a few decorating changes in mind.

"I'd take you up there if I could, but I don't have access," Todd says. "Just Gibson, the artist and her assistant are allowed."

"Her?" It shouldn't surprise me, but everyone I've met from the Company so far has been male.

"Yeah, the artist is the only lady in the building," he adds nervously.

"What's her name?" I ask.

"Daisy Bristol. But everyone here calls her 'the artist.' She came from the robotics company Wayne bought." Todd pauses and points at the body that just arrived with Wayne. It's still waiting on the gurney to be connected to his capsule's life-support system. "I know this has probably blown your minds, but I can't stay here while you guys try to figure everything out. You heard Gibson. I need to hook up the new guy and go home. Wayne knows when anyone accesses the elevator. Fortunately for you guys, I work a lot of late nights. I knew he wouldn't think it was strange if I came here. But he won't be happy if I don't leave when he told me to."

"Is that right?" I'm skeptical. "Seems to me like you guys have a pretty friendly relationship."

"You think?" Todd replies. "I always got the sense he liked Rory better. Funny thing is, that didn't stop him from murdering the guy. Look, Wayne's paranoid. He's got a plan, and he's not going to let anyone get in the way—no matter how much he likes them."

"What's his plan?"

"Dude, your guess is as good as mine," Todd says. "All I know is that it involves the vice president of the United States."

Elvis snorts. "You guys haven't figured it out? Seems pretty obvious to me. Wayne's using OtherEarth to compromise people in positions of power. Then he brings them here, downloads their memories and makes a robotic clone. As soon as the tech is good enough, he plans to switch them."

I'm starting to suspect Elvis thinks I'm a complete moron. "Yeah, I got all of that. The question is *why*?" I say.

Elvis shrugs. "To take over the world?"

Now it's my turn to be a dick. "This isn't a comic book," I tell him. "World domination doesn't motivate people in real life."

"Maybe Wayne's latest patient will give us a clue." Todd clearly wants us to stop arguing and get moving. "Shall the three of us have a look at the new arrival?"

Todd steps around Elvis and makes his way to the gurney. When he pulls the sheet off, I expect to see someone famous, but I don't recognize the new guy at all. He's got the paunch of a sixty-year-old truck driver, but his face is that of a man in his late thirties. I'm looking at the results of a seriously sedentary lifestyle. Wayne's found the only person around whose health could benefit from a stay at the Company's capsule spa.

"Whoa." Todd rears back and grimaces. He obviously knows the guy.

"Who is it?" I ask.

"His name's Ronald Wahl. He's the guy who sold Wayne the robotics company. He's supposed to be off saving orangutans in Borneo or some other do-gooder crap with the fortune he made."

"Must not have read the fine print on the deal," Elvis quips. "Hope you've had a good look at *your* contract, Todd."

"Wait, this is one of the Company's business associates?" I'm finding it a bit difficult to wrap my head around this one. "Why would Wayne want to bring *him* here?"

"Tech support?" The joke must be a reflex. Todd isn't even grinning. If anything, he looks physically ill. This is the price of doing business with the Company. I think it's finally dawned on Todd that he's far more likely to end up in one of these capsules than on the deck of a yacht. "Do you really think you can stop this?"

He's looking straight at me, but I'm not prepared to answer the question. "Me?" I must sound incredibly stupid.

"Yeah, you. Everyone who's gotten in Wayne's way is gone," Todd continues. "Except for *you*. Why do you think I'm showing you all of this? I always thought you were a jackass, but you're the only one Wayne can't seem to beat. You remember that kid who survived being killed in Otherworld?"

Just when I was warming to Todd, he goes and reminds me he's a psychopath. "The kid's name is *Declan*. He's a friend of mine and you did your best to kill him." I can still see him stabbing Gorog, Declan's ogre avatar, even though he knew the real person controlling it could die.

"Yeah, that's the kid." Todd doesn't bat an eye. "You know, he had a pretty crazy theory about you."

"Stop." I put my hand up. "I've heard it a thousand times."

Todd looks confused.

"No, seriously, he has," Elvis helpfully explains. "It's kind of a running joke with our crew."

"Well, the kid didn't think it was funny." Todd refuses to stop. "One day we'd just finished an OtherEarth test. Man, he did *not* like those. Anyway, the kid's got tears and snot and all sorts of stuff running down his face and he says, 'Simon's going to make you pay for this. You can't stop him. He's going to destroy the Company. He's the One.'"

I want to punch Todd in the face so badly that my right fist is literally throbbing. What kind of animal tortures a thirteen-year-old kid?

"You know, I always liked Declan," Todd muses. He can't see that I'm about to explode. "He was a feisty little turd. And I hope he was right about you. I hope you burn this place to the ground."

I get right up in Todd's face. "And after all the shit you've pulled, I hope your friend AJ on the second floor designs a killer experience just for you."

Todd seems more annoyed than intimidated. "Gee, that's not very nice," he snips. "After I risked everything to bring you here. And to think I was just about to give you an update on your little friend."

"Declan is safe now." I gave him a bag filled with more money than I'd ever seen and told him to take his parents and lie low. "I made sure of that."

"Did you?" Todd asks. "You sure he didn't ditch his parents and come back to New York looking for you?"

I can feel the blood draining out of my face. That is exactly the sort of thing Declan would do.

"Where is he?" I spin around. "Is he here somewhere, too?"

Todd keeps his hands in the pockets of his sweatshirt when he shrugs. "Nope," he replies. "You'll have to ask Wayne. Gibson's the only one who knows where the kid's at now."

I glower at Todd. I don't trust him, but I do believe him. "Why would Wayne have Declan?"

"My guess is he's keeping the kid as an insurance policy in case you ever show up again. You mess with him and he'll mess with Declan."

"And why are you telling me all of this?"

"For the same reason I let you see the lab. This is *my* insurance policy."

"How do you figure?" I ask.

"I'm betting on you," Todd says. "And now you owe me one."

HOMECOMING

The sun is rising. We've got to get to Wayne and we're running out of time, but Nasha refuses to act. They may look nothing alike on the outside, but she and her daughter share the ability to drive me completely insane.

"Absolutely not, Simon." She's really putting her foot down now. Literally. The woman's stomping like an angry bull. "Do you know how close we are to taking down the Company? We've got the location of the lab! We know what's inside it. We tip off the right authorities and it's game over!"

"If the lab gets raided, Wayne might hurt Declan. We have to save him first."

"But if we go after your friend first, Wayne could get spooked and move the whole lab. And as I *think* you know, that lab is the key to taking down the whole Company."

Now it's my turn. Immovable object, meet irresistible force.

"Declan comes first. You can either offer to help or you can get out of my way. But you're not going to stop me."

"You mean *us*," Kat chimes in. "I'm coming with you." I'd argue if it would make any difference—but it won't. I sneak a quick peek at her. With that halo of copper curls, she resembles a warrior goddess. Man, I love this girl.

"We're all going with Simon." When Busara steps forward, Elvis joins her.

It's going too far now. As much as I appreciate the vote of support, their company is not what I had in mind. "No. You and Elvis have to stay here. If something happens to me and Kat, you guys have to keep up the fight."

Elvis catches my eye and subtly raises an eyebrow. He must think I just did him a favor by giving him a few hours alone with Busara. The truth is, Elvis's romantic troubles are the very least of my worries. I've proposed a mission that's unbelievably danger-ous. I wish I could come up with something less risky, but there's no time to lose. Wayne is the only person who knows where De-clan is. And Kat and I know where Wayne lives.

It's a trap, of course, and we're walking right into it. Wayne took Declan because he knew I'd do exactly what I'm about to do. He'll be expecting us. I'm just hoping he's feeling cocky enough to spill a few beans when we see him. All I'm after is a single clue, and there are two things I know about Wayne. The first is that he thinks I'm a moron. The second is that the man can't resist the urge to hear himself talk.

"We're just going to have a chat with Wayne," I tell Nasha. "We won't say a word about the lab."

"This has got to be the dumbest idea I've ever heard! You really think I'm going to let you commit suicide?" Nasha's right about one thing. The odds of us surviving this operation aren't exactly stellar. She squeezes her eyes shut and rubs her temples as if her brain might explode. "Maybe you don't understand. We're trying to save the world here. And you want to risk everything for one kid? Do you know how insane that sounds?"

Does it? It makes perfect sense to me. "Would it make a difference if Declan were *your* kid?" I demand.

"Probably not," Busara snorts. Her mother stays silent.

"Look, Nasha, I don't care if you think it's crazy. If you want my help, this is how it has to be. Every person counts," I tell her. "No one gets left behind. *No one.* The day you start seeing people as expendable—the day you start thinking a single human sacrifice might be worth it—that's the day you become Wayne Gibson. Declan is a thirteen-year-old boy who saved my ass on multiple occasions. I am not going to let him die."

The room is so quiet I can hear my friends breathing. They're all staring at me like they're not sure who I am.

"What?" I bark at Elvis.

"That was fucking beautiful, man."

If he's screwing with me, he chose a weird time to do it. I roll my eyes and turn back to Nasha. My outburst made an impact on her, but it hasn't won her over completely.

"You're playing right into Wayne's hands," she warns me. "He knew exactly what you'd do. That's why he took the boy. You go after him and he'll be prepared."

"You think I haven't figured that out?" I ask. "It's all part of my plan. Now are you going to get out of the way or not?"

Nasha's phone rings. I recognize the ring tone. It's a call from her boss. She holds the phone to her ear without saying a word. Three seconds later, her face is grim as she lowers the phone again. She's received her orders, and she isn't happy at all.

"Let's go," Nasha snaps at me. "I'm coming with you."

There's a black SUV with tinted windows waiting for us outside the building. Behind the wheel is another of the freakishly bland men who always seem to be at Nasha's beck and call. I wonder if they grow them all in a lab somewhere. The three of us take our seats in the back, and Nasha picks up a slim black suitcase that's been left on the floor. Inside are three guns cradled in foam, along with matching silencers, an unmarked syringe and a plastic bag filled with zip ties.

"Those will come in handy." I grab the zip ties and shove them into my pocket. "You guys really do think of everything."

"Yeah, and we think you're going to need a lot more than zip ties. You two know how to shoot?" Nasha asks us.

"Yes," Kat confirms. I've only held a real gun once in my life, but I knew exactly what to do with it. I wish someone would tell my dad. Video games are good for something, as it turns out.

"Sure you do," Nasha drones. She's not convinced. "Katherine, after your mother married Wayne, how long did the three of you live in the same house?"

"Almost a year. But my mom and I lived in that place for ages before he showed up. I know every inch of it by heart."

"Do you have any sense of his security arrangements?" Nasha inquires.

"I watched Wayne install his system," Kat says. "He's got the entire place covered. He'll see us the second we set foot on the property."

Nasha leans over Kat to give me a look that screams, *What do you think of that you crazy little bastard?*

"It's okay. We aren't going to hide. I want him to see us," I say. "We'll drive right up to the house and Kat and I will go in through the front door."

"You're going to get shot," Nasha says. "Wayne's probably got an arsenal in there."

"I don't think he'll shoot us. We'll have tripped his security alarms. I think he'll try to keep us talking until the police arrive. I'm hoping he'll let something slip that will help us locate Declan."

"Or he could just splatter your brains all over the wall," Nasha offers.

"If he wanted to kill us, why did he frame us for the Scott Winston shooting?" I ask. "He doesn't want us dead. He wants us to rot in jail."

"So how are we going to avoid being arrested?" Kat asks.

"Once we're inside, do you think you can shut down Wayne's security system?"

"Probably," Kat replies. "But we'll have already tripped the alarm."

"Doesn't matter," I say. I turn to Nasha. "The house I grew up in is on the other side of the woods from Wayne's house. You and the driver drop us off at Wayne's and then wait for us outside my old house. Kat and I will have our chat with Wayne, and as soon as we hear sirens, we'll head through the woods. With the security system down, they'll have no way of knowing which way we went."

Nasha still isn't satisfied.

"Even if you don't get killed, you figure Wayne's just going to come right out and tell you everything you need to know?" Nasha scoffs. "This is never going to work."

"That's your opinion," I say with a shrug. "Seems like your employer has confidence in my abilities. Shall we give the boss a call?"

In an instant, all expression is wiped from Nasha's face. She doesn't offer even the slightest twitch to confirm my hunch.

"I know I'm right," I tell her.

"You don't know anything," she says.

I catch a quick nap in the back of the car. It's seven in the morning by the time we reach Brockenhurst, New Jersey. It's only when we pass the cute wooden sign that welcomes visitors that I realize I never planned to return. The twee little shops that line Main Street are still shuttered and dark. It's hard to believe that anyone actually works here. The whole town feels like a Hollywood stage set. If you opened one of the doors and stepped inside, you'd discover it was all just a plywood façade with nothing behind it.

"Home, sweet home," Kat jokes. She doesn't want to be here any more than I do. I take her hand in mine. As much as Brockenhurst unnerves me, I can't quite hate it. After all, this is where I met her.

At the far edge of town, just past the town's only gas station, is a narrow gravel road that leads through Brockenhurst's last patch of forest. At the end of the drive lies Wayne Gibson's house. Kat and I know every inch of these woods. When we lived here, this was our own little world. Now, as our driver turns onto the drive, I feel like we've crossed into enemy territory. I wouldn't be surprised if Wayne has a hidden camera positioned on every tree.

Soon the white cottage appears ahead of us. Less than a year ago, it was little more than a hovel with rotten siding and rusted appliances on the porch. Now the place is storybook cute, with a fresh coat of paint and green shutters. Wayne's done a lot of work to the house, but it's still the last place you'd expect to find one of the world's most powerful men. Half a mile away, on the other side of the forest, lies my old neighborhood, a gated community filled with mansions modeled after French châteaux. There, Wayne could live alongside his peers. Instead he appears to prefer the company of the half-coyote wild dogs that make their home here in the woods.

The second the car comes to a halt, Kat and I are out of the backseat. There's not a moment to lose. I half expect to see Wayne appear on the front porch with a shotgun in his hands. It wouldn't be the first time he's greeted me in that way. But the cottage door stays closed until we reach it—and find it unlocked. I turn the knob and Kat and I walk right inside. When I was a kid, the front room of the house was filled with shabby furniture and knick-knacks. Now the walls are a bare, brilliant white, and a boxy couch sits facing a television set. There's no other furniture in the room. Wayne must be worth a fortune, and yet he lives like a monk.

"Come on back, guys," a voice calls out cheerfully from the kitchen.

Kat and I separate. While she goes off to work on the security system, I head toward the voice. I find Wayne sitting alone at the kitchen table, a steaming mug in front of him. He's wearing pale blue pajamas and slippers, and his gray hair is still mussed from sleep. I've never seen anyone who looks less dangerous.

"Little early for a visit," Wayne notes, taking a sip from his mug. "Worked late last night and didn't get up at the usual hour. I haven't even finished my first cup of coffee." He cranes his head as if to look around me. "Where's my lovely stepdaughter? Feeling shy? Tell her to come on in and say hello to her stepdad."

"I think we'll both pass," I say, brandishing my gun with one hand while I pull two zip ties out of my back pocket with the other. "Put your arms behind you."

Wayne doesn't argue. After he sets down his coffee cup and complies, I quickly tie each of his hands to the chair. Then I take my place in front of him.

"Straight to business, eh? I admire that in a young man." Wayne gives me a nod of approval. He thinks he's got me right where he wants me. "Your face sure is looking better than the last time I saw you."

I take aim with my gun. Now that I have the weapon pointed at his head, the urge to shoot is overwhelming. I learned to like killing in Otherworld. And there's no one I'd rather put a few holes in than Wayne.

"Hold up, son." Wayne's still cool as a cucumber. "You might want to think twice about shooting me."

"Oh, believe me," I say. "I've thought about this *a lot* more than twice."

"That's a shame. Maybe you should have spent less time

thinking about me and more time worrying about your friend Declan," Wayne says.

I was right about everything. This is all going just as I planned.

"Declan's safe," I say, playing dumb. "I made sure of that."

"Oh, I know you tried," says Wayne. "But kids do stupid crap. Your friend heard you were being framed for a murder and tried to come back to save you."

"You're full of shit," I say, acting as if this is all news to me.

"Just have a look on my phone." Wayne nods at a phone that's been sitting facedown on the table. When I pick it up and turn it over, I see that the home screen is a photo of Declan on a hospital bed.

"Where is he?" I demand. "Tell me, goddamn it, or I'll shoot."

I think Wayne may have missed his calling. He really would make an excellent actor. In a flash, his expression shifts from amusement to pity. "You haven't really thought this through, have you? As long as I have the kid, there's not much you can do to me. I like to think of Declan as my guardian angel. The boy really cuts down on my security bills, that's for sure."

"Oh, there's plenty I can do to you," I tell him, moving my gun so it's aimed right at his groin.

"You talking torture?" Wayne laughs. "Son, I was held by the Taliban for six months in 2003. If those evil fuckers couldn't get a thing out of me, I don't think a little prick like you stands a chance. But who knows? You go right ahead and do what you like. Just know that I'll have one of my people do the exact same things to Declan."

I lower the gun. "How do I know you haven't killed him already? How do I know he's okay?"

"I guess you're just going to have to trust me. Declan's perfectly safe. I've got a very nice lady who checks in on him regularly and makes sure he's having fun."

I feel an electric jolt shoot down my spine. That's the clue I've been looking for. As soon as Kat's finished with the security system, it's time to go.

"Well, if you're not going to tell me where he is, I might as well go ahead and shoot you. I'll find him one way or the other."

Wayne tsk-tsks. I know I'm playing a game here, but his lack of respect is really starting to piss me off. You'd think he'd take me a little more seriously at this point.

"You won't take the risk," he says. "You forget, Mr. Eaton. I've been inside your head. I know what that kid means to you. When he and his parents disappeared, I thought I might need to make do with your mother. Can you imagine what kind of pain in the ass that would have been? But then I got lucky. Declan showed up back in town, and kidnapping Irene Eaton was no longer necessary."

I hear someone enter the kitchen behind me. I assume it's Kat coming to inform me she's done.

"You're right, Wayne. Simon won't hurt you," I hear Nasha say. "But I will."

What the fuck is she doing here? Did she think I couldn't handle this? I'm trying not to show it, but I'm absolutely fuming.

Wayne leans back in his chair. "Why, if it isn't Nasha Ogubu!" How the hell does he know her? I suppose it's possible he met Nasha through James. But he doesn't sound shocked in the least to see her here. "I was wondering if it might be you behind the wheel of that big SUV parked outside. Whatever are you doing in beautiful Brockenhurst?"

"I'm looking for Declan Andrews." Nasha's very good at this, too. I almost believe her. Maybe I should. "Tell me where he is or I'll put a bullet through your head."

"No, you won't," Wayne scoffs. "Mr. Eaton here is never going to let that happen."

"I don't work for Simon," Nasha says. "We have other reasons for wanting Declan. We're told he has a remarkable brain."

"Indeed he does," Wayne agrees. "But if I'm not mistaken, the boy standing here with us right now is the one who interests your mysterious employer the most. After all, you took a pretty big risk sending a team to Company headquarters to rescue him. How many men were you willing to lose for his sake? My guess is you wouldn't even be in Brockenhurst at all if someone hadn't ordered you to keep him happy."

My hunch was right. Someone really has been telling Nasha to go along with whatever I want. And Wayne might know who it is. It takes all the restraint I can muster to avoid looking over at her.

Nasha laughs. "You've got to be kidding. Simon brought us to you. That's all we wanted from him. Now he's no longer of use to us."

"So you don't care what makes him happy?" Wayne challenges her. "Then prove it. Kill me. Or torture me. Whatever you like. Just know there's a very good chance that the same will be done to Declan Andrews. I'm sure you won't mind—as long as that precious brain of his isn't harmed."

I see Nasha raise her gun. Wayne has called my bluff. I'm not sure what's going to happen next. I'm not entirely convinced that Nasha and I are still on the same team.

"Don't worry, son," Wayne tells me. "She's not going to do anything. She wouldn't shoot me even if I told her I was the one who disposed of her husband."

My head spins back in her direction. Oh, shit. My plan just went totally off the rails.

"That's right," Wayne says. "I found James in his office with an Otherworld disk plastered to the back of his head. Killing him couldn't have been easier. Just cut off his airflow and a couple minutes later it was all over. Let Milo think it was all his fault, and he took it upon himself to dispose of the body."

Nasha says nothing.

"Why would you do that?" I ask.

"Figured I was doing humanity a giant favor. Look at all of the trouble James's inventions have caused. He never even stopped to think what any of it would mean for the rest of us. The only thing that mattered to him was preserving his own DNA. He was willing to sacrifice everything just to save his daughter. You see, Simon, you think I'm the bad guy, but I'm not. It's people like James Ogubu who are destroying the world."

Nasha hasn't moved. Her hand hasn't so much as twitched. I can't tell if she knew all along.

"Now would you look at that," Wayne says. "I just informed Mrs. Ogubu that I murdered her husband, and she still hasn't shot me. You know why? Because *you* don't want her to. Now why is that, do you suppose?"

Two shots ring out, one right after another. I hear Wayne's chair topple over, followed by a grunt of pain. Nasha's face is a mask as she lowers the gun to her side. The world seems to be moving in slow motion as I turn toward what I'm absolutely convinced will be a hole-ridden corpse. Instead, I see Wayne's legs twitching in the air. He's alive.

I take a step forward and realize the bullets have blown off the back legs of the chair he's still strapped to. I'm duly impressed. Even in Otherworld I was never that good with a gun.

"Was that really necessary?" I ask Nasha.

"He's lucky I let him live," she says. "He won't be so lucky the next time I see him."

"What the hell just happened?" Kat rushes in. She's still holding a screwdriver in one hand.

"Nasha got trigger-happy. You finished with the security system?" I ask.

"I think so," she says.

"Then let's get the hell out of here," I tell her.

I can hear sirens in the distance as we sprint through the woods toward my old house. It's an obstacle course, but Kat and I know the way. Wayne demolished the fort we built when we were kids, but everything else is the same. I still dream about this place. All of my fondest memories took place right here, with Kat. This will always be where I feel most at home.

A flash of garish checked pattern catches my eye. The Kishka is standing in the distance, leaning against a tree, smoking a cigarette. He touches the brim of his hat in a greeting right before he vanishes from view.

Just ahead, I can see the roof of the fake mansion where I grew up. Soon the rest of the building and the pool come into view. Nasha's colleague will be waiting for us in front of the house. I spot my father standing just on the other side of the sliding glass doors. He should be on the way to his office in Manhattan by now, but he's not. He's still in his bathrobe, and it doesn't look like he's shaved in days. He watches the three of us sprint past. He doesn't seem to believe what he sees. I know the feeling.

Our driver is parked in front of the house. Kat, Nasha and I jump in and the vehicle takes off at a leisurely pace.

As I catch my breath, the rage begins to build inside me.

"How dare you?" I shout at Nasha. "We had a plan. You agreed to it. Then you did what you wanted to anyway. You could have gotten Declan killed!"

"I was trying to help. You weren't making any progress," Nasha says. "The whole trip was a waste of time. Just like I told you it would be."

"That's what you think. I got what I wanted. I could have gotten more if you'd butted the fuck out."

"What exactly did you get?" She doesn't believe me.

"I'll tell you when you tell me who you're working for. Does Wayne Gibson know?"

This time Nasha has nothing to say.

"Who is it? What are they after? Why are they making you do what I want?"

Nasha looks out the window and ignores the question.

"Fine," I tell her. "Keep your little secret. But don't you ever get in my way again."

A VERY NICE LADY

A very nice lady checks in on him regularly and makes sure he's having fun.

I could be wrong—there's always that chance. But after my little chat with Wayne, I have a strong hunch that while Declan's body is lying in a hospital bed somewhere, his mind's been sent to Otherworld. Wayne says he has a woman check in on him there, and I think I may know who she is. All it takes is a few quick Internet searches to find her.

According to Todd, Wayne has ten people working at the lab, and only one of them is female. The woman Todd called the artist. She came to the Company from the robotics shop Wayne acquired—the one whose founder is currently occupying a capsule. Wayne may have kept the acquisition a secret from Milo, but the online financial press was all over it at the time. Ronald Wahl's company was called Skin Job. According to Bloomberg, its robots were designed to function as human companions.

"You know what that means, right?" Elvis cackles over my shoulder. "Wayne bought a dirty-doll factory."

It's starting to make sense. Their whole business model depended on robots that looked human up close and personal. I type "Skin Job" and "artist" into Google and a video interview on YouTube appears at the top of the search results. It dates from earlier this year, around the time Otherworld headsets went on sale. Elvis, Kat and Busara gather around as I click Play. A man with a scruffy beard and spectacles is standing beside a pretty, petite blonde in a flowery dress.

"Oh man, I *hate* that guy," Busara says of the interviewer. "He's a total pig."

"If by *pig* you mean *sexist pervert*, then yeah," Kat says.

I have no idea who the dude is.

"I'm David Evans from TechSpot, and I'm standing here with Daisy Bristol, head of product development at Skin Job," the man says, and I immediately hit Pause.

"*That's* the artist? Daisy Bristol? She looks like a kindergarten teacher," I say.

Busara gives me the stink-eye. "You too? And here I was thinking you were the One. You really disappoint me, Simon. I'm gonna have to go find some other boy hero to worship."

Kat cracks up, but I'm so used to the *One* shit by now that I barely hear it. "What? I just expect evil-genius sex-doll designers to look a little more . . ." I search for the right word.

"Male?" Busara turns to Kat. "See what I mean? Totally sexist."

"Yeah," my girlfriend chimes in. "Not to mention inaccurate. *My* kindergarten teacher was a guy."

"Give me a break! I'm just trying to say that Daisy Bristol looks harmless," I argue.

"Which makes her even more dangerous." Elvis decides to keep rubbing it in. "Man, Simon, you really have been drinking the patriarchy Kool-Aid."

There's no point in arguing my innocence any further. I keep my lips sealed and hit Play once again.

"Skin Job is a startup based here in Brooklyn," David Evans says. "You guys specialize in what you like to call robotic companions, isn't that right?" There's a lurid grin on the interviewer's face, and he appears to be directing his question to Daisy's breasts.

"That's right, David, but I'm not one of them," Daisy says in a lovely Australian accent. She bends her knees just enough so the interviewer's eyes land on her face, not her chest, and gives him a girlish wave. His head jerks up immediately and his face flushes with embarrassment.

"Oh my God." Kat laughs and gives Busara a high five. "You go, girl."

David Evans clears his throat. "You've brought something to show us today, have you not?" He's clearly referring to whatever's beneath the black box that's sitting on a table behind them, but he keeps his eyes glued to the camera. I think he's worried he'll slip up again.

"Yes, I have, David," Daisy announces confidently. "I've been following your show for ages, and I know you've always been a big . . . fan . . . of the women in our industry, so I created something just for you."

David's head jerks in her direction. This clearly wasn't what he had planned. "You did?" he asks.

"It's a tribute of sorts," Daisy tells him as she moves toward the box. "I hope you're flattered."

Beneath the box is a head on a silver platter. It's David's. Everything about it is perfect—from the vaguely pubescent beard to the hipster eyeglasses. You can hear the cameramen laughing as they zoom in on the face. The eyes blink lazily and the lips form a sultry pout.

"Holy shit," Elvis says. "Daisy Bristol is one badass chick."

Kat is awestruck. "No joke. That lady may be my new hero."

I for one will never judge a woman—or a kindergarten teacher—on their appearance again.

"The head is perfectly operational," Daisy says. "It can be attached to one of our six classic male body types. We'll make sure the body comes with your preferred amount of manscaping, and we can even program it to repeat your favorite phrases."

"You—you copied me," David sputters. "How did you do this?"

"I'm an artist," Daisy tells him. "I watched your videos—trying very hard not to vomit at your revolting treatment of women in the tech industry, of course. Then I sculpted a model of your head using clay. Afterward I scanned the model and used our 3-D printers to create a head made from the most skinlike material available. This is a custom creation, of course. Orders like these will only make up a small segment of Skin Job's offerings. A custom business isn't scalable at this point, and a head like yours would be too expensive for all but the richest consumers. But if there are any billionaires out there who'd like to keep David as a companion, feel free to place an order today!"

"This can't be legal," David croaks. I'm actually starting to feel sorry for him now.

"Oh, it's perfectly legal," Daisy informs him. "It takes a while for legislation to catch up with technology."

"Even if it's legal, it's wrong."

"Is it?" Daisy doesn't appear to care.

David is stunned. "How would you feel if you'd been cloned for use as a sex doll?"

"Meh." Daisy dismisses the question with a wave of her hand. "It's not my job to worry about such things. I leave the deep thinking to the ethicists. *My* job is to create and invent—to push the limits of what can be done. It's society's role to figure out whether it *should* be done."

Her argument sounds perfectly reasonable until you actually stop and think about it. Once a technology's out in the world, you can't stop it from spreading. The interviewer doesn't look all that convinced, either.

"But—" David Evans starts to say.

"Have you played Milo Yolkin's new game, Otherworld?" Daisy asks out of left field, and I sit up straight.

"Of course. I tried it out last week," David replies hesitantly. He doesn't see where the conversation is going.

"Yeah, I read your fawning review," Daisy says. "I bet it was hard to write with your head stuck so far up Milo's ass. Are you going to ask *him* if his innovations are good for the world?"

"Otherworld is a game," David says. "It's just for fun."

Daisy strokes the hair on the robot's head. "So is this," she says with a smile.

The video ends and the four of us sit in silence, staring at the screen.

"I can't decide whether Daisy Bristol should have a statue built in her honor or if she needs to be tossed in jail to save humanity," Busara says.

"Both?" Kat offers.

"We have to talk to her," I tell the group. "I think she's the one Wayne has checking up on Declan in Otherworld. Remember how Todd used to control the Elemental of Imperium? The last time Kat and I were there, Imperium had a new ruler. An Empress. I'm pretty sure it's Daisy."

"How is that relevant? It doesn't matter what games she plays. You cannot confront that woman." Nasha's been standing behind us the whole time, just waiting to poke more holes in my plans. "There's no guarantee she'll know where to find your friend's body. And if you reach out to her, Wayne will know you've discovered the lab."

After the incident in Brockenhurst, I'm not really interested in hearing Nasha's perspective. Her recklessness could have gotten Declan killed.

"You can't confront her, but we *can* have someone pay her a visit." Nasha holds out a slip of paper. "I took the liberty of locating her address. I'll send one of my guys to do a little snooping"

I think it's meant to be a peace offering, and I'm not interested in a truce. I take the slip of paper. "We aren't *sending* anyone. Two of us will go. My friends and I don't need your help anymore."

Nasha really is trying her best to be civil. She'd love to kick my ass. I can see it in her eyes. Instead she offers a tight smile. "There aren't two of you who *can* go," she argues. "Busara shouldn't risk straining her heart. And you and Kat have been all over the news again."

It's true. After Kat and I were reported in New Jersey, every cable news channel camped out in Brockenhurst. They don't actually have any news to report, so they're running the old videos back to back. Everyone in America's been reminded what we look like.

"Then I guess that leaves me," Elvis announces. "I'll go by myself."

"No. You can't go alone." Busara refuses to entertain the idea. "None of us goes anywhere solo anymore. That's the deal."

I've only seen Elvis truly angry a couple of times. Back in school he kept his distance from most of our classmates. He didn't care about anything—so there was no reason for him to get mad—except for that one time he was reported for being unhygienic. That has all changed. Now there's someone who's able to get under his skin. I don't know exactly what happened while Kat and I were in New Jersey, but it seems like Busara may have finally pushed him too far.

"You're awfully concerned about my welfare for someone who's barely spoken to me in days," Elvis responds without looking in her direction. "If you don't mind, Busara, I think I'll take my advice from people who actually want me around. The rest of you guys have any objections to me going to Daisy's house alone?"

The unexpected fury in his voice keeps Busara quiet. I guess their alone time did not go as Elvis had hoped. Whatever's going on, I don't want to be in the middle of it. But when no one answers, I have to speak up. "I don't have any problem with you going to Daisy's," I say. "Anyone other than Busara opposed?"

Kat and Nasha both remain silent.

"Great." Elvis stands up and addresses Nasha. "Then I guess it's decided. Now, how are you going to get me inside?"

According to Nasha, the high-rise apartment building where Daisy lives in on the Upper East Side of Manhattan is known for its excellent security. A doorman is always on duty. Cameras monitor every hallway. You even need a special key to operate the elevator. The apartment doors all feature biometric locks. There's no way to break into a resident's apartment if you go through the front door. Yet, like many fancy buildings in the city, there's often no one watching the back door. Dozens of domestics pass through the service entrance each day. Daisy's cleaning lady is one of them. Today, in exchange for a wad of cash big enough to let her finally retire, she'll be bringing along an assistant.

"We're approaching apartment 38H," we hear Elvis whispering. "I feel my sphincter clenching with excitement. So I guess this is your last day on the job, Rosemary. How ya feeling?"

The camera moves and the cleaning lady's face briefly appears on the screen before a rubber-gloved hand shoots up to hide it. "Don't point that damned thing at me," she says.

"Reluctant star, huh?" Elvis asks. "I don't blame you. Or maybe you're worried this is going to be like one of those buddy movies where the cop who's retiring gets pulled into some big case on his last day on the job?"

Busara leans forward. "Is the commentary really necessary?" she hisses.

"If you don't like the show, you don't have to watch," Elvis snaps.

Busara looks to Kat and me. We shrug in unison. We aren't getting involved.

The cleaning lady unlocks Daisy's door and pushes it open to reveal the apartment. "Whoa," Elvis says.

The three of us who are still back in Queens nearly bump heads diving in for a closer view. Daisy lives in a large, loftlike space that's brightly lit by floor-to-ceiling windows. The island of Manhattan lies spread out below. The apartment is so high up that a plane passing by feels too close for comfort. I thought Wayne's house was sparsely decorated, but at least he owns a sofa. The only furniture in Daisy's living area is a tall wooden table that stretches across the center of the room. Arranged on its surface are over a dozen heads. The head facing the camera belongs to Abigail Prince.

"They don't call her the artist for nothing," Elvis remarks as he reaches out to stroke Abigail's cheek. "Daisy's got some serious talent. Though I don't really think she captured our former hostess's sneer. You know—the one that let you know you're nothing but a filthy peasant."

"Keep moving," I order him. "Let's see the rest."

"Well, now, here we have the vice president of the United States," he says, passing over the head of the man with the second-highest post in the land. "And how about that? It's the host of TechSpot, David Evans."

"So why does she have all of these?" Kat asks. "Is she sculpting her models at home?"

"Naw." Elvis instantly rejects the idea. "She said she made a model of David Evans. But if she has a real body to work from, she probably just scans the face and uses a 3-D printer to create the model. I'm pretty sure she's doing this stuff for fun."

The camera begins to pan to the next head. We get just a

glimpse before he quickly moves away. "You know what? Why don't we see what else she's got here in the apartment?" Elvis says nervously.

"No, go back," Kat orders.

"Yeah, I don't think that's a good idea," Elvis says.

"Do it!" Kat's voice is firm.

Elvis reluctantly focuses on the head he tried to avoid. It's a sculpture of Kat's face in repose. Her eyes are closed and her lips slightly parted.

Kat turns to me. "Does this mean the Company made copies of us too?" she asks, but I can't find the right words to answer. "Damn it, Simon, you knew, didn't you? You must have seen our clones at the lab. Why didn't you tell me?"

The horror of it all is coming back to me. If I could, I'd cut out the part of my brain where that memory will always be lodged. "I was ashamed," I say. "I had to leave you there. I couldn't get you out."

Kat blinks, but otherwise her face gives nothing away, which in my experience means she's furious. "We'll discuss this more later," she says before she returns her gaze to the screen.

"Let's see the rest of the apartment," I tell Elvis. "Daisy has got to have an Otherworld headset in there somewhere."

The camera begins to move toward a door. We see Elvis's hand reach out and turn the knob. The light flashes on. It's a bedroom with no bed. It's entirely empty—aside from a pile of clothes and a capsule.

It's the proof I've been waiting for. Daisy is a regular visitor to Otherworld. But she doesn't wear a headset. With a headset, there would be no need for a capsule. Daisy goes to Otherworld with a disk. If Wayne's told her about the danger, Daisy is definitely a total badass. Not many people would willingly risk their lives for a game.

"This isn't the same model as the capsules at the lab." Elvis opens a latch and the top of the capsule opens up. "This one was designed for personal use. Looks like you just climb inside."

"She sleeps in that thing?" Busara asks.

Elvis pans the room. There's a closet filled with clothes and shoes, but no bed in sight. "I don't see anywhere else for her to lie down. And she doesn't seem like a person who'd sleep on the floor."

"Does that mean she's going to Otherworld every night?"

"Must be," Elvis says.

"She's hooked." It's suddenly making sense to me. "Just like Milo. I bet you that's how Wayne got her to work for the Company. He offered to give her Milo's capsule and disk."

"So—what's our next step?" Busara asks.

"Kat and I go to Otherworld and see if Daisy can lead us to Declan. He might be able to tell us where to find his body."

"What's the difference between hunting Daisy down in New York and going to see her in Otherworld?" Nasha demands. "Either way, Wayne will know."

"We're not going to look for Daisy," I say. "We're going to let the Empress of Imperium find *us*."

THE RESCUE

We wait until evening. We need to be sure the Empress will be there when we arrive. This time, when I enter Otherworld, I'm back at setup. The seamless white environment is empty, aside from the mirror in front of me. The reflection I see is my own. A glowing blue amulet hangs around my neck. Other than that, I'm entirely naked. I need to get moving, but I can't resist.

"Older," I order, and I'm suddenly a man in his thirties.

"Much older," I say. My hair turns gray and my skin sags in ways I'm not looking forward to.

"Checked suit. Fedora. Cigarette."

The Kishka stares back at me from the mirror. "Hey, kid," he says. "Figured out who you are yet?"

"Back!" I bark. I'm eighteen and buck naked again.

Every time I've visited Otherworld, I've worn the brown robe of a Druid. Now I don't have time for that crap. I give my avatar jeans, a T-shirt and a pair of sturdy boots.

When you leave setup, you're supposed to begin your Otherworld adventure at the gates of Imra. I look around, but Imra's nowhere to be seen. The gates and buildings are gone. There's nothing here but a mountain of lava. At some point in the past, the volcano that once housed Imra erupted. The city and its walls must have been completely destroyed. I hope it was Pomba Gira's revenge.

Otherworld's air is cleaner than it was the last time we were here. Without the smog, I can see skyscrapers in the distance. I wonder which city they belong to.

"Like the new outfit." Kat appears beside me, wearing her favorite camouflage jumpsuit.

"Thanks," I tell her. "You ready to rumble?"

"Nope. Now that we're alone, you're going to explain why you didn't tell me the Company had cloned us."

God, I was *really* hoping we wouldn't have to finish that particular conversation.

"Our clones were naked inside the capsules. I didn't want you to feel embarrassed," I say.

"Embarrassed? About *what*?" Kat demands. "That I was a victim of a crime that hasn't made it into any lawbooks yet? Don't worry. I'll make sure justice is served. What really pisses me off right now is that my boyfriend thought he needed to protect me from the truth."

Now that she mentions it, I can see how that might piss someone off.

"I mean, when exactly did I ever give you the impression that I'm a fragile little flower that needs to be handled carefully?"

"Never," I have to admit. "I know you could kick my ass if you wanted to."

"Damn straight. Keep that in mind, would you?" She gives my avatar a kiss. I can't feel her lips, but it still sets me on fire. Kat grins as she steps back. She knows what she's done. It's an unbelievably cruel punishment.

"Wow." Kat's taking in the landscape that surrounds us. "I gotta tell you, after our last trip, I was a little worried Otherworld wouldn't exist at all anymore."

Down below, a cloud of dust races across the red desert wasteland. Maybe I'm mistaken again, but it sure looks a lot like a buffalo. They seem to have made a miraculous comeback.

"Get down!" a high-pitched voice shrieks behind us.

Something has poked its head out of a hole in the volcanic rock. It's a tiny creature with skin the same shade of gray as the rock, and a face with the features of multiple Earth species—the giant eyes and ears of a lemur and the scales of a lizard. Otherworld's children have been getting busy.

"You don't want them to see that you're back!" it says.

It seems smart to do what we're told since the creature apparently knows who we are. Kat and I drop down, pressing our chests flat against the rock. The dust cloud travels past the volcano, and I can see a hairy body in the center of it. Still, Kat and I wait until the creature has passed before we begin to rise.

"It was just a buffalo," I tell the creature.

"Yes, but the buffalo here were once beasts," he says. "Now they are something else altogether. That was one of the monster machines that she makes."

"She?" Kat asks.

The creature looks at us as if he suspects we're high. He has a surprisingly somber personality for something that looks like a stuffed animal from a museum gift shop. "The Empress of Imperium, of course."

Of course.

"And who are you?"

"My name is Ilo," he says. "I have been waiting for you to return to Otherworld for many years. Now that you are here, I can escort you back to Albion."

I almost laugh at the thought of this guy escorting us anywhere. He's barely knee high.

"Albion?" Kat asks. "Why Albion?"

"All but two realms have fallen to the Empress," says Ilo. "The White City will be conquered any day now. Then Albion will be the only free and safe realm in Otherworld."

After my first and last visit to Albion, I'm in no rush to go back. I can't imagine how it could be one of the last two realms to resist invasion. It was nothing but an enormous garbage dump with a starving giant, a grizzled old Elemental and . . .

"Have you heard of someone named Bird in Albion?" Kat takes the question right out of my mouth.

"Heard of her?" Ilo snorts. "She is our protector. She is the reason we are not slaves to the Empress like the rest of Otherworld."

"The rest of Otherworld?" Kat repeats in astonishment.

Ilo seems to have serious doubts about our intelligence.

"I'm sorry, it's been a while since we've been here," I explain. "We don't know what the Empress has done while we've been gone."

"She has ruled Imperium for ages," Ilo says. "Before she arrived, the city was swimming in refuse and poisoned by its own pollution. The Empress brought Imperium back to life, it is true. Once the skies cleared and the streets were emptied of garbage, other realms came asking for help. She would only save them if they would accept her as their leader. One by one, the realms of Otherworld began to fall under her control."

So far, the Empress isn't sounding all that bad. Last time we were here, Otherworld was a disaster. Someone had to clean the place up. "Where do the NPC slaves come in?" I press.

Ilo looks around nervously before he answers. He seems to feel exposed up here on the rocks. I wouldn't mind having this conversation elsewhere myself, but it doesn't look like there's anywhere we can go.

"Her slaves are not NPCs. They're *Children*. Every inhabitant of the realms had to take part in the cleanup," Ilo says, his words spilling out faster. "Monitors placed on their bodies ensured compliance by reporting their location and activity. Once the job was finished, however, the monitors were not removed as agreed. The Empress now controls every creature in her empire. If she wants something built, they must build it. If she wants someone found, they must find them. If there's a realm that won't submit to her rule, they must conquer it.

"There is no crime in the Imperium empire," he continues. "Everything is beautiful. The Empress has even built beasts to replace those that went extinct. But it's all come at the expense of the Children she's enslaved."

The Children agreed to a bad deal. When they accepted the trade-off, they didn't know what they were trading. The Children got what they wanted in the short term. And now they could end up paying for it forever.

"That is why I must guide you to Albion. The Empress knows that Otherworld is still visited by others like her. She's put a bounty on all human heads—including yours and that of the White City's Ancient."

Even though we want the Empress to find us, I'm not exactly thrilled to find out I'm a wanted man in this world, too. But it's something else Ilo just said that concerns me far more. Kat's face says she's worried too. "She put a bounty on the White City's Ancient?" It feels unbelievably weird to refer to James Ogubu in that way, but I doubt Ilo will know James's real name.

"The Empress has been trying to breach the White City's walls for years. The residents have fought back, but the Empress's slave army has become too large to resist. The White City residents won't be able to hold out much longer."

"And if the Empress manages to capture the Ancient? What do you think she will do?"

Ilo shakes his head. "I do not know. She has not been kind to those she sees as rivals. Bird has tried to rescue the Ancient many times. She has never been able to find a way to bring him back safely to Albion."

There's still one thing I don't understand.

"What makes Albion so safe?" Kat asks the question I had in mind.

"You don't recall?" Ilo seems both shocked and a little offended. "It's Albion's most beloved story, and the two of you are part of it."

"We are?" I ask.

Ilo sighs at my ignorance. "The day the Empress's soldiers were defeated, the Elemental of Albion offered Bird a wish. She wished that the realm would be forever free of the technology that had brought such devastation to Otherworld. As a result, the technology the Empress uses to enslave the Children does not work in Albion. The Children she's sent to defeat us have found themselves free to join us. The monitors simply fall away. The Empress does not dare send any more."

Kat turns to me. "We've got to go to the White City. We need to get James out."

"No, no, no!" Ilo interrupts. "You must come with me to Albion. Your friend Declan is there. He's been waiting!"

"Declan?" I ask. "He's in Albion?"

"Yes. He arrived many years ago."

"And he's not in danger?" I ask.

"Of course not. Albion is perfectly safe."

"Then he can wait while I take a quick detour to the White City."

Ilo stomps his foot in frustration. "Have you not been listening? The city is surrounded by the Empress's troops! You will never be able to get inside!"

He doesn't know I have a trick up my sleeve. I reach down into my shirt and pull out my amulet. It belonged to the Clay Man, and there's nothing else like it. It allows the wearer to transport from realm to realm. The only problem is, I won't be able to take anyone with me. Only one person can go.

"Simon, let me use the amulet this time," Kat says. "I can pull up the hood of my jumpsuit and disappear. I'll get James out of the White City without being seen."

I don't think Kat's being noble. She really wants to go. So do I. I'm curious to see what's become of the White City. The technology they had was far more advanced than ours. I wonder if it was what saved them for so long.

"Rock, paper, scissors?" I ask.

"You're on," she says. She almost always wins.

This time, her luck runs out. My rock smashes her scissors.

"Damn it!"

"Don't be a sore loser." I give her a quick kiss before I take the amulet in my palm and close my eyes. I tell the stone where I want to go, and when I open my eyes, I'm in James Ogubu's living room. There's nothing left but the walls. The windows have shattered, and a thick layer of dust and dirt blankets the floor. Who knows where the furniture has gone? Outside, half the balcony has crumbled away. The surrounding buildings haven't fared much better. It's hard to believe there could be anything living inside the hollowed-out shells, but I can see figures scuttling around within them. There are still Children left in the White City. A bright flash of light is followed by the sound of an explosion. I watch as one of the tallest buildings in the White City crashes to the ground.

James Ogubu is sitting on the floor with his back against the wall. There's no telling how long he's been there. His eyes are closed. His face and clothing are coated with dust.

"James." I rush toward him in a panic. We should never have left him like this.

"Hello, Simon," he says as his eyes slowly open.

I take the amulet off and place it around his neck.

"Tell the amulet you want to go to Albion. Bird is there. She will care for you."

"So it's true?" he asks. "I wondered what happened to Bird when she didn't return. There were rumors about a safe haven in Albion, and I thought she might have something to do with it. She must be very old by now."

It's an odd time to strike up a conversation. You'd think James would be eager to leave. Then again, he probably hasn't spoken to anyone in years.

"Go see for yourself," I urge him. "Tell Bird that Kat and I are here and we found Ilo. We'll meet you in Albion. We can talk more when I get there."

James nods and closes his eyes and his avatar disappears in a flash, leaving me alone in the shell of the apartment he's inhabited for so many Otherworld years. I can't imagine how miserable it must have been. On Earth, solitary confinement is reserved for only the most hardened criminals. I've heard that most of them crack. I don't know how James could have endured the isolation. How did he manage to stay sane? What has he been waiting for?

Even after a few short minutes in the apartment I'm depressed as hell, but I'm still not quite suicidal. Which is unfortunate because I need to die in order to get back to setup. I could jump out the window, but that seems like a waste. If I'm going to go out, I'd rather do it with a bang. So I head downstairs and outside in search of the front line in the White City's battle against the Empress. The vehicles that once flew through the sky, zipping around buildings, have all been abandoned in the streets. They're piled in heaps as if they plunged to the ground midflight.

I pass the site of Bird's old business. The flashing signs have all dimmed. I see no lights in the buildings. The entire city has gone dark. I walk by an alley where three emaciated Children stand huddled around a flickering fire. I have no idea what's kept the Empress's troops out of the White City. Whatever powered the realm must have run out long ago. A new, dark age has begun.

When I finally reach the realm's border, I see what has saved it. When the city became a part of Otherworld, it was fortified to keep out the residents of Otherworld. Now those old protections have been put to use again. The Empress's army has gathered at the base of the city's walls. I see a few NPCs mixed in with the mob, but most of the soldiers are Children. There are thousands of them, all pressed into service by the monitors they wear somewhere on their bodies. The gates have held and the walls haven't been breached. Buzzing flying machines form another front line in the sky. As they advance toward the city, they're shot out of the air one by one. Each crashes into the mob below, incinerating the Children they've hit and sending balls of fire shooting upward.

I don't know how long the White City's inhabitants have managed to keep the Empress's army at bay. Even a day would be a miracle, and it looks as though their luck might change very soon. The Children who stand guard at the wall appear thin and sickly. I watch as one slumps down against the battlements. By the time I reach him, he's already dead. As I bend down to double check, I spot movement out of the corner of my eye. While the White City's fighters defend their realm against the threats from above, another attack has been launched from below. Mechanical creatures are scaling the wall. The first reaches the top a few feet from me. I've never seen anything like it before. It looks like the mechanical skeleton of an apelike beast the Empress decided was too bizarre to finish making. My hand goes for my dagger before it occurs to me that it will do me no good. A long arm shoots forward, gutting me with the claws it used for climbing. Blood splatters the ground, and one of my lives disappears. He drops me to the ground and stomps on me. The move would have killed a Child, and the mechanical beast seems to think I've been eliminated as a threat. It wasn't designed to fight someone like me.

Before it realizes I'm not down for the count, I hurl myself at the monstrosity, sending it sailing back over the wall. I hear the crash, but I don't have the satisfaction of watching. Two identical beasts have appeared farther down the line. They're immediately surrounded by the Children manning the wall, giving a third creature the opportunity to climb up unchallenged. I charge straight at it, using my right shoulder as a battering ram. It, too, flies backward off the wall. This time, I look over the edge to see the impact, only to see another one climbing toward me. I stand up, position myself and jump. My body collides with the beast's metal skeleton, knocking it off the wall. When we both hit the ground, my second life disappears. My third and last life begins lying atop the mangled carcass. I've landed in the center of the Empress's army. Children of all shapes and descriptions surround me. I wait for one of them to deliver the coup de grâce, but none does. They just stare down with empty eyes. Then the crowd parts, giving me a brief glimpse of the wall. Three more of the metallic skeletons are beginning to scale the rocks. If the Empress's army doesn't bother to stop me, I figure I might have a shot at taking one of them out. Then an NPC appears in front of me.

"The Empress would like to meet you," he says.

Not without Kat. "Tell her I need a rain check," I say. Then I pull out my dagger and plunge it deep into my own chest.

I'm back at setup, staring into the mirror at my naked avatar. This time, the amulet is gone. With a few quick orders, I dress myself once again.

I finish the process and head back to the pile of hardened lava that was once the City of Imra. I couldn't have been in the White City for more than an hour, but I know in an instant that I was gone too long. Kat's here, crouched over what I now realize is Ilo's body. It's hard to believe that the puddle of blood beneath it could have come from such a tiny creature. Kat tore off the hood of her jumpsuit and attempted to use it as a tourniquet. But she wasn't able to save him. Ilo's giant amber eyes stare up at the bright Otherworld sun. Kat stands and takes my hand. The two of us are surrounded by NPC warriors wearing armor emblazoned with the insignia of Imperium.

THE EMPRESS OF IMPERIUM

Kat and I are marched down the volcanic mountain and loaded onto a transport vehicle—a small pod made of a dense transparent material. From a distance, it looked like a bubble floating atop the sand. Once we draw closer, we can see the bench that circles the interior. There's no room for soldiers inside the vehicle, but there's no need for them either. The door we entered through seals invisibly. Even if I had the foggiest idea of how to unseal it, I doubt I could find it again if I tried. I feel terrible about what happened to Ilo. The order to kill him was cruel and unnecessary. Kat and I wouldn't have put up a fight. We're headset players now, and our own safety is guaranteed. There's nothing even an Empress could do to us. The two of us are completely invulnerable. Ilo wasn't.

Kat and I sit in silence on our way to Imperium, as we glide across the Wastelands between the realms—over deserts and through swamps. For a few minutes outside Imra, we're joined by a herd of the mechanical beasts the Empress created. She gave these ones skin and hair, and they look every bit as real as Otherworld's originals. Maybe they are. It's hard to know where the line gets drawn. One group of beasts was digital and the other's mechanical, but both were created by humans playing God.

I'll give it to the Empress, though: Otherworld has never looked better. The garbage that once littered the Wastelands is gone. The burned-out realms are green again. Smog no longer smothers the cities. There are Children everywhere, erecting new structures and working in the fields. They look remarkably healthy and well fed. It all seems idyllic until you notice the sinister black monitors they all wear.

We're traveling through the swamp where Alexei Semenov's avatar once lived when our vehicle is joined by a flying machine. It bears no resemblance to any drone or plane you might see on Earth. It appears to be a mechanical bird without feathers or skin. It stays with us long enough to give us a good look—then suddenly veers off to the side and dives beneath the murky water. When it resurfaces, it holds a struggling Child in its beak. The creature's silver skin sparkles in the sunlight, like the scales of a fish. A black monitor around its tail is flashing. It must have thought it could hide, but even the swamps aren't safe anymore. We continue on our path while the machine flies back in the opposite direction. Wherever the Child is being taken, it's certainly not Imperium.

Soon the skyline of the Empress's realm appears on the horizon. The city is built at the base of a cliff. We can only see the upper stories; it resembles a forest that's sprung from the wasteland's barren ground. The highest tower still bears the name Moloch, though the sign is no longer illuminated. There's no land for farms or vegetation in the realm, so the Empress has installed vertical gardens. Those were the patches of green that Kat and I saw when we flew past with Bird. I haven't set foot in Imperium since Moloch's time, when towers were under constant construction and hundreds of players were vying to build the tallest. Now the workmen are gone, and lush vegetation hangs from the windows and climbs the walls.

"It's beautiful." Kat's voice is flat rather than filled with awe. She thinks the city's looks are deceiving. I agree. It's all too perfect. The place is extremely dangerous. There's no doubt about it.

Our vehicle glides down the side of the cliff and into the city's canyons. The towers above still crowd out the light, leaving the streets unnaturally dark. But the bottom floors of the buildings around us have been put to good use. Crops grow beneath multicolored lights, forming a neon layer cake of farms. I only recognize mushrooms and asparagus. The rest must be unique to Otherworld.

Just as on my last visit, a door rises, and our vehicle descends into the basement of one of the towers. But this time, Kat and I don't need to leave our bubble. It enters an elevator shaft and shoots upward until it reaches an open floor that's surrounded on all sides by the sky. We glide out into a flower-filled meadow. A beautiful tree grows in the center of the floor. Someone is sitting there, her back leaning against its trunk. She's wearing a straw hat with a bow, and I recognize her flowered dress. It's the same one she wore in her interview.

Kat and I watch in silence as Daisy finishes tinkering with

something in her lap. Then she looks up. When she smiles at the two of us, an opening appears in our bubble, and Kat and I are able to step out.

"Hello," the Empress says. "Welcome to Imperium. Did you both enjoy the trip? I thought it might be nice for you to travel by ground so you could have a good look at all the improvements I've made."

It's hard to believe this is the same woman who's enslaved the Children and who murdered Ilo. Daisy's changed nothing about her physical appearance. She looks exactly as she does in the real world. Short, pretty and dainty as a doll. I have to force myself to remember that when it comes to Daisy Bristol, all is not what it seems. As she draws near, I can see she recognizes us too.

"You know who we are?" I ask.

"Certainly." She sounds amused. "You two are the Tech Avengers. I made copies of you both."

I feel myself blush when I realize this woman has seen me buck naked. The perfect little birthmark on my clone's right thigh? That was *her* handiwork.

"Tech Avengers?" Kat asks.

Daisy smiles. "You must not have time to watch much news. That's what they're calling you back in New York. Silly, isn't it? Wayne came up with the name, and somehow it caught on. He's got a real knack for PR. Now that I've answered your question, maybe you can answer one for me. What are you two doing in Otherworld?"

"We're looking for someone," I tell her. I don't think it's a good idea to lie unless it's necessary. There's something in Daisy's eyes that tells me she knows far more than we do. And the cutesy crap is all a façade. Inside, the woman's a monster. She's wearing a disk, but she doesn't seem scared in the slightest. She's got something up her sleeve.

I glance down at the item she was toying with when we arrived. Daisy's holding it like a softball. It looks like a tiny mechanical head.

"The person you're looking for—is it the boy or the man?" she asks.

"Actually, both," says Kat. She's obviously chosen the same strategy I have. "But we need to find the boy's body back on Earth. Can you tell us where it is?"

"I have no idea," Daisy says. "I wish I did. The kid's brain holds secrets I'd kill to have. But even if I did know, I wouldn't share that information with you. The kid belongs to my boss, and I'm not going to mess with Mr. Gibson. I have no intention of losing everything I've built here in Otherworld. Did you ever visit Imperium back in the old days? When that idiot engineer was masquerading as Moloch?"

I'd rather keep her on the subject of Declan, but I don't think she'll go back right away. "You mean Todd?" I ask.

"Is that his name? I've heard he was supposed to clean the place up. Then he got kicked out and the whole world fell apart. The Children got their hands on the tech that was left behind and went nuts with it. Imperium was a total shithole when I arrived. It's taken me decades and decades in Otherworld years to restore the place."

"Yes, it's amazing what slave labor can accomplish." My head spins in Kat's direction. She's decided not to play nice after all.

I'm expecting the worst, but Daisy laughs. "Oh, come on. Do

I look like I enslave anyone?" she asks. "I come to Otherworld to work. The extra time has proven to be a great advantage. I can make years' worth of progress every Earth night. I wish I could show you what've I've accomplished back in New York. But no one will ever know about it, I'm afraid. That's all part of the deal. Mr. Gibson takes care of that world, and I get this one."

So that's the bargain? I want to know more, but Kat jumps in. She's utterly furious.

"How can you say you haven't enslaved anyone? The Children in your realms all wear monitors on their bodies. You're watching them every second of the day."

"Me?" Daisy titters as if the suggestion is ridiculous. "That system was automated ages ago. The Children's leaders helped me come up with the work requirements. We agreed on the laws and hours each inhabitant would have to contribute. I merely created the systems that enforced the rules. Now, at least in Imperium, everything runs like clockwork. I can leave Otherworld for years at a time. When I return, things are even better than I left them. I've never had to crack a whip, and I certainly don't want to!"

"Then set them free now!"

"And have things return to the way they were? When I first came to Otherworld, half the realms were at war. The Children were starving. Chaos is just as powerful a force in Otherworld as it is back on Earth. I've had to conquer the other realms just to ensure Imperium's quality of life. I can't let things return to the way they were—for everyone's sake! But . . ."

She looks down at the head in her hands and toys with it for a moment as if she's considering another option.

"But what?" Kat demands.

"I might consider easing some restrictions and reducing the Children's mandatory work hours if you agree to help me with something in return."

"What?" I ask warily.

"My troops have been unable to take the White City. The citizens of the realm are harboring an avatar they call the Ancient. I would like to meet him."

"Why?" Kat demands. "What do you want to do to him?"

"Nothing at all! I'm James Ogubu's biggest fan!"

So Daisy knows. "Did Wayne tell you he was here?"

"No, he insisted I inform him if I encountered any unfamiliar avatars. I figured that meant someone important was here. At first, I thought it might be Milo, but when the Ancient was described to me, I knew it had to be James Ogubu instead. I met him once at a conference. I had *so* many questions that I wanted to ask him, but he said he had to get home to his daughter. Now he and I will have all the time in the world to talk shop!"

Kat raises a skeptical eyebrow. "You're telling us you've been attacking the White City just so you can talk shop with James Ogubu?"

"I'm dying to find out how he managed to download his consciousness into an avatar. My dream is to live on in Otherworld after my human body has expired."

I think of the bombed-out apartment where James had been trapped for God knows how long. That's probably not the kind of existence that Daisy has in mind.

"Why do you need James for that?" Kat asks. "Wayne already has the technology."

"There's a big difference between having the tools and knowing how to use them," Daisy says. "We still haven't figured everything out. Look at what happened with you two. Wayne wanted a simulation so he could see what you'd seen, but the whole thing turned out glitchy. Now he's worried that the robots won't be ready."

"For what?" I ask.

Daisy smirks. "Who knows what that creepy old man has planned. Why do you think I'm itching to get downloaded into an avatar?"

"Yeah, well, that's not going to happen," Kat tells her.

"Oh, I think it will." Daisy sounds confident.

"Are you threatening us?" Kat responds. "Go ahead and kill us if you want. It won't do you any good."

"I'm not going to *kill* you, sweetie," Daisy replies. "I'll simply confiscate your avatars. You guys can come to Otherworld as often as you like, but you'll always find yourself locked up here in Imperium. It might make it quite difficult to reach your friends in the future. How badly do you want to find the boy?"

"It doesn't matter how much we want to help you. We can't take you to see James," I tell her. "He's in Albion now. I sent him there myself."

Daisy shakes her head in confusion. "Why can't I visit him in Albion?"

Kat and I share a look. "We heard you were at war with Albion."

"Who on earth told you that?" she responds. "I have no beef with Albion, as long as my people stay out of the realm. Their leader, the Bird, has done well for herself. She's taken a different tack, of course, but the results have been the same. The land has healed and the citizens are healthy."

"And free," Kat notes bitterly. "Bird didn't need monitors to spy on and punish the Children of Albion. She cleaned things up on her own."

"You're so cute," Daisy laughs. "She didn't do it on her own. She had powerful magic to help her. I had technology. Take a step back and you'll see they're the same."

Maybe she's right. Perhaps the means by which she and Bird control their realms are the same. But the results definitely are not.

"So you want us to introduce you to James Ogubu so you can ask him about the tech. And in return you will make life easier for the Children?"

"Of course!" Daisy replies. "That seems a fair trade for ever-lasting life, doesn't it?"

"What do you think?" I ask Kat.

Kat clearly doesn't want to be anywhere near Daisy Bristol. "I think it's what James would want us to do," she says through gritted teeth.

BIRD

Daisy sits primly across from me in the vehicle. Kat is by her side. The two of them couldn't be more different. My fierce, wild-haired girlfriend with her camouflage jumpsuit and ever-present quiver—and the little blond doll in her flowered dress. If the two came to blows, everyone would put their money on Kat. Except, perhaps, for Kat. I can see she takes Daisy very seriously. She's nervous about the trip.

Daisy, on the other hand, doesn't seem worried at all. Which is odd, since she's wearing a disk. Unless Wayne lied to her, she must know that any injuries she suffers on our journey could prove fatal. James Ogubu spent an eternity holed up in an apartment in the White City because he couldn't risk his avatar. And yet Daisy walks around like she's completely invincible.

We take the pod back downstairs to the basement. There, a new vehicle is waiting—one large enough to carry the three of us and our new companions. Two large NPCs will be joining us, each one the size of a bear and armed with enough ammunition to take over a small country. Otherworld NPCs aren't supposed to leave the realm in which they were generated. I wonder how Daisy found her way around the rules.

The shimmering silver vehicle is the shape of an elongated bullet, with two seats facing forward and four plush chairs in the back. The NPCs take their places at the front of the vehicle. The rest of us claim seats in the back. Within minutes, we've left the steel forest of Imperium behind and sped into a neighboring realm. I have no idea what it might once have been. Under the Empress's control, it's an endless orchard. We speed past trees, their branches drooping with fruit I don't recognize. It's stunningly beautiful for the first few minutes. Then the monotony begins to gnaw at me. No matter where I look, I see the same thing.

"Which realm is this?" I ask.

"Summerland. It was my first big project," Daisy tells us. "When I arrived, it was still a war zone. Land mines made the terrain unpassable. The inhabitants were sick and starving. Now look at it! This place is heaven! When other realms saw what I'd accomplished here, they welcomed my soldiers with open arms."

"Must have been a lot of work to turn a war zone into a farm," Kat says. "How many enslaved Children did it take to do it?"

Daisy's getting tired of Kat's comments. "There's a difference between being enslaved and being asked to work hard to improve your own life."

"So you *asked* them to work, did you?" Kat says. She points up ahead to a group of Children who are plucking fruit from the trees. "Those Children can just stop whenever they like?"

"Slow down," Daisy orders the vehicle. Our speed is reduced to a crawl as we pass the orchard's workers. They freeze and watch us, clearly frightened of what might happen next. There must be fifty of them here, all dressed in identical uniforms that have been altered to fit their unique bodies.

"Do these look like unhappy creatures to you?" Daisy demands.

It's such a bizarre question that I can't figure out how to answer it. I'm starting to think that Daisy might not be able to tell the difference. The Children here are fit and strong. Their clothes are clean and well made. They have all the basic requirements of life—except for the one thing that actually makes life worth living.

"You're insane," Kat says. It's not an insult—just a statement of fact.

"Stop!" Daisy shouts at the vehicle, which immediately puts on the brakes. "Open."

The door opens, and the Children outside stand at attention. No one moves a muscle as Daisy steps out into the grove. They don't know what to expect from her. At this point, neither do I.

"Hello!" she calls out in a cheerful voice. "How are the citizens of Summerland today?"

The crowd remains silent, but a current seems to pass through it. Something is very wrong here. Daisy's chosen the wrong moment to stop. But she can't see that. She may be able to build mechanical creatures, but the ones composed of flesh and blood seem to make no sense to her.

"Has it been so long since I've visited this land?" I think she was expecting far more fawning. "Do you not recognize your Empress?"

One of the Children steps forward—a small, bald female with dark green veins that spread down her muscular limbs like vines. "We know who you are, Your Highness. Do you know us?"

The Empress glances over her shoulder at Kat and me and scrunches up her face and mouths, *So cute!*

"She really is batshit crazy," Kat says as soon as Daisy has turned away.

"Yup," I agree.

"You are my beloved subjects, descendants of the Children who worked with me to bring this realm back to life."

The small green Child isn't done. "Last week, my brother was gathering fruit from the treetops when he fell from his ladder," she says. "He was badly injured, unable to work. We sent word that he would not be able to make his quota. We begged you to make an exception. The next day, one of your mechanical beasts came for him. We have not seen him since. Why didn't you answer us?"

Daisy's face is a blank. This little detour isn't going as she'd planned, and she can't figure out what to do. "I must have been away from the realm at the time," she tells the Child. "The systems here are all automated. I did not personally order your brother's punishment."

"Where has he been taken? May we please have him back?"

Daisy shrugs her shoulders. "The punishments have been clearly posted for all Otherworld residents to read. Those who are unable to contribute labor for a significant period of time are relocated to the Ice Fields."

Relocated. An injured Child would stand no chance of survival on the Ice Fields. She might as well have put a bullet through his head.

The meaning of the Empress's words has not been lost on the Children. A murmur spreads among them. Then a second female breaks through the crowd and rushes at Daisy before anyone can stop her. She's wielding a pair of pruning shears with sharp, daggerlike points. With one lightning-fast move, the Child lifts the shears into the air and then brings the point down hard right where Daisy's heart should be. A split second later, the Child's head explodes. One of the NPCs has taken out the assassin. The Empress, for her part, appears completely unharmed. Something has protected her.

Kat rushes over to the body of the fallen Child, but nothing can be done. As the body waters the ground with its blood, the remaining Children scatter, rushing away from the scene through the trees.

The NPCs start to take off in pursuit, but Daisy stops them and waves for them to come back. "Don't bother," she calls out. "Let's get to Albion. We've wasted enough time already."

Kat stands up from the Child's lifeless body. Her face is cold. "She should have killed you."

Daisy smirks. She thinks Kat wants to know how she did it, and she's proud of herself.

"Electrical body armor." She pulls a thin, virtually transparent layer of fabric away from her skin. "Next best thing to eternal life. I'd love to design something like this for use back on Earth, but we're not quite there with the tech yet."

I glance over at Kat. I can't read her mind, but I'd bet a million dollars she's trying to come up with a way past that armor.

"What?" Daisy laughs. "You didn't really think I trusted you guys with my avatar, did you?"

With our vehicle careening across realms at top speed, the rest of the journey takes less than an hour. What I see through the windows looks much the same—until Albion appears in front of us. With its tangle of trees and dense foliage, the realm resembles a briar patch in the middle of Daisy's carefully tended garden.

"Not much curb appeal. I really do wish the Bird creature could convince her followers to tidy the place up a bit," Daisy says with a sigh. "I'm sure some of them would rather not live like savages."

I feel our vehicle begin to slow. It almost seems to be straining against some invisible force. Before we reach the border of Albion, it comes to a complete stop and the doors slide open.

"Albion's no-technology rule applies to vehicles too?" Kat asks.

"Apparently," Daisy reports. "The Bird's a real hardass about it, from what I've heard. Nothing is easy in Albion."

One of the NPC soldiers exits the vehicle first. Daisy follows with the second soldier right behind her. Kat and I take up the rear.

As the first NPC soldier attempts to cross into Albion, he bounces off an invisible barrier.

"Your Taser," Daisy says. "Leave it here."

The NPC drops the Taser at the border and passes through

with a massive machete still strapped to his back. Daisy attempts to follow him and bumps up against the same barrier.

"Damn it," she mutters. "Let's try that again." The second time, she's allowed through. Nothing about her appears to have changed, but I think I know what the difference is. She had to deactivate her body armor.

Kat and I make it through with no problems. My dagger and her arrows are acceptable in Albion. We step through the thick line of foliage that forms the realm's border and discover ourselves in the Albion from Max Prince's play-through. The trees around us are gnarled, their bark black. Golden flecks of sunlight sprinkle the ground, which is carpeted with multicolored leaves. This part of the realm has been allowed to return to its natural state. I remember the terrifying wildlife that once lived in these woods, and I wonder if the bear, deer and wolves have made a comeback too.

I hear hooves in the distance, and my adrenaline surges. It sounds like horses, but in Otherworld you never know what you're going to get. Even the horses here are probably best avoided. Soon the three largest stallions I've ever seen appear with Children atop them.

"State your business," orders one of the Children, a giant covered in luminous golden fur.

"I am the Empress of Imperium," Daisy replies boldly. "I have come to visit one of your residents."

"You must leave at once," the Child orders. "We are a free realm. We do not welcome those who enslave our kind."

Daisy looks over at me, raises an eyebrow and clears her throat. I guess that means it's my job to state our case. I reluctantly step forward. "My name is Simon Eaton. My companion is Kat Foley. We were both here the day Bird saved this realm. We've come to visit her, as well as our friends Declan and James. The Empress would like a word with one of them. We would not have agreed to escort the Empress if she hadn't promised to improve the lives of the Children in return. Bird will vouch for us."

The Child's eyes flick back and forth between Kat and me. "You are the Ones?" he asks skeptically.

Kat catches my eye. "OMG, does this mean I get to be a One, too?" she teases me.

"You can be the *only* One as far as I'm concerned," I tell her.

"Yeah, thanks, but no thanks," Kat says. "I already have enough stress in my life."

The Child on horseback doesn't seem amused by the banter. "So are you the Ones or not?" he demands.

"I guess so," I tell him. "But we really prefer Kat and Simon."

"Climb on, Kat and Simon," the Child says, reaching down from his saddle to help us up. The beast he's riding is big enough for the three of us.

"No," I hear Daisy say haughtily. "I'm afraid I need to have my own horse."

The sound of the Children laughing is loud enough to launch a flock of crows from the branches overhead. I look back to see Daisy reluctantly pulled up onto a horse, sandwiched between a Child and an NPC.

My ass is completely numb by the time the trees clear and a village appears. If my internal compass is accurate, it must have been built in the location of the castle where Kat and I found the drag-on's skeleton. In fact, I have a hunch that the stones from the old building were used to construct the village's houses. They're small structures with thatched roofs and brightly painted doors.

"Oooh, this is so adorable!" Daisy exclaims. "I'm going to have one of these built as soon as I'm back in Imperium."

"How Marie Antoinette of you," Kat mutters.

The Children who are out on the street have stopped to watch us pass. They or their ancestors must have arrived here from countless other realms. You can see evidence of every creature in Otherworld in their faces and bodies. Several little ones, whom I take to be children, race behind us. Their parents' DNA has blended together beautifully.

Soon, the horses come to a halt in front of one of the houses. It's the same size as all the others—the home of an average vil-lager. As I slide off the back of our mount, the door opens, and a female appears before us.

Bird has grown old, though I'm not sure how I know that. Her hair hasn't grayed as a human's would. She doesn't appear to be stooped or frail. But her face feels wiser and her eyes have seen more than the rest of ours have. She steps forward and embraces Kat and me in turn.

"I was told you were coming. We've all been waiting." Her eyes shoot toward Daisy and the two NPC soldiers. There's no sur-prise. "I see you've brought company."

"Bird, meet the Empress of Imperium. Empress, this is Bird," I say.

Daisy slips off her horse and walks toward Bird with her hand held out. Bird doesn't take it. Either she doesn't want to shake the Empress of Imperium's hand or she isn't familiar with the custom.

"I love what you've done with the place," the Empress says, letting her hand fall. "From the outside, the realm looks like a jungle, but this is very attractive. And you did it without the help of technology? It must have been very time consuming."

"Yes," Bird says. "But those who choose to come here are willing to work. I don't need to force them."

Daisy sniffs haughtily but doesn't bite back.

"We sent James Ogubu to you earlier today. Now the Empress has come to meet him," I explain. "She's a really big fan."

Bird's eyes linger on my face. She knows there's far more to the story. "If that's the case, she may come inside. Her guards may not."

The two guards stand rigidly by Daisy's side. They give no indication that they either heard or understood.

The Empress frowns. "I'm afraid I can't leave them." Without her body armor, she's utterly defenseless. I'm not sure that her guards have caught on.

"It's okay," says a voice. A tall dark man emerges from the dwelling. I've never seen him wearing anything but the same jeans and button-down. Now James Ogubu is dressed in beige linen pants and a matching shirt. The outfit would look like a potato sack on most people, but James appears regal as always. "I will speak to her."

Daisy heads straight for him, her hand outstretched. "James Ogubu," she gushes like the ultimate fangirl. "Such an honor to meet you. My name is Daisy Bristol. I've been trying to reach you for ages."

"By laying siege to the city in which I was living?" James notes as Daisy's eyes take him in. She's inspecting his avatar like she's buying a new car. "You have an interesting way of making new friends, Ms. Bristol."

"My apologies," Daisy says with a toothy smile. "I suppose I might have been a little too eager. I'm sure you don't remember who I am back on Earth. I worked for a company called Skin Job that was recently purchased by the Company—"

"Skin Job?" James inquires.

"We made lifelike robotic companions," she explains, eager to get to the main topic. "Now the Company is using our tech for other purposes."

"I can only imagine," James drones.

"I'm such a big fan of your work that the only thing I asked for as a signing bonus was access to Otherworld. And—"

James cuts her off. "I'm sorry, Ms. Bristol. What is it that you want from me?"

"What you have!" Daisy gestures toward his avatar. "I want my memories and personality and everything else uploaded into an avatar. I want to live on here in Otherworld after my real-world body perishes. I want immortality."

James's eyes scan her avatar. "Am I correct in assuming that you are currently using a disk?"

"Yes, I've been told that it's the same disk Milo Yolkin once used," she brags, as though it's some kind of badge of honor that she's got the disk that Milo died wearing.

"Have you ever wondered why you haven't encountered any other people here using disks?" James asks her. "Headsets are in short supply, but there must be quite a few disks still floating around the Company. Didn't Wayne tell you why no one else uses them?"

"Of course he did!" Daisy says with a laugh. "He doesn't want me to die in here! I'm critical to his success. He made it perfectly clear that I can be injured or killed in Otherworld, so I fixed the problem."

For the first time, James appears genuinely intrigued. "You fixed the problem? Are you telling me you managed to debug the disks?"

"No, no, that's far too complicated. I just built electronic body armor for my avatar," Daisy replies humbly. She pinches the invisible fabric that covers her body and pulls it out for him to see. "Something like this probably wasn't an option when you arrived in Otherworld. I've heard you've been here since the Dark Ages. But with the tech available to us today—"

"You made your avatar invulnerable," James says. "Very clever."

"Thanks!" Daisy chirps.

"The armor isn't perfect, though, is it?" James notes. "Technology is forbidden in Albion. Your invention must not work here."

I swear I just saw one of the NPCs twitch. They must be listening after all.

Daisy laughs. "That's why I brought the boys. They're programmed for hand-to-hand combat." She glances over at Bird. "Your realm is peaceful, I'm sure. But you can never be too careful, am I right?"

Bird doesn't dignify Daisy's question with an answer.

"You want me to tell you how to achieve digital immortality," James says. "So you can rule Imperium forever and keep Otherworld's residents enslaved."

"Yes," Daisy says. "And in return for that information, I'll cut back on the Children's work requirements and allow them more free time to do . . . whatever it is they do."

James shakes his head. Her offer is nowhere good enough. "I will give you the answers you seek if you agree to free the Children and help my friends Simon and Kat destroy the Company back on Earth. That is my only offer."

James Ogubu knows how to play hardball.

"You want me to free the Children?" Daisy's aghast. She doesn't seem nearly as concerned about the Company. "Did you see what they were doing to this place before I arrived? What's the point of immortality if you have to spend an eternity in a hellhole like that? Look, it's like Mr. Gibson says—sometimes someone has to step up and take charge. Isn't that what Bird's done in Albion? Nobody here has a choice when it comes to technology."

"They have a choice whether they come to Albion or not," Bird says. "And they're able to leave whenever they choose. Can you offer your citizens that?"

"Are you kidding?" Kat can no longer hold her tongue. "She won't even give them a day off when they're injured. On the way here, we met the sister of a Child who fell from a tree while he was working. When he couldn't make his work quota, the Empress here had him killed."

Bird has been silently listening. Now she gasps in horror. "Is this true?"

"Absolutely not!" Daisy snaps. "I didn't have anything to do with what happened to that creature. I thought I told you—everything is automated. His band informed the system that he hadn't been working and the system sent a mechanical beast to deliver him to the Ice Fields. I didn't press a single button. I didn't even know about it."

"But you designed the system," James Ogubu points out. "That makes you responsible, does it not?"

"Fine," Daisy huffs. "I promise I'll change it as soon as I'm back. I'll even send these two thugs out to the Ice Fields to search for the kid just in case he managed to survive." She gestures to the two NPCs who've accompanied her.

I see Bird studying the two soldiers. They're standing side by side, their backs rigid and their eyes focused on an invisible horizon. "They're that loyal, are they?"

"What?" Daisy asks. "Them? Of course. Don't you have NPCs here? They're digital sl—" She catches herself before the word slips out. *"Servants."*

I see a familiar twinkle in Bird's eye. She knows something. "No, we don't have many of their kind here in Albion," she informs the Empress. "They're bound to the realms in which they were created. They may not leave without the permission of the realm's ruler."

"Well, they're here with me, so permission granted." Daisy's getting bored. "Do you mind if we get back to the reason for my visit?"

"I told you. I have already provided my only offer," James reminds her. "Unless you free the Children, we no longer have anything to discuss."

Daisy sighs. "I was really hoping we could come to an

arrangement. I am such a huge admirer of yours. I don't want to have to hurt you."

"It's come to this, has it?" James asks as though he's suspected it would all along.

"First I ask nicely. Then I take what I want," Daisy says.

Kat instantly pulls an arrow out of her quiver, but James only laughs at the Empress's threat. "I know I don't have the physique of a soldier, but I don't think your avatar will stand much of a chance against mine, Ms. Bristol."

"I don't do my own dirty work," Daisy tells him. Then she points to the NPCs. "They do."

This time James and Bird both laugh. The Children passing by on the street all turn in our direction. From a distance it must look like we're all having a jolly good time.

"They'll do what you want in Imperium, certainly," Bird says. "But not in Albion. The old magic rules this world. When you brought your . . . *servants* into my realm, you set them free. It will be their decision whether to do your bidding."

My mind is reeling. Are NPCs capable of making decisions like that? If so, what does it mean? All along, I've considered them part of the game, each NPC designed to play a specific role. Milo gave them the ability to improvise, which made them seem life-like when you encountered them in their realms. But if they're capable of what Bird just described, I can no longer say for sure whether they're real or unreal.

Out of the corner of my eye, I see one of the NPCs standing behind the Empress take a quick step forward. In a flash, my dagger is out. Kat still has an arrow nocked. But the soldier isn't going for James or Bird. Instead, he comes up behind Daisy. Before we know what's happening, he's taken her head in his hands. With one fast twist, he breaks her neck.

The Empress of Imperium falls to the ground. Somewhere back in the real world, Daisy Bristol has died too.

The assassin turns back to his fellow soldier. "Come," he says. "Let's go home."

We watch in shock as the two giant soldiers march toward the border.

THE BOY

The shock keeps me frozen in place. It hasn't had the same effect on Kat. In an instant, she snatches the dagger out of my hand and drops to her knees beside the Empress. With her back to me, I can only see her arm pumping back and forth as though she is sawing. I can't even begin to guess what she might be doing to Daisy's avatar.

Then she stands up in triumph, a swatch of strange fabric in her hand.

"Sorry," she says when she sees our stunned faces. "I wanted to get this before the Empress's body disappears."

Kat holds out the piece of fabric for James Ogubu to take. He glances down at it and then back up at Kat.

"You can use it to reverse engineer her body armor," Kat explains. She waves the swatch in the air. "With something like this, your avatar will be safe from now on."

James smiles at her but doesn't take it. "Thank you," he says. "But that won't be of much use to me, I'm afraid. If Bird will let me, I would like to stay here in Albion. The armor will not work in this realm."

"I would be honored to have you remain in Albion," Bird says. "As for the armor, I could make an exception."

"Allow no exceptions that aren't necessary," James insists. "I saw what happened to the White City. If you want to preserve Albion as it is, no technology is safe. You must monitor it all closely, or it will develop in ways you can neither control nor predict."

"But what about you, James?" Kat argues passionately. "Someday you may need to leave Albion. What will you do then?"

"I don't know," James replies. "And that's perfectly fine with me."

Kat still isn't prepared to accept his answer. But before she can say anything, her attention is drawn away. The Empress's avatar is flickering. James gently plucks the scrap of fabric from Kat's fingers and lays it on Daisy's chest. When her avatar disappears, her invention will go with her.

I don't know how to feel looking down at her body. Daisy was a danger to everyone here and on Earth. With her death, the enslaved Children of Otherworld can finally be free. And yet I can't celebrate her passing. There's no doubt Daisy was a genius. Skills like hers could have made life better for her fellow creatures. But she never understood humans or Children. To her, we were all just flesh-covered machines.

With her death also comes a new urgency. Back in Manhattan, Daisy Bristol's corpse is lying inside a capsule. How long before it's discovered? When Wayne finds out, he'll know something is up. There's a good chance he'll shut down the lab—and move his hostage.

"We've got to get to Declan right away," I tell Kat.

"Follow me and I'll take you to him," Bird says. "He's with the beasts."

As she guides us through the village, the residents on the streets stop to stare. I see eyes peering out at us in wonder from the windows of every building.

"They're still not used to seeing avatars in Albion," Kat notes.

Bird's rumbling laugh sounds rich with experience. I'm reminded that she's seen far more than we have. "Yes, but that's not why they're watching. You don't know how important you've been to all of us. Everyone here has come to Albion seeking a safe haven. Without the two of you, this realm would not be what it is today."

We pass the last building in town and find ourselves facing a wide-open prairie. Golden grass sways in the wind. In the distance, a herd of elephants wades peacefully through the tall stalks. It's hard to believe this is the same dystopian realm Kat and I visited only a few Earth days ago.

"It's incredible what you've done here," I tell Bird.

"I wish I could take the credit," Bird says. "Volla is responsible for bringing Albion back to life."

"Volla? The Elemental of Gimmelwald?" If she's alive, it's the best news I've had in ages.

"Yes. She and her offspring were among the first to arrive," she responds. "They'd been wandering the Wastelands for ages. Our Elemental restored her power. Now she and her children tend to the four corners of the realm. This prairie occupies the western corner of Albion. There are jungles to the north, mountains in the east and forests to the south."

Startled by something hidden from view, a deerlike creature springs out of the vegetation a few hundred yards in front of us. We watch its horns cut through the grass as it makes its escape.

"The beasts seem to be thriving," Kat says.

"We send scouting parties out to the realms and Wastelands to search for them. In some cases, we found the last of their kind. We've managed to save some species. But I'm afraid that many are gone for good."

Bird turns up a path toward a hut at the edge of the prairie, and Kat and I follow her inside. Sitting on the straw-covered floor is a young man feeding a creature from a bottle. It's the size of a large sheep, with coarse red hair and a long, elephantine trunk.

"Oh my God! Is that a woolly mammoth?" Kat marvels.

"She was smuggled to Albion from the Ice Fields," Bird says. "When she arrived she was small enough to hold in my arms. I didn't think there was much chance she'd survive, but Declan dedicated himself to saving her life."

"Declan?" I guess I was expecting to see the ogre who accompanied me on my first trip to Otherworld. But now I recognize the boy I met back on Earth. His new avatar is a few inches taller and years older than his real-life body.

He rises to his feet and gives me a bear hug. I can't find the words to tell him how happy I am to see him. I think some people were born to be on your team. It doesn't matter who they are; you know them when you find them. I recognized Kat and Elvis for that almost instantly. It took a little while longer with Busara. I didn't even know who Declan was when I first met his ogre avatar. But I knew he was someone I was meant to meet.

Declan lets go of me. "Sorry, Simon," he says, sounding more mature than he looks. Suddenly it strikes me. Declan's been here for so many Otherworld years, he's now far older than me. "I went back to New York to help you, and you've had to save my ass again."

"Everything happens for a reason." I can't believe those hokey-ass words just came out of my mouth—or that I actually believe them. "If Kat and I hadn't returned to Otherworld to find you, James Ogubu could have died. You did us all a big favor."

"You're serious?" he asks skeptically. "You're not trying to make me feel better?"

"Nope," I say. "How'd you end up getting captured, anyway? Bet you didn't go down without a fight."

"I went to Columbia Presbyterian Hospital," Declan says. "They got me there. Still don't know how they did it."

The hospital? "What were you doing there?"

He seems to think that the answer should be obvious. "I went to see Scott Winston."

I can't imagine why Declan thought visiting the man I'm supposed to have shot would somehow help me. "Why?"

"When I saw the video of the shooting, I knew it had to be a fake. I don't have any idea how they did it, but the Company obviously switched the real assassins' faces with yours and Kat's. I figured there was also a pretty good chance that Scott Winston's bodyguard was in on it all, since he never said anything. But there was one person who saw the shooters that day who might be able to prove you're innocent. Scott Winston."

I think back to the video. Declan's right. Winston was looking directly at the assassins when he was hit. If he'd died as the Company had planned, it would have been a perfect crime. But Winston survived. The Company left a loose end. It was a brilliant piece of detective work on Declan's part. If only his rescue plan had been as good.

"And you thought the hospital would just let you in to see him?"

"It's not as dumb as it sounds. I figured I stood a decent chance. I was so young back then that people didn't see me as threatening."

"So it worked?"

"Hell no," Declan admits. "I never even got past the lobby. It's like the Company saw me the second I stepped through the door."

"They probably did." Wayne must know that Scott Winston's a liability. He needs to get rid of him, but Winston's probably under heavy guard. I bet the Company has people hanging around the hospital, waiting to finish the job.

"Some guy came up to me and grabbed my arm. Next thing I knew I felt him stab me with a needle right in the ass." Then Declan grins. "I did get a few good kicks in before I passed out. Might have broken the guy's nose, too."

"Nice," I say. "Any idea where they're keeping your body?"

"If I had to guess, I'd say I'm still at the hospital," Declan tells me. "Last thing I remember is being hauled up to the third floor. I'd bet I'm still there somewhere. They're probably pulling the same bullshit they did before, keeping me in a coma."

I hope he doesn't notice me cringe. It's not going to be easy to get him out of the hospital. The Company clearly has the place staked out.

"All right. We'll have you out in a couple of hours' Earth time."

"Just—" Declan seems to be struggling to find the right words.

"What?"

"I've spent decades here in Otherworld, but back on Earth, I still look thirteen. Please don't treat me like a child. Don't send me back to my parents."

"Why the hell would we send you back?" I ask with a smile. "We're going to need you."

THE LAUNCH

The second I remove my headset, I can hear arguing from the next room.

"I'm not going to talk about this now. We don't know who's listening." The voice belongs to Busara. I imagine her sitting on the living room sofa, arms crossed and eyes focused on a wall in front of her.

"You do what you want." This time it's Elvis. "I'm not going to shut up. I want to know why you've gone cold. Back on the island, everything was fantastic. Then we get to New York and you're a different person. What happened to you?"

"I don't know. I guess I'm just not cut out for this sort of thing."

"What sort of thing?" Elvis's voice is rising in frustration. "What in the hell are you talking about?"

I climb off the treadmill and head to the door. They'll have to finish their fight later. The four of us have a life to save.

Then Busara shouts, and I freeze with my hand on the knob.

"I don't want to talk about it!" I don't hear anger in her voice. I hear anguish and terror.

"What the hell is going on out there?" I hear Kat whisper. She's returned from Otherworld too. She sets her headset down softly and comes to join me at the door. I don't feel comfortable eavesdropping like this. But something tells me we shouldn't enter the room.

"You know Simon used to hate me, right?" Busara says, taking me by surprise.

"He didn't hate you. He thought you might be a robot. It's not the same thing," Elvis says.

"Has he told you what I did?" She sounds so guilt-ridden. I honestly have no idea what she's talking about.

"Annoy the hell out of him?"

"He didn't tell you, did he?" Busara says miserably. "I tricked him into going to Otherworld for the first time. I even gave him a disk. I thought Milo had killed my father. I wanted Simon to kill Milo's avatar."

Oh, *that*.

"Simon told me he went to Otherworld to find Kat," Elvis says.

"Yes, but I was the one who gave him the disk. And I didn't tell him how dangerous it could be."

"Good God, Busara. Simon would have put on a bacon Speedo and jumped into a piranha-infested swimming pool for Kat. You should have given him a heads-up, but it wouldn't have stopped him for a second."

He's definitely right about that. I feel Kat interweave her fingers with mine and I squeeze her hand.

"That's not the point," Busara says. "Don't you see? Back then I would have done anything. I didn't think twice about putting Simon's life in danger. Something came over me, and all that mattered was getting what I wanted—revenge."

"Why are you dwelling on all of this when Simon's obviously forgiven you? People make mistakes, Busara. That's part of being human."

"I'd almost convinced myself that was true," Busara says. "I thought maybe it was a onetime thing. Maybe that wasn't who I really was. And then I met my mother."

"What does your mother have to do with our relationship?" Elvis demands.

"She lied to my father. She spied on him for money, and she acts like it was no big deal. It was what she wanted to do, so she did it. It didn't make any difference who ended up getting hurt."

"You don't know how much of that is true," Elvis argues. "And for the record, I don't think your mom is a bad guy. I have a hunch you don't know the real story."

"I know she lied to *me*," Busara cries. "I know how much she hurt me. And now I know that's where I get it from. If she can do it to me and my father, I can do it to you too."

"What do you mean?" Elvis says.

"I mean someday, I'll end up having a choice between doing what I want and what's best for you. And I'll end up choosing myself. Just like my mom did."

"You're wrong." Elvis sounds completely certain. "About everything, Busara."

"No." I can hear her crying. "I'm not."

Kat takes advantage of the pause that follows to whisper in my ear. "We shouldn't be listening to this." She pulls me back toward the treadmills, where she picks up a headset and drops it.

The clatter is loud enough to draw the attention of the two people in the next room.

"They're back," Elvis says. "We'll finish this conversation later."

"It's already over," Busara replies.

I hear footsteps approaching the door, and I quickly grab my headset and hop back on the treadmill.

The door opens and Elvis steps inside. If I hadn't heard what just happened, I'd wonder if he had a terrible case of food poisoning. His face is a pasty white and he looks like he could vomit at any moment. I can't think of anything to say, so I blurt out, "Daisy Bristol is dead."

Elvis bows his head as if it's too much for him to take. In the background, Busara bursts into tears. I should act surprised. That's what I'd do if I hadn't heard their conversation.

"I had no idea you guys were so fond of Daisy," I say awkwardly.

"Yeah, she was a real badass," Elvis says.

"If it makes you feel any better, she turned out to be a sociopath," I mutter helplessly.

"Did you find Declan?" Busara asks as she wipes her tears away with the collar of her shirt.

"Yep," I say. It's only just dawning on me that we're in a bit of trouble. "He's at Columbia Presbyterian Hospital."

"Well, come on, let's go get him!" Elvis is already retreating to the other room.

"It's not that simple," Kat says. "The Company has the building under surveillance."

"So we'll wear disguises," Busara says.

"You know that won't work, and there's no time for it anyway. As soon as Wayne finds out that Daisy's dead, he's going to know something's up. We have to get Declan out of the hospital before Daisy doesn't arrive at work in the morning."

"Okay," Elvis says warily.

"Which means you two will have to go in to get him out on your own. Kat and I would be spotted in a second."

Busara clears her throat. "Is this really a two-person job?" she asks.

"Yes," Kat tells her, firmly. "It is."

There's a black SUV waiting downstairs for us. Our hosts have been listening, but Nasha herself is nowhere to be found. Maybe she's asleep. After all, it is two o'clock in the morning. But I have a feeling her absence has something to do with her daughter's confession. It must have been hard to hear that your daughter's worst fear is becoming like you. The whole thing is weighing heavily on my mind as well. If I could find a few minutes alone with Busara, I'd tell her I don't blame her for introducing me to Otherworld. It happened for a reason. I would have gotten there one way or another.

There won't be any heart-to-heart convos on this ride, though. Busara and Elvis are busy staring out the windows on opposite sides of the car.

"It's Tuesday, isn't it?" Elvis muses. "Lot of people on the street at two o'clock on a Tuesday morning."

Tuesday? I have to think for a moment. It's been a while since the days of the week made much difference to me.

"Technically it's Wednesday," Kat says.

I see Busara's spine stiffen. "Wednesday the what?"

"No idea," I tell her.

But the question seems to have a special meaning for Elvis as well. "Could it be the fifteenth?"

"Sounds about right," Kat says. "What—"

Her question's cut short when we're all thrown violently forward against our seat belts as the car comes to a screeching stop. Through the windshield I see a young man caught in the glare of our headlights. He's standing in the middle of the road, less than six inches from our front bumper. A hipster type with a nicely trimmed beard and chunky black glasses, he seems oddly unfazed for someone who was just a few inches away from becoming roadkill. He smirks as he lifts one arm, his hand shaped as if it's holding an invisible gun. He aims the imaginary weapon at our driver and shoots. Before he sprints away into the dark, a triumphant smile spreads across his face.

"August the fifteenth at two twenty-five in the morning," Elvis says. "OtherEarth went on sale at midnight."

The chunky black glasses. I should have known. I wonder how many OtherEarth players are going to get themselves killed tonight.

We spot hundreds of gamers before we leave Queens. There are dozens more on the bridge to Manhattan. Most are on the south side of the bridge, aiming invisible firearms at something in the distance. I'd bet anything it's Godzilla.

But the shit doesn't truly hit the fan until we reach the island of Manhattan. Everyone we pass is sporting a pair of OtherEarth glasses. People are sprinting down the sidewalk as if something terrifying is right on their heels. Others have ducked down behind cars clutching invisible handguns.

"Oh my God." Elvis points upward to where a man in glasses is scaling the side of a brick building. He's at the fifth floor. If he falls, there's little chance he'll survive.

"This is incredibly dangerous. The cops need to shut it down," Busara mutters just as a police car speeds past and pulls over in front of the building that's being used as a climbing wall. I turn around to watch through our rear window. The cops get out and stare helplessly at the man high above them.

"How is anyone going to stop it?" Elvis says, taking the words right out of my mouth. "Most of this isn't illegal."

Up ahead we can see the hospital. It's a tall modern structure with a brightly lit lobby that appears almost completely empty. Every security guard seems to be stationed outside on the sidewalk, all of them keeping at least three gamers at bay. The building must play a role in some OtherEarth game. As we arrive at the main entrance, one of the gamers pushes through and a battle breaks out among the blue-clad guards and the mob in glasses.

"Go now," Kat urges Elvis and Busara. "While they're all distracted."

The two hop out and head toward the entrance. Kat and I stay behind in the car and turn our attention to a tablet computer. A camera in Elvis's hat lets us see what they see.

"You okay?" we hear Elvis ask.

"Don't," Busara snaps. "Everyone is listening."

"Don't *what*?" Elvis asks.

"Never mind," Busara huffs.

"Oh, did you think I was going to say something about our conversation earlier? Don't you think Simon and Kat deserve to know you're an impostor?"

"Impostor?" The word seems to have hit her hard. She sounds devastated.

"Of course. The girl I'm in love with would never believe anything as insane as the crap you told me."

"Insane!" Now she's shocked. I doubt anyone's used that word in reference to her before. "How can you say that?"

"Because I know the real Busara, and she loves me too," he says. "That's how."

"But—"

"I have nothing more to say to you," Elvis tells her. "Let me know when the real Busara is back, would you?"

"But—"

"Shhhhh!" he orders. "Everyone is listening! Right, Simon? You hearing all of this?"

God, this is painful. "Yep," I say. "Loud and clear."

Shortly after they remove his IV and peel the disk off the back of his skull, Declan should be able to get out of the hospital on his own two feet. There are clothes in Busara's backpack for him—the sweat suit that Nasha gave her daughter back on the boat. It's the only outfit we had that might come close to fitting a small thirteen-year-old boy.

The guards are so busy with the gamers outside the hospital that there isn't much security inside the building. The only people Busara and Elvis pass are another couple dressed in dark workout gear. Their faces aren't familiar at all, but something about them grabs my attention.

"Elvis, turn around for a second," I say into the mike. His camera turns back in the direction he and Busara just came from. The guy is tall and thin and his girlfriend curvaceous with wild, curly hair. They're headed toward the intensive care unit on the other side of the building.

"Who do those two people look like from behind?" I ask Kat.

"Us," she says. "Do you think they're trouble?"

I watch them walking away. "Probably, but I don't know how. Pretty hard to hide weapons under those skintight gym clothes."

"Hey, can we keep going?" Elvis says. "It really looks like I'm ogling that dude's girlfriend."

"Sure," I tell him. "Keep going." I don't know what else we could do.

Those are the last two people they pass in the halls on the way to Declan's room. The elevator is empty, and on the third floor, the medical staff and the patients who are able to get out of bed are all standing at the windows, looking out at the mayhem in the street below.

We find Declan on the third floor in room 321. The scene brings back memories I wish I could forget. The feed from Elvis's camera shows a kid lying in a hospital bed, a sheet pulled up to his chest.

"He's smaller in real life," Kat notes. "He barely looks twelve."

As Elvis moves closer, I can see Declan's eyes moving beneath his eyelids. If you didn't know any better, you'd think he was dreaming. A plastic tube inserted into his right arm delivers a steady drip of sustenance. Mixed in is the chemical that's responsible for his comatose state. Busara steps into view. She bends over and slowly pulls the IV needle out of his skin. Then she gently lifts his head and removes the boy's Otherworld visor and the disk from the base of his skull.

Busara returns his head to the pillow. A few moments later, Declan's eyes open.

"What the—" he starts to say when he lays eyes on his visitors. He's never seen Busara or Elvis in real life.

"Relax!" Elvis whispers. "Simon sent us."

"Where is he?" Declan asks.

"Watching," Elvis tells him.

"And waiting," I say. "Now that Declan's awake, get the hell out of there!"

There's a flash of bright light, followed by the sound of an explosion. I'm still watching the camera feed. I see Busara grab Declan. She pushes him down to the floor and covers his body with her own. Then all I can see is a close-up of the floor.

"Shit!" our driver blurts out. It's the first time I've heard any of Nasha's men speak. I look up just in time to see a wall of the hospital collapse. An entire corner of the building follows.

"Elvis!" I shout in terror. "Are you guys all right?"

The camera rises from the floor. "What happened?"

"There was an explosion on the other side of the building," I tell him. "You guys need to haul ass right away."

"There's a nurse on this floor who works for the Company," Declan says. "If he sees us trying to leave, we'll never escape."

I see Busara dump the sweat suit they brought for Declan in the trash. What in the hell is she doing?

"Busara?" Elvis says.

"I've got an idea," she tells him. "I'll be right back."

She ducks into the room's bathroom and emerges seconds later wearing a hospital gown and a paper mask. She hands her shirt, jeans and shoes to Declan.

"Put these on," she tells Declan. "I think they should fit."

"Busara—" Elvis tries again.

"Trust me," she says. "Declan and I are the same size. We have the same hair. If the nurse gets a quick look, all he'll see is the hospital gown and the back of my head. He'll assume I'm Declan."

Elvis starts to argue, but Busara stops him.

"No, Elvis. I need to do this. For you and Declan. And for myself. I'm serious," she says, but she doesn't look it. She's practically beaming with happiness. This is the chance she's been waiting for—the opportunity to prove to herself who she really is. Busara leans toward Elvis. Their faces are off camera, but Declan's snort in the background makes it perfectly clear what's going on.

"I love you," I hear Busara tell him.

"I know," Elvis tells her. "It's nice to have you back. Please don't die."

"I won't," she tells him. "My mother always told me I was bound for great things."

Then she opens the hospital room door and disappears.

Down on the street, sirens and flashing lights surround our SUV. The fire and police departments have arrived on the scene.

Now that Elvis and Busara have been separated, there's no way to know where she is. Elvis and Declan are still making progress. They're coming out of the emergency exit with a terrified crowd of doctors, nurses and patients. A few people are crying, but most seem stunned silent. I wonder what will happen to those who are trapped in their beds.

I spot Elvis among the people who've made it out. He ferries Declan across the street to us and the two of them climb into the SUV.

"I'm going back in to get Busara," Elvis announces.

"That's not going to be necessary." Kat points out the window. "She's right there."

A man in a nurse's scrubs has just exited the building, holding Busara tightly by the arm. The man definitely works for the Company. If I had to guess I'd say it's one of Wayne's ninjas. Busara didn't get away.

Elvis lurches for the door handle but finds it locked. "Let me out!" he shouts at the driver.

"No!" I order. "Don't open it." Then I take Elvis by the shoulders. "You go out there and you'll end up getting taken too. You don't want to go through what happened to Kat and me."

"I don't give a shit!" Elvis struggles to break free, but I'm much stronger than he is. It seems strange. I wonder if that's always been the case.

"Listen to me! If we want to save Busara, we're going to have to give that guy something he wants even more."

"What?"

"Unlock the doors and get ready to move," I order the driver. We hear the locks open and I start to slide out.

"Holy shit, Simon! Where are you going?" Kat shrieks.

"The only thing that guy wants more than Busara is me," I say.

I slam the door and start off toward the man. He sees me coming and drops Busara's arm. I give him a wink and take off to the right. He shoots after me like a bullet. Every police officer I pass does a double take when they see me. At least one joins the chase. I know I'm not going to get away. I just want Busara to have enough time to make it to the car. Less than a minute after I took off down the sidewalk, I'm tackled from the side by a female police officer with a body that feels like molded concrete. I'm lying facedown on the ground with my arms cuffed behind my back when I catch sight of the black SUV I arrived in. No one else even seems to notice as it speeds off in the direction of Queens.

EYEWITNESS

The door opens and a man in an old-fashioned check suit enters the room. He takes off his fedora and places it on the table before he takes a seat on the opposite side of the table. I watch him dig in his breast pocket for a pack of cigarettes. Then he props his feet up on the table, the dirty soles of his wingtips facing me. He lights his cigarette and exhales a cloud of pale blue smoke that hovers in the middle of the interrogation room.

"Gotta say, it feels damned good being on the other side of this table." He takes another drag off the cigarette. "What's the matter? Cat got your tongue?"

I glance over at the two-way mirror. There are people behind it, no doubt.

The Kishka laughs. "You worried the cops will think you're bananas?"

I nod.

"You don't need to move your lips, kid. I can always hear you, remember?"

Sure would have been nice to know that a little bit earlier. "Is this normal?" I ask in my head.

"Having conversations with someone who's supposed to have died forty years ago?" He shrugs and offers me an impish grin. "Probably not."

No shit. "No, I meant this. I've been in here by myself for hours now. Is this some kind of mind game?"

"I have a feeling they're busy with other things. Something big is going down."

And I'm stuck in a fucking interrogation room with a hallucination.

"I heard that," the Kishka says. "I prefer to think of all this as a glitch."

What?

"*Glitch* comes from *glitsh*. You know that word? With an *s* at the end instead of a *c*? Of course you don't. Your mother married a WASP. It's from Yiddish. All the best words come from Yiddish. It means *slippery place*. That's where we are right now—you, me and the whole fucking world. A very slippery place."

I'm almost positive I've never heard the word *glitsh* before. If the Kishka's a hallucination, how could he know words I don't?

"I'm not a fucking hallucination," he sighs. "Why is it so hard to get that through your skull?"

Suddenly this conversation seems way more important than it did a few seconds ago. If he's not a hallucination, what the fuck is he? If he knows things I don't, what can he tell me?

I don't get to ask. The door opens and a woman enters. I recognize the suit before I realize who's inside it. In an instant, she has her arms wrapped around me. The smell of her shampoo brings back memories.

"Mom. How did you get in here?" I whisper.

"I'm your lawyer." She steps back and wipes away a tear. Once it's gone, it's hard to imagine it was ever there. "So you know, whispering won't do any good. If anyone's on the other side of the glass, they can hear anything you say."

She walks around the table and takes the Kishka's seat. He's gone, but he's left his mark. My mother sniffs the air.

"Has someone been smoking?" she asks. "They're not allowed to do that in here."

"Not while I've been waiting," I tell her.

"Good." She sounds unconvinced.

This is not the mother I grew up with. She may be wearing my mother's suit, but the two women are not the same. This is the woman I saw on Nasha's spy cameras. The one I saw wearing jeans and boots. Nasha told me my mother has changed. I'm starting to suspect that this is who she really was all along.

"What's going on?" I ask her.

"There was a terrorist incident at Columbia Presbyterian Hospital early this morning."

"Yeah, I know, I was—"

"Stop." My mother holds up a hand like a crossing guard. "Let me do the talking for now."

"Okay."

"A bomb was detonated in the intensive care unit. Five patients and three members of the medical staff are dead."

"Oh God." My head drops into my hands. What's wrong with me? I saw it happen, and I never thought about the humans inside.

"A camera in the lobby captured a video of the two suspects entering the building and walking toward the intensive care unit. The people in question resembled you and Katherine Foley."

She must be talking about the couple in black workout clothes who caught my eye at the hospital. "It wasn't us. It was—"

All my mom needs to do is raise her hand again.

"It is believed that the suspects' target was Scott Winston, CEO of Chimera Corp. Until recently, he had been staying in the ICU directly above where the bomb was positioned. The blast killed the new patient who'd been moved into the room."

"But Scott Winston survived?" I asked.

My mother nods. "He did," she says. "He regained consciousness yesterday evening and was taken to another part of the hospital. Apparently, the move was done in secret. The people who attempted to murder him weren't aware it had taken place."

"Wow," I say.

"Wow indeed," my mother agrees. "But that's only the first bit of information I need to give you."

Good God, there's more?

"Scott Winston has released a statement to the press. He claims that the video that captured the shooting last week was forged. He says that he saw the two people responsible. He is one hundred percent certain that they were not the same couple shown in the video."

Declan had the answer all along. Scott Winston was the only person on Earth who could exonerate us.

"Winston's statement got the police searching for new footage. They found a video posted on some tourist's Twitter account. The real assassins appeared to be two men in their late twenties."

"So they know Kat and I are innocent?"

"They do."

"Then why am I still here?" I ask.

"I've asked them to keep you here," she says. "Until it's safe for us to move you."

"Us?" I groan. "Don't tell me Dad's here too."

My mother chuckles. "No," she says. "I traded that family for another."

My dad's a douchebag. If I were my mom, I'd get rid of him too. But what is she trying to say?

"Come on," my mother says, cocking her head toward the door. "They don't need to keep you in here anymore. You can wait somewhere that's a bit more comfortable."

"I'm free to go? Don't they want to interview me?"

"Of course they do. I've arranged for you to speak to the FBI later today. You can walk out the front door of the station any time you like," my mother tells me. "But I wouldn't recommend it just yet. The Company will have people watching the building." She leads me out of the interrogation room and through a room filled with cops at their desks. A few hours ago, I was number one on the most wanted list. Now, no one even looks up as I pass. It's as if they're all doing their best to pretend I'm not here.

I want to ask my mother how long I'll have to wait before I can safely leave, but there hasn't been an opportunity. She passes an elevator and opens the door to the fire stairs instead. I don't know whether I'm supposed to follow. My mother catches the door just before it swings closed. "Let's go," she says, waving me over.

We descend three flights, passing no one on the stairs. "Can you please tell me what's going on?" I ask.

"You'll find out in a second," my mother says.

We emerge in a basement where a beat-up Subaru is idling. The man behind the wheel is indescribably bland. I know in an instant that he must be one of Nasha's men.

"Get in," my mother orders. "She'll be here shortly."

"She—you mean *Nasha*?" My mother nods. "How the hell do you know Nasha?" I never introduced them. As far as I know, they never met back in Brockenhurst.

"Nasha and I have a mutual friend."

Just when you think your mind can't be blown. I guess my mother's contact list includes professional spies as well as mobsters. "Who?" I blurt out.

"Her employer." My mother is smiling. This is so unbelievably weird. My mother knows Nasha's boss but I don't. "You'll meet him soon too."

"Just tell me who he is," I plead.

My mother shakes her head. "I promised I wouldn't yet. Just get in the car, Simon. I'll see you when all of this is over."

I watch her walk back to the stairwell door. She gives me a little wave before she vanishes inside. I think she's doing this to torture me.

I open the door of the Subaru and slide inside. There's a tablet computer on the backseat. Its presence cannot be an accident. Nasha's employer must want me to have it. I tap the Home button and the screen comes to life. Live feed from a cable news network is playing. I can see a reporter broadcasting from the hospital that was attacked. The volume is turned down, but a chyron reads, *Thirty people now presumed dead.* All so the Company could murder a single man. I wonder if Wayne is feeling proud of himself right now.

The video switches over to a man sitting in a hospital bed holding a microphone. I assume it's one of the people who survived the bombing. And it is. At the bottom of the screen a new chyron introduces the man as *Scott Winston, CEO of Chimera Corp.*

"When I saw the footage of my attempted assassination, I immediately knew that the video had been altered. I *saw* the two people who shot me. Their faces are still etched into my memory. I know with absolute certainty that the two teenagers who have been accused of the crime are not the people I saw that day. I also knew that I had been the victim of a very sick joke."

"Joke?" the reporter scoffs.

"Sorry—poor choice of words, I know. There's only one software that can alter video so seamlessly. It's produced by my corporation. The people who attempted to murder me used my own tools against me."

"Had you ever considered that the software might be used in a situation like this?"

Scott Winston stays silent for a few seconds as the reporter patiently waits for his answer. "The idea had been raised by people within my corporation. At the time it seemed strictly theoretical. I did not take the threat seriously. I do now. I've ordered a review of all products currently in our innovation funnel. Projects that are deemed unethical or dangerous will be terminated. I hope it doesn't take another tragedy for other businesses to do the same."

The camera cuts back to the news anchor. "That was Scott Winston speaking from his hospital bed earlier today—"

The door on the other side of the backseat opens, and I jump halfway out of my skin.

"I'm surprised you still get nervous." Nasha pokes her head into the vehicle. "Haven't you figured out you're the hero of this story? Nothing's going to happen to you."

"Heroes get killed off sometimes," I say. "Besides, who says *I'm* the hero?"

Nasha laughs as she slides in next to me. "Everyone, kid. Took me a while to believe it too. You don't exactly look the part."

I yawn. This shit has gotten so boring. I don't even have the strength to argue. "Is Kat back at the apartment? Are you taking me there?"

"Not yet," Nasha says. "I need to make a quick detour. I'm hoping you'll agree to come with me."

I'm not sure I want to go anywhere alone with Nasha. "Where?"

"To the Company's lab. It's time for me to get paid."

"I don't get it," I say. "What's at the lab?"

"You'll see," she says.

"I hate to disappoint you, but I can't get you in there."

"I don't need you to," Nasha says. "He's going to let us in." She points her thumb backward.

There, lying on the row of seats behind us, is Todd.

THE DOWNLOAD

"Hey, buddy," I say. "How ya doing back there?"

Todd can't say much with the gag stuffed in his mouth, but he manages to give me a very meaningful stink-eye.

"Is it really necessary to keep him tied up like that?" I ask Nasha.

I can tell by her grin that it isn't. "We take all available precautions when dealing with Company employees."

Seems wise. I'm not going to argue.

Nasha leans forward and taps the driver on the shoulder. "Let's get going." Then she turns back to me. "It's seven-thirty. Todd says lab employees start arriving at work around eight-thirty. We need to be finished and out by nine."

"Nine? Don't we want to be out of there *before* the employees start showing up?"

"We'll be on Todd's floor. The other employees won't bother

us. We need to be done by nine because that's when the authorities are going to raid the lab. This is the day the Company goes down."

I should be thrilled. This is what I've been working for, and I hope Nasha's right. But something inside me is telling me it won't be that easy.

"You bet your ass it won't." My head jerks toward the front passenger seat. The Kishka's sitting there.

"Simon?" Nasha asks. "Is something wrong?"

"What?" I force myself to turn back toward her.

"Did you see something? Or some*one*?" The way she asks the question makes me think she might know—and her expression tells me that might be okay. But I'm not going to spill the beans about the Kishka with Todd lying in the backseat.

"No," I tell her. The Kishka has vanished. "We just need to be careful."

Nasha studies my face. "We will," she says.

Now that the sun has come up, there are more OtherEarth players on the streets. Half of New York must be planning to call in sick from work today. I'm sure this would be the biggest story of the day if not for the hospital bombing. Riding down Park Avenue, I count four ambulances pulled to the side of the road where EMTs are caring for injured players. Around Fifty-Second Street, I spot a sheet-covered body being loaded onto a gurney. Nearby, there's a pool of blood on the sidewalk. The guy must have fallen from one of the buildings that line the avenue. His plunge doesn't appear to have disturbed the other players in the vicinity. A woman sprinting down the sidewalk runs straight through the blood splatter, ignoring a furious cop who's trying to protect the scene.

This is bedlam. Did Wayne know what he was unleashing on New York? Was this part of his plan—or just an unintended consequence?

Once we pass Grand Central Terminal on our way downtown, Nasha reaches back and snips the ties binding Todd's arms and legs. As soon as his hands are free, he removes his gag.

"Jesus, lady!" he says. "I don't know why you'd expect me to help you. First you kidnap me and then you keep me hog-tied for hours. That's not exactly how you make friends. Who the hell is this woman, Simon?"

"I'm the only thing between you and the death penalty," Nasha says. "I think you're the one who needs to be busting their ass to make friends."

Todd looks over at me.

"She's right," I say. "Be nice, would you?"

Todd slumps back angrily and keeps his lips shut for the rest of the drive. When we arrive, he lets us in. We walk through the dark lobby to the elevator.

"Good morning, Todd," says the elevator. "Starting early today?"

"You know me, Dot," he drones. "I never quit."

"I sense an extra three hundred and nineteen pounds."

"I'm bringing two in for downloading," Todd says, punching the number three.

"All right, we're here," Todd grunts when we step off on the third floor. "What is it you want?"

Nasha's eyes are roaming the room, taking in the equipment that surrounds the two dentist chairs and the strange helmets suspended above them. At last her gaze settles on Todd. "I need you to download everything you can—my memories, my personality, everything," she tells him.

I can't have heard right. "You want him to *what*?" I blurt out before Todd can utter a word.

"Once it's all downloaded, Elvis will upload it all into an Otherworld avatar," she says.

"Elvis doesn't know—"

Nasha stops me. "He does. I taught him how."

"How do you—" This time, I stop myself. There's only one answer that makes sense. "Did you and James have this planned all along?"

"As much as I'd love to tell you the whole story, this isn't the time or the place." Nasha sits down in one of the white leather chairs. "We need to get started."

When Todd walks over to Nasha's chair, her arm darts out. She grabs a fistful of Todd's shirt and drags him toward her. "I'm trusting you with my brain, boy," she warns him. "Anything goes wrong and Simon's going to make sure you end up frying in a different kind of chair. We clear on that?"

"Crystal," Todd tells her. "Go ahead and get comfortable. The procedure will take about thirty minutes."

"Awww. Look at you making nice," Nasha replies, letting him go. "I appreciate that." She adjusts her position and Todd lowers the helmet into place. Soon Nasha's entire head has disappeared inside it.

The sight of Nasha's motionless, black-clad body makes me uncomfortable. This is how I must have looked when the Company raided my brain. Utterly defenseless.

"What do we do now?" I ask Todd.

"Wait," he says, taking a seat on the only stool in the room. I could sit down in the empty reclining chair next to Nasha's, but I'd rather stand.

"How's all this stuff work?" I gesture toward the machinery.

"You really think you'd understand if I told you?" Todd asks. "Or was that just an attempt at small talk?"

"Never mind," I say.

"So this is James Ogubu's wife," Todd says. "I guess I should have recognized her. She's been working with you to take down the Company?"

Todd takes my silence as confirmation.

"It's pretty ironic, don't you think?" he asks. "Ogubu started all of this. Now his wife has to clean it all up."

Now he's got my attention. "What are you talking about?"

"Without James Ogubu, there would be no disk. Without him, we wouldn't be able to download memories. If you think about it, every shitty thing the Company has done can be traced right back to him. I'm going to end up dead or in jail because of James Ogubu."

"He created the disk to help his daughter. He figured out how to download memories because his life was in danger," I argue, feeling offended on James's behalf.

"Yeah," Todd says. "*His* daughter. *His* life."

I see his point. "James never meant to do any harm."

"I'm sure he didn't," Todd says. "But the road to hell is paved with good intentions."

Todd stops and his spine stiffens. The elevator has been called down to the ground floor. My heart literally skips a beat.

"Fuck," Todd mutters. "We've got visitors." Last time we were here, Todd had a plan ready in case someone showed up. This morning it's clear that he doesn't. I quickly scan the room around us. There's literally nowhere to hide—not even a desk to crawl under.

"What should I do?" I ask.

"Lie down." Todd points to the chair beside Nasha's. "Close your eyes and don't open them until I tell you to."

"What about Nasha?" I ask.

"She has to stay where she is," Todd tells me. "We can't interrupt the download."

I follow Todd's order and lie down on the white leather chair. My heart is racing. When I hear the elevator come to a stop on our floor, it nearly bursts out of my chest.

There's a ding and the doors open with a whoosh.

"There he is," says an all-too-familiar voice. "It's not even eight o'clock and he's already hard at work. Son, you are a genuine asset to this organization."

"Thank you, sir." Todd's voice cracks. Something is very wrong and he knows it. "Hello, AJ. How nice to see you in my part of the building." AJ's presence can't be a good sign. He's the guy who develops Wayne's custom experiences.

"Hello, Todd," says a voice I've never heard before.

"I see you got your robot sidekick with you this morning,

Todd," Wayne says. He must be referring to me. "You boys sure are inseparable."

Todd tries to laugh and fails miserably. "That's how they learn, sir."

"Of course," Wayne replies. "And who do we have here? Looks like a lady, if I'm not mistaken."

"I made a few tweaks to the machinery, sir. I needed to give it a test run, so I found a volunteer."

I cringe on the inside. If that's the best Todd could come up with, we're both dead.

"Well, how about that?" Wayne drawls. "What do you suppose the odds are? You need a volunteer and the kind soul who offers to help you out just happens to be Nasha Ogubu."

Yep. We're screwed.

"I'm sorry, sir." Todd's backpedaling furiously. He didn't expect Wayne to recognize her. "She made me bring her here. She wanted her memories downloaded. I'll go ahead and stop—"

"No need to do that," Wayne says. "Let it run. A copy of Mrs. Ogubu's memories will come in handy, I'd imagine. Now do me a favor, son, and wake up your robot friend for me."

There's a long, terrifying pause before Todd says, "Simon. Open your eyes and sit up."

I obey, doing my best not to show my panic. Wayne is standing with his hands in his pockets. AJ is by his side. Like Todd, AJ is slim and youthful, though he's dressed more like a man Wayne's age in pressed pants and a checked oxford. He's holding a disk and a pair of black glasses in his right hand. One of Wayne's tough guys has come with them. Dressed in what can only be called badass black, he's casually crossing the room toward Todd.

"What would you like Simon to do?" Todd croaks, keeping an eye on the man coming his way.

"Nothing. I just want your friend to see what I'm going to have done to you." Wayne nods to the ninja. In a flash, the man takes Todd by the head and rams a thin steel blade under the base of his skull. Todd's eyes roll back and his knees buckle. The man releases him and he falls to the ground. Todd's eyes are still open as a small pool of blood forms a halo around his head.

"Really is a shame," Wayne says, looking down at the corpse. "That boy was a hard worker. Too bad he turned out to be a traitor."

I don't say a word in response. I try not to show any emotion at all.

"Oh, come on!" Wayne smiles broadly as if it's all a big joke. "Isn't the robot act getting old? Stand up, Mr. Eaton."

He knows. My only hope is to play for time. Nasha said the authorities would be arriving at nine. That can't be too far away. I silently watch as Wayne's smile transforms into a scowl. He glances at the ninja, who steps forward and points his blade at the back of my skull. I feel something drip onto my shirt. I know without looking that it was a drop of Todd's blood.

"*Now,* Mr. Eaton," he demands. "The three of us are taking a little trip downstairs."

THE KILLER EXPERIENCE

The ninja stays with Nasha while Wayne and AJ escort me down to the glass room on the first floor. Wayne holds the door open for me and the three of us go inside. AJ hands me the disk and glasses and waits for me to put them on. He gives me a smile before he leaves. I watch as he makes his way down the stairs toward one of the leather armchairs in the lobby. Whatever's about to happen, AJ intends to watch.

"You just keep going around sticking your nose where it doesn't belong, don't you?" I turn my attention back to Wayne. There's a single stool inside the otherwise empty room, and he's taken it. He's wearing a pair of OtherEarth glasses, too, and pointing a gun he didn't have before.

"Sticking my nose where it doesn't belong? How do you expect me to take you seriously when you talk like a Scooby-Doo villain? And *that*"—I gesture toward his gun—"that isn't a real weapon."

"You're wearing a disk, son. This may be a fake gun that fires fake bullets, but it will kill you just as quickly as any other gun would," Wayne informs me. "And this way we won't leave a huge mess in the conference room if I'm forced to use it."

"Gee, you're awfully squeamish for someone who murdered thirty people earlier today."

"Their deaths were unfortunate but necessary," Wayne says. "It's a shame the operation was not a success."

"Why were you trying to kill Scott Winston anyway?" The only way to survive this is to keep Wayne talking until the authorities arrive at nine.

"Killing Winston was the only option I had left. I offered him a trial of OtherEarth and he turned me down. I invited him to visit the lab, but he wouldn't come. The man has been releasing dangerous technology into the world, and I'm afraid the only way to stop him was to kill him."

"You really think Winston deserves to die?"

"His company created software that blurs the line between real and fake. He was going to make the technology available to every criminal, terrorist and anarchist on Earth. I couldn't allow that to happen."

"I still don't understand what good would killing him do."

Wayne's wide grin is that of a man who's thought things through. "The number two honcho at Winston's corporation is a big OtherEarth fan. And he's got some interesting proclivities that I'm pretty sure he'd rather not be made public. Once Winston's gone, the number two guy takes over as CEO. I don't think I'll have much trouble getting him to see my point of view. If I do have any trouble, he'll end up in one of the capsules upstairs."

"What exactly is your point of view?" I ask. "I heard you used to run Cyber Command. Your job was defending the country, and now you're setting off bombs and assassinating CEOs."

Wayne leans forward, his elbows on his knees. "My point of view is that I see the chaos that lies in humanity's future unless

someone takes decisive action. I didn't notice anyone else stepping forward. You see, I've figured out who this country's real enemies are—and they're not Russian kids hacking government servers. I spent my whole government career going after bad guys who were just using tools that bigger bad guys were making. These men like Scott Winston who've been willing to fuck up the world just to make a few bucks? I'm taking them down one by one. I started with Milo Yolkin."

I'm not buying this shit for a second. "So you really think you're the good guy in all of this? You beta tested disks on helpless hospital patients. You used my friend, a thirteen-year-old boy, as a guinea pig."

"It's awful. I agree. I wouldn't have gone to such lengths if the disk weren't so important. I figured if I was going to fight the tool makers, I was going to need the ultimate tool. The moment Milo Yolkin showed me the disk, I knew it was exactly what I'd been looking for. But I had to figure out how best to use it. Some people were harmed in the process, it's true. But the world will be better off because of their sacrifices."

"So other people get to make all the sacrifices, and you're the one who ends up in charge of the ultimate tool. Is that right?"

"Someone had to take charge," Wayne says. "I'm not perfect, but my motives are purer than most. I have no interest in hoarding money. I'm a champion of law and order."

"Are you kidding? Have you seen all the OtherEarth gamers out on the streets tonight? They're tearing the city apart!"

"Yep," Wayne says smugly. "I imagine the game will probably be banned. Regulators will get more involved in the industry. Other corporations will think twice about introducing augmented reality products in the future."

"If OtherEarth gets banned, the Company will go under financially."

Wayne chuckles. "I don't think so. There's very strong demand for our custom product. We've been getting calls from all over the world. Oligarchs. Prime ministers. Despots and dictators. They all want what we're offering. We've also acquired a very important new investor. Her resources are practically unlimited, and they've been put at our disposal."

I know what he's getting at. "You're talking about Abigail Prince."

"Never meant to add Ms. Prince to the collection. That was just a little piece of good fortune that practically fell right into my lap. Not only has she brought an end to the Company's financial problems, she's brought you and me together again. I'll admit— you've had me a little worried, Mr. Eaton. Now I can put all those worries to rest."

"By killing me," I say.

"Well, here's the deal, son," Wayne tells me. "I'm going to give you one last chance, just for sport. See if you're everything they say you are. I had AJ put together a special experience just for you. If, at any point, you attempt to remove your disk or glasses, I'll shoot you. If you can't handle your custom experience, you can ask me to put you out of your misery, and I'll gladly comply.

But—if you manage to make it through to the end, I'll allow you to live."

I laugh. "I don't believe you."

Wayne holds up a hand as if taking an oath. "You've got my word of honor. Now—what do you say we get started?"

I glance downstairs into the lobby. A few more people have joined AJ. The lab's employees are arriving for work. I don't know how long it will be before the police arrive. No more than half an hour, I'd estimate. Whatever horrors Wayne has in store for me, I can survive for thirty minutes.

Wayne signals to AJ, who taps a device in his hand. Nothing changes. Wayne's still sitting on his stool in the corner. I watch as he lifts a finger and twirls it, as if to tell me *turn around*. I don't want to. Then I hear someone clear their throat impatiently behind me.

I take a peek over my shoulder. There's an operating table in the center of the room, and Kat is lying on top of it. Thick leather straps hold down her arms and her legs. There's a gag in her mouth. A vein throbs in the center of her forehead, and her eyes are wide with panic. Her midsection has been prepped as if for an operation. I spin around.

A man in a doctor's coat stands next to a rolling cart on which an assortment of surgical instruments is displayed. The man is thin and pale, with dark hair and old-fashioned wire-rimmed glasses. Perfectly calm and composed, he practically radiates evil. "Shall we begin? This is a timed experience. You really don't want to waste another minute." He picks up a large scalpel and tries to hand it to me. When I don't take it, his eyes close and open in a slow, lizardlike blink and he places it back down on the tray.

"In twenty-nine minutes, this room will fill with a poisonous gas that will kill the three of us. The disk you are wearing will ensure that you die a very real and extremely painful death. However, there is a key that will allow us to escape. This young woman has swallowed it. If we want to retrieve the key, one of us must cut her open to find it."

"No," I say. "Not going to happen." Game or no game, there is no way I'm going to do anything like that.

It seems the man was expecting that response. "There is always a chance, however slim, that your friend will survive the operation," he tells me. "However, if you do not start within the next nine minutes, I will be forced to perform the procedure myself. Unlike you, I do not care how much the girl suffers—or whether she lives or dies."

"I'll kill you if you touch her," I growl.

"Not if I shoot you first," Wayne says behind me.

I spin around to face him. "You sick bastard."

"Don't look at me," Wayne says humbly. "AJ deserves all the credit. He spent time digging through your memories and came up with this experience all by himself. The kid's a goddamned genius."

"It's my job to inform you that you are wasting valuable time." I turn back to find the man in the lab coat checking his watch. "You only have eight minutes left to decide."

There's no chance of anyone arriving to rescue me within the next eight minutes. I can stall until then, but I'll eventually have to act.

It's not real, I tell myself. The girl on the table isn't Kat.

I take a step toward her. She's looking up at me with terrified eyes. I tug at the straps on her arms and legs. They're locked down. There's no way to remove them. The panic building, I reach for the gag. As I do, my hand brushes her cheek. It's soft and hot and wet with her tears.

"Are you certain that's wise?" the man in the lab coat inquires.

I don't give a shit. I pull out the gag.

"Simon!" Kat gasps, and I have to clutch the side of the table to avoid falling to the ground. "Please, Simon, don't hurt me!" It's her voice. Those are her lips. But the words don't belong to the girl I love.

"I like the real Kat so much better, don't you?" someone says. I look up to see the Kishka leaning against the glass wall near Wayne. "This one's like someone's idea of a girl. In my experience, real-life ladies aren't that helpless." The Kishka looks completely unperturbed by the scene. My mouth must drop open, because he puts a finger to his lips. "Probably best if they don't know I'm here," he tells me.

My eyes pass from him to Wayne and then back to Kat. I'd swear on my life that they were all flesh and blood. I can see the red, raw marks that the restraints are leaving on Kat's wrists. I watch as tears stream from her eyes and her chest heaves with each breath.

"You know what's real and what isn't. You always have." The Kishka sticks his thumb out at Wayne. "He can make as many copies as he likes. They won't fool you unless you let them. That's not your girlfriend. The man in the coat isn't real. Look at them. You can see the difference."

I can now. They're empty. There's nothing inside them.

And you? I think.

"I'm part of you. I'm as real as it comes."

You're inside my head.

"I'm inside every cell of you."

What am I supposed to do?

"What would you do if those glasses weren't on your face?" he asks. "Do that. It's how you've survived so far. You haven't let the bastards change you."

"Your time is running out," the man in the white coat interrupts, as if on cue. "What are you going to do?"

The Kishka is gone, and the panic has faded. There are only two real things left in this room. Me and the man holding a fake gun. Now that I've realized that, I know this is what I've always wanted. I'm alone in a room with Wayne Gibson. He raises the gun as I take a step toward him.

"Sounds like you've got a big decision to make," he says. "Better get cracking before it's too late."

I smile at him and keep walking in his direction. For the first time in a long time, I feel fucking *great*. Wayne, on the other hand, looks concerned. He rises from his seat, holding his gun out in front of him.

"Another step and I'll shoot," he informs me.

"You do what you gotta do," I tell him. I'm in control of this experience now.

Wayne's back is pressed up against the glass wall when he shoots. I feel a blast of pain in my heart. It's not real, I tell myself, and the pain quickly begins to fade. Wayne is staring at the hole in my chest as it seals and disappears. Within a second, even the tear in the fabric of my shirt is gone. I know what is real. I am, but the bullets are not. As thrilled as I am to have figured it out, I still feel a little bit pissed at myself. I've seen *The Matrix* at least twenty-five times. I should have tried this shit ages ago.

"You missed," I say. I'm almost in arm's reach when Wayne fires three more times. I hear the shots, but the pain I feel lasts only a moment before it goes away. I reach Wayne before he can fire a fifth bullet. I grab him by the throat with one hand and wrench his gun away with the other. I feel stronger, more powerful than ever before. Wayne's eyes roll back in his head as I begin to squeeze the life out of him.

Beyond the glass walls of the conference room, in the lobby downstairs, the lab employees are watching in awe. Most don't seem to know if this is all part of the experience. AJ's the only one who knows for certain that it's not. I see him begin to inch toward the exit, careful to avoid causing a panic among his colleagues. He's almost to the door when I see him lurch forward and fall flat on his face. Every head in the room turns in the direction of the elevator. Nasha emerges, a gun in her hand. The soundproof walls of the conference room prevent me from hearing anything, but I see her shout something at the lab employees in the lobby. They back up against one of the walls—all but AJ, whose left femur appears to have been shattered.

Then Nasha looks up at me. My hand is still around Wayne's throat. I can feel a weak pulse in his jugular, but he's no longer fighting. Nasha's eyes go wide and she shakes her head furiously and waves her arms in the air. It's me she's worried about. Not Wayne and not her mysterious employer. I can read her lips. She's telling me not to kill him. I don't know what reason she'd offer, but I do know that the police who will soon be arriving might have a hard time understanding why I murdered someone who'd threatened me with an imaginary gun. More importantly, I also know that I am not a killer.

I let Wayne drop to the ground. His body collapses into a pile so pathetic I don't even bother to give it a kick. When I turn around, the man in the white coat is preparing to operate on Kat. Before he slices her open with his scalpel, I reach around and rip the disk off the back of my skull. I toss it and the glasses onto Wayne's unconscious form. And then I leave the room.

I'm descending the stairs to the lobby when I realize I've lost track of AJ. The other employees are still clustered together against the back wall, but AJ has slithered away. All he's left behind is a small puddle of blood on the floor.

"Nasha!" I call out.

She turns her head, aims her gun and fires right at me. The two shots, milliseconds apart, echo through the lobby. I hear a thud as something heavy falls to the ground, but I feel nothing. I glance down at my chest. There's no hole. Not even a trace of blood. I look behind me and see Wayne lying at the top of the stairs. The weapon he's still holding is definitely not imaginary. I spared his life, and he was going to kill me anyway. Now he's taking what appear to be his last breaths. I wish I had something to say to the man who thought he alone could save the world, but I don't. I rush forward, kick the gun out of his hand and watch as his eyes flicker and close.

"Hands in the air!" someone shouts. I turn back toward the lobby to see a SWAT team swarming in through the front door. One of the officers drops to a knee next to a body on the floor.

It takes me a moment to realize that it's Nasha. That's when I remember the second shot. The officer checks her pulse and rises so quickly that my own heart seems to stop.

Then the cop motions to me. "She wants to speak to you!" he shouts.

I rush over to find that Nasha's still alive. I kneel beside her, wishing I weren't so familiar with scenes like this. Too many people have died in my arms. But when I take her hand and look down at her face, I know this isn't going to play out like the others. Nasha is glowing as if she's lit up from the inside.

"It's okay, Simon," she tells me. "I knew my time here would end this way. I've been waiting."

"Nasha—"

"No, no, none of that. Don't you see? We did it. We took them down. Here." She holds out the hand she's kept clenched in a fist. When it opens, I see a small drive. "Give this to Elvis. He'll know what to do with it."

I look down at the device in my hand. A human being is on it. "Are you sure?" I ask. I know Elvis is a genius, but I'm not sure I'd trust him with something so precious. I'm not even sure if I trust myself to transport it.

"You know, when I heard about you, I thought none of it could be true. I thought the old man had finally lost his mind. But he was so certain that I knew I had to take a chance. Turns out he was right all along."

Her body is dying. Even I can see she doesn't have much time left. I don't know if she's delirious. She hasn't said a word about her daughter. I'm not sure I'm the one she should be talking about on her deathbed. Still, I can't help but ask.

"What old man? Who are you talking about?"

Nasha smiles. "My boss," she says. "You'll meet him soon."

There are a thousand questions I'd like to ask, but none of them are important at this moment. "Is there anything you'd like me to say to Busara?" I ask her.

"Yes," Nasha says. "Give my baby a hug and tell her I'll see her soon."

The police are ushering the lab employees past us out the door. I can hear ambulance sirens drawing closer. When I look down and plead with Nasha to hold on for a few more minutes, I find she's already gone.

THE REUNION

Kat leaps on me the second I walk through the door and presses her lips against mine. As much as I'd like to spend the rest of my life kissing her, there are a couple of things that need to come first.

I gently push her back. "Where's Declan?" I ask.

The tone of my voice dampens her excitement. "Asleep in one of the bedrooms," she says. "Poor thing was exhausted when we got back."

"Good," I say. At least Declan's safe.

Elvis approaches me. I can tell he knows.

"You're alone," he says somberly. "She didn't come back with you."

All I can do is nod.

"What's going on?" Busara's face has gone ashen. "Did something happen?"

"Do you have it?" Elvis asks me.

I hold out my hand. In the palm is the single most valuable thing I've ever held. Elvis takes it from me.

"She said you'll know what to do with it," I say.

"I do," he responds. "She taught me."

"What is it? Who said that?" Busara grabs Elvis's arm. "Elvis, tell me."

Elvis looks over at me. I suppose I have some explaining to do.

"After I was released from jail, your mother made me take her to the lab," I say. "She wanted to download her memories."

Busara's eyes widen. "Why?" she whispers.

This time, Elvis answers. "So she could be with your father if something happened to her."

"So something happened?" Busara croaks. "Are you saying my mother is dead?"

"Yes," I tell her. "I'm so sorry."

"No." Elvis holds up the drive. "She's right here. I'm going to reunite her with your father. That's what she wanted."

There's a knock at the door. The four of us go silent. The knock becomes a pounding. Then the door caves in. Four FBI agents enter the apartment with their guns drawn. When they see us, they holster their weapons. I'm still on the verge of a heart attack, but Kat's kept her cool.

"You know you're going to have to fix that, right?" she says.

"Does this mean we're under arrest?" Elvis asks.

"No, sir," one of the agents assures us politely. "We just got worried when you didn't open the door."

*   *   *

I've spent the past six hours being interviewed by an FBI agent. Somewhere in the same building, Kat is being interviewed as well. Elvis and Busara stayed behind with Declan. They'll all be interviewed at a later date. I've told Agent Brick everything I know—leaving out only the details that might make him question my sanity.

It's a pretty bizarre story nonetheless, but Agent Brick has spent most of the time listening quietly and taking notes. The follow-up questions he's asked have been simple and straightforward. It's almost as if he's heard the story before. My account is just further confirmation.

Then one of his questions takes me by surprise.

"What exactly was your connection to Abigail Prince?" the agent asks.

I've been through all of this. "When Kat and I were kidnapped by the Company, she helped us escape," I repeat, wondering if he was really listening the whole time. "She wanted to help us bring down the Company because they framed her son for murder."

"How did you first get in contact with her?"

I hesitate. I distinctly remember recounting this part of the story. "An anonymous person sent us Abigail's phone number."

"And you don't know who it was?"

"No." That's what I told him the first time around, and technically it's truth. It was someone connected to Nasha Ogubu, but I don't know exactly who it was.

"Hmmm." The agent looks down at the information before him. "Abigail Prince was found dead this morning inside the Company's lab."

I suspected as much, but I'm still saddened by the news. "I'm sorry to hear that," I say. "I wish she could have lived to see what she helped us accomplish."

Agent Brick closes his notebook and looks up at me. "Can you think of any reason why you are listed in Abigail Prince's will as her sole heir?"

I have to stop and replay his last sentence inside my head. "What?" It doesn't even make any sense. Abigail barely even knew my first name. She definitely didn't know my last.

"Abigail's son, Max, predeceased her. In the event of both of their deaths, her fortune will pass to you."

I don't know what to say. "I've only known her for the past few weeks. She changed her will in that time?"

"No," says the agent. "According to the information I've been given, her will was written months ago."

"And it has *my* name on it? Simon Eaton? That's impossible. How did she even know who I was?"

"That's a question we'll be trying to answer in the coming days," the agent says. I get the distinct impression that he thinks I know more than I do.

"I can't wait to find out the answer," I respond.

I sit silently as the agent makes a few notes on his pad.

"Am I free to go?" I finally ask. I'm dying to get out and talk to Kat.

"There's one more pressing issue to discuss before you go. In the course of searching the Company's laboratory on Franklin Street this morning, we discovered an automaton designed to re-semble you."

This shouldn't be news. I went through all of this earlier. "I told you—when Kat and I were kidnapped, they scanned our bodies and stole a month's worth of memories. They used them to make the robot clones."

"Yes, I was listening. I wanted to let you know that the—ahem—robot clones were both taken into evidence. When the Bureau has finished—"

I leap in before I realize what I want to say. "Don't destroy them yet."

The agent raises his eyebrows. I've finally managed to surprise him. "I'll make sure your preferences in this matter have been communicated. In the meantime, do not discuss the Company with anyone, including the press."

"People deserve to know what's happened," I argue.

"The public will panic if the truth is told," Agent Brick tells me.

"You're asking me to keep my mouth shut about all of this?" I ask, stunned.

"It wasn't a request, Mr. Eaton," the agent says.

It's after midnight by the time Kat and I are allowed to leave. We grab a cab and head across the Queensboro Bridge, back to the apartment we've been calling home. We find Elvis, Busara and Declan on the sofa when we arrive. A news program is playing on the television.

"Have you been sitting here all this time?" I ask.

Elvis snorts. "Not exactly. Declan climbed down the fire escape and went for a walk while Busara and I were . . . napping."

I look down at Declan. "Where did you go?"

"There," says Busara. She's pointing at the television.

Elvis picks up the remote and turns up the volume. Declan is on the screen, speaking to a group of reporters gathered outside the Company's lab on Franklin Street. He's reading from type-written sheets of paper. He keeps his eyes on the pages, as if he's too nervous to look up.

"Several months ago, I was hit by a car while riding my bike. When I was taken to the hospital, the doctors told my parents that I was suffering from something called locked-in syndrome. In other words, I was conscious, but my body was completely paralyzed. I could neither move nor speak. I was locked inside my body. The doctors convinced my parents to let me test a new therapy for patients with locked-in syndrome. A disk was attached to the back of my skull and a visor was placed over my eyes. Together, they communicated with my brain and allowed my mind to enter a virtual world. There, I could not only walk and talk again, I was able to use all of my senses." Declan looks up at the camera. His confidence is growing.

"My parents were told the disk had been invented by Milo Yolkin, the founder of the Company. They trusted that it would be safe. What they couldn't have known was that I didn't have locked-in syndrome at all. The Company was keeping me—and other patients like me—in a comatose state so they could beta test their new technology. You see, the disks Milo Yolkin invented had a bug.

"If you were hurt in the virtual world, the disk would convince your body that the injury was real. If you were hurt badly enough, it would kill you. In order to identify the source of the problem, the Company needed guinea pigs. I ended up being one of them."

Declan puts down his notes. He's standing on a busy street in Manhattan, but there's silence all around. It's as if the whole world is listening. "People died testing the disk. I don't know how many, but I can give you the names of two people who were murdered by the Company. Carole Elliot and Marlow Holm. I only survived because there's something different about my brain. For some reason, the disk wasn't able to kill me. When the Company discovered this, I became their favorite guinea pig. At first, they were hoping to fix the disks. Then they decided they didn't need to.

"Rich and powerful people were lining up to buy custom OtherEarth experiences. When paired with a disk, OtherEarth could make any fantasy come true—no matter how dark or perverted. The disks let users feel, smell and taste everything that's happening. Some people have already died playing OtherEarth. Other people have stopped being able to tell the difference between the game and real life.

"OtherEarth made Max Prince kill his stepfather. The director who beat up his lead actress? He was playing OtherEarth, too. Other famous people have had their secrets stolen and used against them. And that's not all the Company's been up to. They have bodies stored in a lab on the fourth floor of this building. Some of the bodies belong to powerful people—and some of them are those people's robot clones."

"I know it sounds farfetched, but it's true. The FBI raided this building this morning. I thought there was a chance they'd cover up what they found. I wanted to make sure that you all know the truth."

Declan looks up at me nervously as the camera returns to an anchorperson.

"You were right about the FBI," I tell him. "They made us swear to secrecy."

"Well, it's all over the news now."

"Is the public panicking?" I ask.

"Yes. But don't you think they should be?" Declan says.

"Absolutely," I say as I sit down beside him. I'm starting to think this might turn out all right. "You did a great job."

I turn my attention back to the television just in time to see seven glorious words appear on the screen. *Is This the End of the Company?*

JAMES AND NASHA

Kat and I left our avatars in Albion, so we arrive ahead of the others. Who knows how many Otherworld years have passed since we last visited? And yet the little village where Bird lived looks exactly as we left it. From the outside, the stone cottages haven't changed. The road that runs between them is still dirt. Beyond are the fields that were home to a herd of elephants. But I can see tall green mounds on the edge of the old town and a glass tower in the distance that tell me life in Albion is not completely the same.

Children come to the cottages' windows as Kat and I walk down the street. A few naughty little ones run outside and follow us. They are beautiful beings—mixtures of every creature in Otherworld. Kat and I try several times to ask them if James Ogubu still lives in town. But whenever we turn to speak to them, they dart away, giggling.

We head in the direction of Bird's cottage. I worry that we may not be able to pick hers out from among the identical dwellings that line the lane. But as we draw closer, I can see there's only one with a statue in front of it—and a quotation written on the wall by the door. *Freedom Is Never Free.* The statue, carved from stone, shows Bird as she looked when Kat and I first met her.

"She died five years ago." The door of the cottage has opened. James Ogubu stands on the threshold. He's wearing the same linen suit, but other than that, he's entirely different. He looks happier than I've ever seen him.

"I wish we could have said goodbye. I'm so sorry we missed her," Kat says.

"You haven't," James says. "Her body is gone, but her legacy is all around you. In all the ways that matter most, Bird is still very much alive."

"Simon and Kat deserve credit too, you know." Nasha has emerged from the cottage. She's transformed as well. Her braids are down and her feet are bare. Even the black workout gear is gone. In its place is a pretty tangerine sundress. "These two helped make all of this possible. They played a big part in saving this world—and the one back home as well."

"Maybe this one's in good shape, but there's still a lot more to do on Earth," I tell her. "The Company's done for—but there are other corporations like it."

"You'll have everything you need," Nasha tells me. "If you don't already."

"Are you talking about Abigail Prince's fortune?" I ask.

Nasha's smile tells me she knows things that I don't. "You still have some big surprises in store," she says. "I wish I could be the one to tell you, but it wouldn't be fair."

"To whom?" I ask.

"Your mother, for starters," Nasha says.

Before I can follow up with another question, James cuts me off. "Speaking of parents and children, where is our daughter?"

"On her way to Albion," I say. "Elvis is with her. Both of their avatars were still in the White City. I don't know how long it will take them to get here."

Nasha laughs. "It should take about an hour, wouldn't you say, James?"

"If they manage to hop on the right transport," James replies.

"There are transport vehicles that travel from the White City to Albion?"

"Oh, yes, there are transport vehicles from every realm in Otherworld."

Kat looks concerned. "Is technology no longer banned in Albion?"

"Some is, some isn't. Following the fall of Imperium, Albion's population multiplied. Before, it had been easy to live this way," James says, gesturing to the surrounding village. "Afterward, we had to look for new solutions. There were too many Children to feed. Too much waste to remove. Before Bird died, she and the Elemental had to relax the rules."

"But I remember you said every technology can come with unintended consequences."

"And it can—unless a society is dedicated to ensuring that doesn't happen."

"Why don't you take them around and show them some of the changes," Nasha suggests. "I'll stay here and wait for Elvis and Busara."

As the three of us walk toward the outskirts of town, a large transport vehicle passes us on the lane. It's similar to the model Kat and I rode in with the Empress of Imperium when we accompanied her here. Last time, the vehicle wasn't allowed past the border.

"Doesn't that look like one of the Empress's vehicles?" Kat asks me.

"We used her technology as our model," James says. "Not everything she created turned out to be dangerous. We discovered that the fuel her transports ran on was remarkably clean and renewable. We made our vehicles larger to allow for more passengers, but otherwise the design is more or less the same. As a matter of fact, Imperium remains Otherworld's center for innovation. You should visit when you have a chance. There may be other ideas you can use on Earth."

We're approaching the tall green mounds that Kat and I noticed when we first arrived back in Albion. They're not hills, though. They're buildings covered entirely in vegetation. Outside the buildings, herds of deerlike beasts nibble peacefully at the grass.

"Here you can see more of the Empress's inventions," James tells us. "As the population of Albion grew, we needed housing and sustenance. The buildings grow all the food that the inhabitants need. In return, the waste of the inhabitants is liquefied and delivered to the plants as nourishment. Each building is a self-sustaining ecosystem that has only a minor impact on the beasts and vegetation around it. Again, we have the Empress to thank for it. The Council approved the technology with very little debate."

"The Council?" I ask.

"Our governing body, the Council, is made up of representatives from every realm in Otherworld. Together we decide whether a technology will be in the best interest of Otherworld's residents. The decision must be unanimous. Anything that is not approved is destroyed. Much has been destroyed."

"Where are the elephants?" Kat asks. "There was a herd here the last time we visited."

"Bird brought them here to save them. Once the population was stable, they returned to their native realm, Karamojo."

The name sends a shiver up my spine. In Karamojo, human headset players once hunted Children for sport.

"That realm and the Ice Fields are now sacred spaces for the Children," James tells us. "The young ones are taken there to teach them about the past. Only by learning history will future generations ensure that it never repeats itself. If they ever forget, hopefully Nasha and I will be here to remind them."

Speaking of which, there's a question I've been dying to ask. Once again, Kat beats me to the punch. Sometimes I wonder if she reads my mind. "You knew your wife was coming, didn't you?"

James gives us a smile. "I hoped it wouldn't be quite so soon," he says. "We wanted Busara to have a few more years with her mother on Earth."

"So the fact that she was a spy didn't bother you?" Kat asks. This time I'm amazed by her boldness. I doubt I would have pushed it so far.

"I knew. Not from the very beginning, but shortly after that. Nasha told me everything. Her boss had made a fortune stealing secrets from tech companies. But he'd grown alarmed when he saw the kinds of secrets his employees were stealing. He realized there was no one in tech looking out for humanity. So he decided to start keeping tabs on the industry. I trusted him and Nasha with all of the information I had. When Wayne took over the Company, the three of us were thrilled. We thought he shared our concerns. Then he revealed just how dangerous he was. When I died on Earth, Nasha had to return to work to ensure that Wayne was stopped and the Company was taken down."

"Who was Nasha's boss?"

James smiles. "A man named Arnold Dalton."

"Max Prince's uncle?" I should have known. How else would her people have gotten access to all of his personal belongings?

"Yes," James confirms.

A transport vehicle glides past noiselessly on its way to the village. There are only two passengers inside. Elvis and Busara have the entire vehicle to themselves, but they're seated thigh to thigh. I don't think they notice us standing outside. They only have eyes for each other.

"Should we head back to the village?" Kat asks.

"You guys go ahead," I tell them. "There's someone here I need to talk to."

A man has appeared in the center of the field. The tall grass reaches as high as his chest. A plume of smoke rises from a cigarette he must be holding, giving him the appearance of a magician who's just appeared onstage. He motions me toward him. There's something he wants to say. I get the sense that it's urgent.

"Who are you going to speak to?" James Ogubu asks, looking around. He doesn't see anyone.

"Go," Kat tells me. "I'll explain."

I leave them and wade through the grass toward my grand-father.

"Sorry to interrupt," he says as I approach. "Can we have a word?"

"Of course," I tell him.

"Not here," he tells me. "I gotta admit—I still find this place creepy as hell."

I have to laugh at that one. "Okay, then where?"

"Take off that gadget and meet me back in Queens. But—" He reaches out and puts a hand on my arm. "I'm going to look a bit different when you get there. This outfit was pretty snazzy in the sixties, but it's not really my thing anymore. It okay with you if I change into something a little more suitable for the twenty-first century?"

How am I supposed to answer that question? "I guess. As long as you're not naked," I tell him.

"You kidding?" the man says. "Last thing you need right now is an inferiority complex."

I'm laughing when I pull off my headset. I stop when I realize I'm totally blind. The apartment is pitch-black. We should have left a light on somewhere. I grope my way off the treadmill toward the switch on the bedroom wall. The bright glare of the overhead light doesn't bother Kat, who's standing on her treadmill and speaking into her headset. I can't make out what she's saying, but I know she's attempting to explain the situation to the others. I wish her the best of luck.

The Kishka is here somewhere. I can smell smoke in the air. I leave my headset on the treadmill and wander out to the living room in search of him. When I flip on the lights, I find a much older man sitting on the sofa. He's wearing a dark blue suit that fits him so perfectly it must be bespoke. His Hermès tie is covered in little blue diamonds. The hair on his head is thinner and whiter. The giant nose tells me this is the Kishka.

"What's going on?" I ask.

"Have a seat," he says, motioning to a chair opposite the sofa.

I drop down into the chair without taking my eyes off the man in front of me. "You look . . . rich," I say.

"You forgot old." He gives me a wink. "I was both. Maybe I still am. To be honest, I'm not entirely sure."

"I don't understand," I say.

"That makes two of us," he tells me. "If you'd told me ten years ago that any of this was going to go down, I'd have had myself institutionalized. I'd be willing to bet that you feel the same way."

"Ten years ago I was eight," I say. "This all would have made perfect sense. But I'm starting to think it might be a good idea to see a shrink."

"Meh. There are better ways to spend your money." He pauses to take a drag off his cigarette. "By the way, I gave these up ages ago. They were just part of the disguise. I'd have been dead a long time ago if I'd kept on smoking." The cigarette disappears, and the Kishka's hand falls to his bony knee.

"The disguise?"

"Well, I wanted to make sure you'd recognize me. You'd only ever seen me in that gangster book, so I figured I'd better look the part."

I tap my own nose. "I think I would have figured out who you were without the cigarettes."

The Kishka beams. "Makes sense," he says. "That's how I knew who you were when I saw you. Apparently, the Diamond DNA is pretty damned powerful."

"Yeah, I guess so," I say. "So what did you want to talk to me about?"

He leans forward, his elbows on his knees, as if he's trying to get a good look at me. "I wanted to tell you how unbelievably proud I am of you."

It takes me by surprise. I don't remember anyone but Kat ever saying something like that to me before. "Thanks," I say awkwardly.

"I mean it," he tells me. "I can't think of anyone who could have done what you did. Even when everything went batshit insane, you held it together. You got the job done."

"I didn't do it alone."

"Of course not. I never bought that One bullshit either. But give yourself some credit. You put together the team," he says. "And that girlfriend of yours—she's one of a kind too."

"Are you saying that because she doesn't think you're proof that I'm losing my mind?"

"Sure. But she's also pretty damned handy with a bow and arrow." He whistles softly. "She's remarkable. I wish I could have had the chance to meet her."

What an odd thing for a hallucination to say.

"I'm not a hallucination," the man says. "Took me a while to figure out that you weren't either. All of this is real."

I hear myself laugh nervously. I really am going insane.

"No, you're not," the Kishka says, reading my mind. "I don't know what happened—how these lines got crossed."

"Grandpa," I say. "You've been at the bottom of the Gowanus Canal for over forty years."

"What? That's not me," he says. "You must be thinking of Shorty."

"Shorty? Who the fuck is Shorty?"

"You'll find out. But if you don't mind, I'd rather not spend our last moments together talking about that rat bastard."

"What do you mean, our last moments together?"

"This is goodbye," he says. "Whoever's running this show let me stick around to see how it ended. Now they're making it pretty clear that it's time for me to go."

"You're not going to visit me anymore?"

"Don't have to," he says. "You have Diamond DNA. I'll be with you all the time."

"What am I going to do without you?"

"You're going to keep up the good work," my grandfather tells me. "I've made sure you have everything that you need."

He teeters as he stands up from the couch. I jump out of my chair and offer him my hand for support, forgetting he's just a figment of my imagination. He ignores my hand and wraps his arms around me. When I hug him back, I can feel the ribs beneath his jacket. He was right. He's every bit as real as me.

THE KISHKA

My mother, Kat and I sit at the back of the funeral home viewing room, watching the people who've come to say goodbye to the Kishka, who's lying in a coffin at the front of the room. Some are mourners. Others seem to be here to ensure that the old man is truly dead. I see one tough-looking senior citizen wearing dark sunglasses stealthily stick his hand into the coffin, lift my grandfather's hand and let it plop back down. Another leans over as if to give him a kiss, but I suspect he's making sure that the Kishka's no longer breathing. My mother let a few of the Kishka's old associates know about his passing. Word must have spread among the rest.

Mixed in alongside the octogenarian gangsters who knew Arthur Diamond are people I assume were associates of Arnold Dalton. Bankers in blue suits. Socialites with laser-smoothed skin. I haven't seen many who look like they might be spies. Either my grandfather's employees chose not to attend his wake—or they're in disguise. There *was* a well-heeled couple earlier this morning who caught my attention. They're still the only two people so far who haven't flinched when they spotted me sitting at the back of the room.

When I came face to face with my grandfather for the first time this morning, it freaked me out too. Lying there against the satin cushions of the coffin was a seventy-eight-year-old version of myself. At first I couldn't understand why I wasn't sad that I hadn't gotten to know him. Then I realized I knew him better than anyone else—because he'd been with me the entire time.

My mother saw him before he passed away. Nasha brought her to him for the first time a few weeks ago. Nasha told my mom she'd be meeting the man who was funding the efforts to take down the Company. Mom said she would have refused to go if she'd know she'd be meeting her father. She recognized him the moment she saw him, and she almost walked right out the door. But something made her sit down and listen.

When the Kishka disappeared over forty years ago, my grandmother told my mother he'd died. My mom was too young to wonder why there hadn't been a funeral—or why none of her father's associates had come to pay their respects. The truth was, the Kishka was still very much alive—and in jail. A man named Shorty Papalardo had been murdered, and the Kishka had helped dispose of the body in the Gowanus Canal. Then he turned state's evidence and put five other mobsters in jail.

My grandfather was kept in solitary confinement for three years—largely for his own protection. While he was in jail, he and my grandmother secretly divorced. By the time he got out, my grandmother had remarried. Her new husband was a banker. She made it quite clear that there was no room in my mother's life for a broke felon who'd be on the run from his enemies for the rest of his life.

The FBI gave my grandfather a new identity and he moved west, close to his older sister in Chicago. When he started his first store, he made her the face of it. As the company took off, he stayed in the background. He never remarried. And though he kept an eye on his daughter back in New York, he never dared contact her.

Later in life, the Kishka grew bored with retail. The only parts of the business that still gave him a thrill were the secret reports he received on his competitors' businesses. When his niece, Abigail Prince, came of age, he turned over the retail empire to her and began a new venture. He hired the finest corporate spies and sent them out to infiltrate the booming tech world. The information they gathered helped the Kishka multiply his fortune tenfold.

"Then, about five years ago, something very strange began to happen," my mother told me. "My dad told me that whenever he would lie down for a nap, he'd see a kid—a boy who looked exactly as he had. It was you he was visiting."

I would have been thirteen. The age I was when I found the book *The Gangsters of Carroll Gardens*. The age when I first realized that the Kishka was my grandfather. It was the discovery that had changed my life forever.

"He couldn't understand what was happening. He was sure he was going insane," my mother said. "He went to see the best neurologists. None of them could explain what he was seeing. Then, on a hunch, he sent one of his spies to Brockenhurst. And he realized the boy he was seeing was his grandson."

As my mother told the story, I could tell she was still struggling to believe it. She'd devoted her life and career to the rational—written laws and irrefutable evidence. Nothing had prepared her for what her father had told her. There was no logical way to explain how our lives had crossed the way they had.

But I never doubted a word of it. Thinking back, I could feel his presence—even when I couldn't see him. The experience changed my grandfather as well. It was around this time that he took his espionage business in a new direction. He'd learned enough to worry about the fate of the world. After he found out he had a grandson, such things mattered more than ever. So he began monitoring the tech industry.

"He said when you discovered Otherworld, he knew it meant something. He'd been following developments at the Company quite closely. But when Nasha's husband died, he lost his main source of information. Then your path and his unexpectedly aligned. You were both being guided in the same direction. He said that for the first time in his entire life, he began to believe in fate."

Fate. The word still makes me nervous. I've seen too much to accept that fate is the only alternative. But I also know there's no point in worrying about the alternatives. My life and my grandfather's intersected for a reason. Neither of us could have taken down the Company alone. Each had resources the other needed. We seemed to be following a plot that was already written. But by whom?

Now it's all on me. I've inherited two fortunes—Abigail Prince's and my grandfather's. I have unlimited resources—more than enough to purchase what little was left of the Company when it went on the auction block. I became the owner and CEO of the Company at age eighteen—six months younger than Milo Yolkin was when he founded it. When I took over, I had no employees. They'd all been arrested, along with the Company's board of directors. But the tech that was left behind belonged to me.

James Ogubu gave me a list of names—people he thought had the expertise and integrity to form a panel. Professors, engineers, ethicists and business leaders. They reviewed each innovation and determined whether it was likely to help or harm humanity. In the end, almost everything was dismantled and destroyed. We kept three important artifacts. The simulation video that the Company created. And the clones they built of Kat and me.

The wake is almost over when an old man stops in the aisle beside me. "You've got to be the grandson," he says to me in a thick Brooklyn accent.

"Yes," I say.

"Your grandfather sent me to jail. If I'd known he was alive, I would have killed him myself."

I feel Kat tense, but I'm not concerned. "I'm sure you're not the only one here who feels that way."

The old man breaks into a smile. "I saw you on television the other day. Knew who you were the second I saw that nose. It was a commercial for that big news show everyone watches. You're going to be on the next episode, am I right? Commercial said you were going to blow our minds. Wanna give me a hint?"

"Wish I could," I say. "But you'll just have to watch."

As he walks away, I catch sight of another older gentleman

paying his respects at the front of the room. He's wearing the same glasses and guayabera he had on the last time I saw him.

"Look, it's the Phantom," Kat whispers in my ear.

He saved our lives back in Texas. Without him, I'd be dead. The same goes for the Kishka. And Kat. And my mother. Nasha, Busara, Elvis, Declan and Carole. They all saved my life at one point or another. Without all of them, the Company wouldn't have fallen.

None of my friends crack jokes about *the One* anymore. We all know there's no such thing. No single person can save the world. We have to band together and save each other.

OTHER YOU

A lanky eighteen-year-old kid and his wild-haired girlfriend sit on a stage in front of a studio audience. He's dressed simply in blue jeans and a T-shirt, while the show's stylist has given her a gorgeous black dress and heels. Doesn't seem entirely fair, if you ask me. Even without the fancy clothes, she already looked way out of his league.

"Can you tell us your names?" the celebrity interviewer asks.

"I'm Simon Eaton," says the kid.

"My name is Katherine Foley," the girl tells the man.

"You're a couple of high school students from Brockenhurst, New Jersey. And the country knows you better as—"

"The Tech Avengers."

"Shall we show the video?" the host of the show asks the producer, who's standing off camera.

The studio lights dim and a giant screen behind the trio lights up. The video shows the tech mogul Scott Winston exiting a

Manhattan office building. Two people in black on the back of a Vespa enter the frame. Guns are produced, and Winston is shot. As the attempted assassins make their escape, we see their faces. The video freezes and zooms in. The faces are clearly those of the two people onstage.

"Is that you?" the host asks.

"No," says the girl.

"You're kidding," the host pretends to scoff. "That's obviously the two of you on the back of that Vespa. Or is it? What do you think?" he asks the audience.

The crowd roars. There's no doubt in their minds.

That's our cue. Kat and I step out onstage, and the audience seems to gasp in unison as we take seats beside our doubles. I hope the cameras don't pick up the streams of sweat that are trickling down my face. This is my first time in front of a crowd this large. We chose the show because it reaches most of America—a fact that's making my stomach churn at the moment.

Below the stage, I spot my mother sitting beside Kat's. Elvis and Busara are right behind them.

"Do you mind telling the folks here who *you* are?" the host asks.

"Umm, sure," I reply, gaining confidence when I hear that my voice is unexpectedly steady. "My name is Simon Eaton."

"And I'm Katherine Foley," says Kat.

"But I don't understand," the host says, gesturing to our clones. "Who are these people?"

"They're not people," Kat informs him. "They're robots."

She reaches over and removes the fleshy panel that forms her robot's face. Beneath it is a mechanical skeleton—not unlike those the Empress made in Otherworld. Someone in the audience literally shrieks at the sight.

"I know," the host commiserates. "I felt the same way. So, Simon and Katherine, are you claiming that *these* are the people we just saw in that video?"

"Nope," I reply.

The host throws his hands up in the air. "Okay, now I'm really confused!"

"The video was a fake," says a man just offstage.

The audience is perfectly silent as a thirty-something man in jeans makes his way toward us.

"And you are?" the host asks.

"My name is Scott Winston," the man says as he sits beside me. "I was the person who got shot in the video."

The audience is eating this up.

"I saw the people who shot me. None of the people or robots in this room were there that day. The people involved in the attempt on my life used a special software to make it appear as if Simon Eaton and Katherine Foley were on the Vespa in the video."

"How do you know that?" the host asks.

"The software they used was developed by the company I own. I gave it the green light—even though it was dangerous—because I knew it would be profitable. Then my company's innovation was turned against me—and against Simon and Kat. If we don't do something about it, technology like this could end up being used against anyone in this room."

"What are we all supposed to do?" the host asks.

"Start paying attention," Winston says. "Force companies like mine to take responsibility for their creations. Make them accountable to society—not just their shareholders."

"Let's get back to the robot clones," says the host, who seems a bit bored by Winston's lecture. "According to reports, the Company made a few of these things. Is that right?"

"At least four that we know of," Kat replies. "They were incinerated."

"Who else did the Company clone?"

Kat glances at me. "We're not able to discuss that." The vice president himself asked us not to speak of it. We agreed—in return for his resignation.

"But you've decided to keep yours?" the host asks.

I look over at the other Simon—and he looks back at me. Kat and I discussed it, and we feel the same way.

"They'll both be destroyed immediately after the show," Kat says.

"You guys done being celebrities now? Ready for your first day on the job?" Elvis asks as our car makes its way from the studio to the old Company headquarters on the opposite side of Manhattan.

"The security sweep is complete?" I ask.

"Our best people oversaw it. They say the place is a fortress."

"And you got rid of all that crappy corporate décor?" Kat wants to know.

"It's at least sixty percent less evil empire now," Busara answers.

"Plus, we made sure there are lots of snacks," Elvis adds. "You've got to have snacks to keep employees happy these days."

"Good thinking," I tell him. "So today's our first meeting with the team. What's on the docket?"

"First up is a biomedical company that's using gene editing to create custom babies for anyone with a million dollars to spare."

I'm stunned. "You're kidding," I say. "They're messing with the human genome? Don't they know how dangerous that is?"

"Like I always say, humanity's just a bunch of monkeys playing with a box of matches," Elvis tells me.

"What does that make us?" Kat asks.

Elvis turns to her. "Monkeys with fire extinguishers," he says.